all round
Isle of MAN
BY FAR THE MOST COMPREHENSIVE GUIDE

Edited by: Trevor Barrett

Contributors: Stan Basnett, Duncan Bridges, Frank Cowin, Yvonne Cresswell, Andrew Douglas, Barry Edwards, John Hellowell and Dawn Maddrell.

Photography by: Lily Publications, Michael Thompson and Isle of Man Department of Tourism & Leisure

First Published
by Lily Publications 1994
First All Round edition 2002
New Second edition 2004
Third edition 2006

Published by Lily Publications Ltd., PO Box 33, Ramsey, Isle of Man, IM99 4LP
Tel: +44 (0)1624 898446, Fax: +44 (0)1624 898449.
www.lilypublications.co.uk   EMail: lilypubs@manx.net

ISBN 1 899602 47 X

D1416075

CONTENTS

Ballaglass Glen

A
PEEP BENEATH
THE CLOAK

Although well patronised since Victorian times by generations of holidaymakers, particularly from the north-west of England – given its location in the Irish Sea, 60 miles off Lancashire's Fylde coast – it's surprising that in this age of global travel the Isle of Man remains relatively 'undiscovered'.

On the other hand, there are frequent visitors who jealousy guard the secret of this holiday gem. Perhaps they fear that too many feet stepping ashore will stampede the Island's quiet, unhurried lifestyle and trample its great natural beauty. Or, more likely, maybe they just want it all to themselves.

In the pages of this guide the Isle of Man is available to everyone. From the comfort of your armchair you can begin to appreciate the Island's many attractions – and the differences which set it apart from anywhere else in the British Isles.

Chief among these is Tynwald – the system of self-government established by Norse

just the motivation you need.

As you turn the pages, you will gradually unravel all that lies beneath Manannan's Cloak. As old as time itself, and conjured up at will by the ancient sea god Manannan Mac Lir to protect the Island from the envious eyes of invaders, this shroud of mist is a local weather phenomenon romanticised in Manx

The hundred feet high Sugar Loaf stack in the south

rulers more than a thousand years ago and still effective today. Empowered to make their own laws, the Manx enjoy a sense of freedom and independence which is reflected in the warmth of their welcome and the easy and relaxed pace of life – one of the Island's most endearing and contagious qualities, encapsulated in the Manx saying *traa dy-liooar*, meaning time enough.

If you are one of the many who enthusiastically admit to being intrigued by the prospect of visiting the Isle of Man, but have never quite made it, this guide could be

mythology – one of many legends, superstitions and tall tales which help make the Isle of Man an even more enigmatic and appealing holiday destination.

ISLE OF MAN FAST FACTS

LOCATION

■ The Isle of Man is in the Irish Sea, off the coastlines of Lancashire, Galloway, Northern Ireland and North Wales.

Northern landscape near Andreas

■ It is well served from airports across the Britsh Isles and by sea from England and Ireland. Travel time by air is as little as 20 minutes and by sea averages approximately 4 hours (conventional ferry) or 2.5 hours (fastcraft).

SIZE

■ The Isle of Man is 33 miles long, 13 miles wide and covers an area of 227 square miles.

POPULATION

■ 76,000.

CURRENCY AND POSTAGE STAMPS

■ The Isle of Man has its own currency – the Manx equivalent of sterling – but accepts all UK currencies (and euros in some shops and other establishments). Manx stamps, much prized by collectors, are produced by the Isle of Man Post Philatelic Bureau, for more details visit www.gov.im/post/stamps.

LANGUAGE

■ Manx Gaelic went into decline in the 18th century but is now being revived. English is the language in common everyday use.

■ The Manx name for the Isle of Man is Ellan Vannin.

NATIONAL DAY

■ Tynwald Day, held early in July (usually 5th) at Tynwald Hill in the village of St John's, is a celebration of the Isle of Man's 1,000-year-old parliament and independence. A spectacle of colour and ceremony, the event attracts a large audience and in 2003 was attended by the Queen and the Duke of Edinburgh.

LANDSCAPE

■ The Isle of Man is very scenic: unspoilt countryside, uncrowded beaches, dramatic coastline, high hills and wooded glens with tumbling waterfalls.

■ The highest point is Snaefell (2,036

feet – 635 metres), accessible by mountain railway.

■ The landscape supports a great variety of habitats and is a haven for wildlife.

■ More than 40% of the Island is uninhabited.

COASTLINE

■ Most of the 100-mile coastline can be walked on the 95-mile coast path Raad ny Foillan (Road of the Gull).

TOWNS AND RESORTS

■ The capital is Douglas, on the east coast. The other main centres are Peel (west), Castletown, Port Erin and Port St Mary (all in the south), Ramsey (north) and Laxey (east).

MOTORING

■ There are 600 miles of roads. Driving is on the left and road signs are in English. Car hire is widely available. Parking discs, available free of charge, are required in towns. Touring caravans are prohibited because of the Island's narrow roads and winding country lanes.

PUBLIC TRANSPORT

■ The Isle of Man is remarkable for its vintage railways and trams. The Isle of Man Steam Railway runs between Douglas and Port Erin, the Manx Electric Railway from Douglas to Ramsey (via Laxey), the Snaefell Mountain Railway from Laxey to the summit of Snaefell, and the Douglas horsetrams along Douglas's 2-mile promenade.

■ Frequent bus services operate all over the Island. Money-saving Explorer Tickets cover all bus and public transport train travel (the Groudle Glen Railway and the Curraghs Wildlife Park miniature railway are separate attractions in their own right).

ACTIVITIES & SPORTING ATTRACTIONS

■ The Isle of Man has 9 golf courses (8 are 18-hole) and the Island is a mecca for angling (licences are required), outdoor pursuits, walking, watersports and many other sporting and leisure activities.

■ Famous the world over, the TT (Tourist Trophy) Festival of motorcycle racing is held in early summer.

ARTS & ENTERTAINMENT

■ The Isle of Man Arts Council is extremely active in promoting the performing and visual arts throughout the year.

■ The magnificent Gaiety Theatre on Douglas promenade dates back to 1900 and is one of the finest surviving examples of the work of Frank Matcham, Britain's greatest theatre architect.

■ Linked to the Gaiety Theatre by its original colonnaded gardens is the new Villa Marina entertainment complex, which opened in 2004.

■ Erin Arts Centre in Port Erin is an important and long-established venue for the performing arts, regularly hosting major international festivals of music and song.

EVENTS

■ The Isle of Man's busy annual events calendar is a year-round celebration of Manx arts and culture.

HISTORY & HERITAGE

■ 10,000 years of Isle of Man history and heritage are told in the award-winning *Story of Mann*, presented Island-wide at Manx National Heritage sites and attractions such as the Manx Museum in Douglas, medival Castle Rushen in Castletown and the House of Manannan in Peel.

EXPLORING THE ISLE OF MAN

■ Whatever your mode of transport, Ordnance Survey's Landranger map (number 95) is an invaluable source of reference and information.

TRAVELLING
TO THE
ISLE OF MAN

Whether you travel by air or sea, crossing the Irish Sea to the Isle of Man is part of the adventure. Flying gives you an obvious time advantage, and several airlines serve the Isle of Man from airports across the British Isles. Sailing, on the other hand, enables you to bring your car, though there is no shortage of car hire companies on the Island.

The information given in these pages was correct at the time of going to press (January 2006), and is a general guide to formulating your travel plans. Obviously, you need to contact individual operators for a completely up-to-date picture. As many readers will also appreciate, it is well worth shopping around by phone or online to cash in on money-saving special offers.

But a word of caution: if you're intending to visit the Isle of Man in the main holiday season, it's wise to book your flight or sailing well in advance to secure your preferred outward and return travel dates.

TRAVELLING BY SEA

Ferry services are operated by the Steam Packet Company, based at the Sea Terminal on Douglas harbour – your arrival point on

To get the best prices to sail to or from the Isle of Man log onto:

ᴡᴡᴡ.steam-packet.com

Our new easy to use website gives you access to the best fares on all our routes to or from the Isle of Man. Get a £10 saving on a return car journey and £5 saving on a foot passenger journey when you book online.

STEAM PACKET COMPANY
175th ANNIVERSARY

the Isle of Man. The company's fleet comprises the conventional ferry the *Ben-My-Chree*, SeaCat and SuperSeaCat fastcraft. All vessels carry cars and foot passengers.

From England you have the choice of two departure ports. Heysham in Lancashire is 9 miles from the M6 and the average crossing time is 3 hours 30 minutes by conventional ferry and 2 hours by fastcraft. Sailing from Liverpool is a longer journey, taking on average 4 hours and 2 hours 30 minutes respectively.

From Belfast (fastcraft only) it takes 2 hours 45 minutes, whereas Dublin gives you the choice of conventional ferry (4 hours) or fastcraft (2 hours 50 minutes).

TRAVELLING BY AIR

As at January 2006, airlines and airports serving the Isle of Man daily were as follows:

- Belfast (Euromanx)
- Birmingham (Eastern Airways & Flybe)
- Bristol (Eastern Airways)
- Brussels (VLM Airlines)
- Dublin (Euromanx & Aer Arann)
- Glasgow (BA Connect)
- Liverpool John Lennon (Euromanx & Aer Arran)
- London City (Euromanx & VLM Airlines)
- London Gatwick (BA Connect)
- London Luton (BA & Aer Arran)
- Manchester (BA Connect, Euromanx & Aer Arran)

CONTACT DETAILS

- Steam Packet Company: tel 01624 661661 www.steam-packet.com
- Aer Arann: 0800 587 2324 (UK) 01 8447700 (Ireland) www.aerarann.com
- BA (British Airways Connect): 08708 509 850 (UK) 1-890-626-747 (Ireland) www.ba.com
- Eastern Airways: 08703 669100 www.easternairways.com
- Euromanx: 08707 877 879 www.euromanx.com
- flybe: 0871 700 0123 www.flybe.com
- VLM: 0207 476 67017 www.flyvlm.com

The Isle of Man is served by regular air services from the UK and Ireland

Going there for you.

Operators of:
Isle of Man Buses
Isle of Man Steam Railway
Manx Electric Railway
Snaefell Mountain Railway

Please ask for details of timetables and fares offers
Bus/Rail information line 662525

Isle of **Man**
transport
Arraghey Ellan Vannin
Transport Headquarters
Banks Circus · Douglas
Isle of Man IM1 5PT
Tel: 01624 663366

WELCOME
TO THE
ISLE OF MAN'S TOWNS AND VILLAGES

TOWNS
AND VILLAGES
IN THE EAST

DOUGLAS

Located in the gentle curve of the bay bearing its name, the capital of the Isle of Man is a grand Victorian resort with a sweeping promenade, a busy quayside and harbour, a great variety of accommodation and restaurants, and plenty of family attractions.

One of the best places to view the town is from the top of Douglas Head, where the whole of Douglas Bay is spread out before you. Fringed by gardens to the front and with a backdrop of Snaefell mountain, this is an impressive scene – not least for the striking new architecture which is transforming this once small fishing port into a stylish and vibrant capital befitting its role as an important international centre of banking, commerce and tourism.

Alongside the tall new office buildings and luxury apartments are developments such as the Tower Shopping Centre, the yacht haven and the new Villa Marina which opened in 2004. Each symbolises the breath of fresh air

breezing through Douglas as the town rises to the challenges of the 21st century with great optimism and confidence.

It was largely due to its sheltered position on the east coast that Douglas became the Island's major port and the focus of trade in salt, herring, hides, soap and beer. During the 18th century it was also a centre for the 'running trade', by which merchants avoided high British tariffs on imported goods such as tea, tobacco, wine and brandy by importing them legally into the Isle of Man, paying lower taxes to the Lord of Mann, and then 'running' the goods to colleagues waiting along the shore on the British mainland.

'Running' increased the wealth of the town, but in 1756 the British government brought an end to the business by purchasing the rights of the Lord of Mann so that all goods entering the Island paid British taxes. The Royal Navy and British customs officials controlled this, and the effect was a drastic drop in the wealth and living standards in the town. Interestingly, a commander of one of the revenue cutters was Lieutenant William Bligh, later of mutiny on the *Bounty* fame, who married a local girl, Elizabeth Betham. Peter Heywood of Douglas was also on the *Bounty* crew as, of course, was Fletcher Christian, whose family had strong Manx connections.

In 1787, during a terrible storm, a gale off Laxey wrecked the Island's herring fleet. Many boats and lives were lost as they headed for the shelter of Douglas's crumbled pier, and in 1801 a new Douglas pier was constructed.

Shipwrecks were a common feature of life for Island sailors. Sir William Hillary, who had moved to the Island after triumphs in the Napoleonic wars, launched the appeal which led to the formation of the Royal National Lifeboat Institution in 1824 after organising the rescue of 97 men from a Royal Navy cutter which had run aground in the harbour entrance at Douglas in 1822.

Sir William was involved in many other

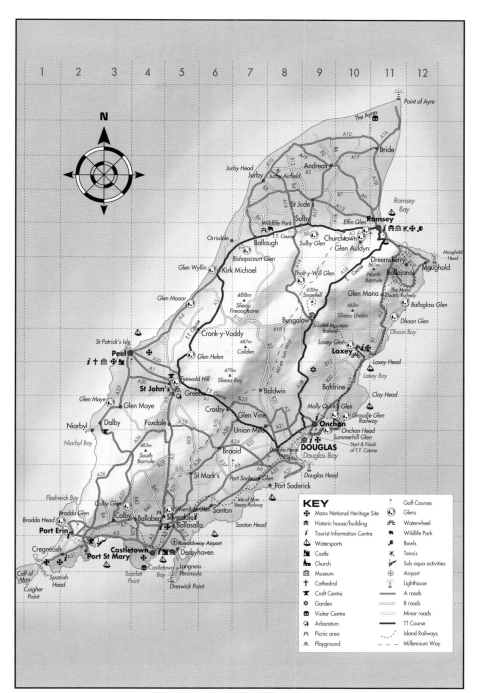

KEY

✠	Manx National Heritage Site	⚘	Golf Courses
⌂	Historic house/building		Glens
i	Tourist Information Centre	✳	Waterwheel
⚓	Watersports		Wildlife Park
▣	Castle	⚘	Bowls
⌂	Church	⚝	Tennis
⛫	Museum		Sub aqua activities
✝	Cathedral	⊕	Airport
⚒	Craft Centre	⚡	Lighthouse
✿	Garden	——	A roads
✿	Visitor Centre	═══	B roads
⚘	Arboretum	═══	Minor roads
⌂	Picnic area	▬▬	TT Course
⚑	Playground	-·-·-	Island Railways
		— —	Millennium Way

rescues, including that of the paddle steamer *St George* in 1832 after it had become stranded on Conister Rock near the entrance to Douglas harbour. Although a non-swimmer, Sir William took out the lifeboat with his crew and saved all 22 aboard. In 1832 he was also responsible for building the Tower of Refuge on Conister Rock – a sight familiar to all ferry passengers arriving at and departing from the Sea Terminal today.

The town spread out from the harbour in the 19th century; first as Georgian residences were built for affluent arrivals from England attracted by the low cost of living, and later for the wealthy holiday visitors from the factory towns of northern England who came on the steamships from Liverpool and Whitehaven. In 1830, to cater for this increased sea traffic, a group of local businessmen decided to build the passenger ship *Mona's Isle* – an enterprise which led eventually to the formation of the Isle of Man Steam Packet Company.

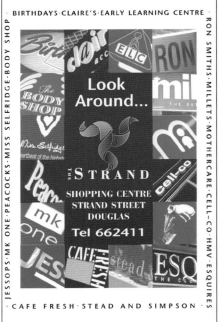

Douglas Bay viewed from the northern end of the two-mile sweep

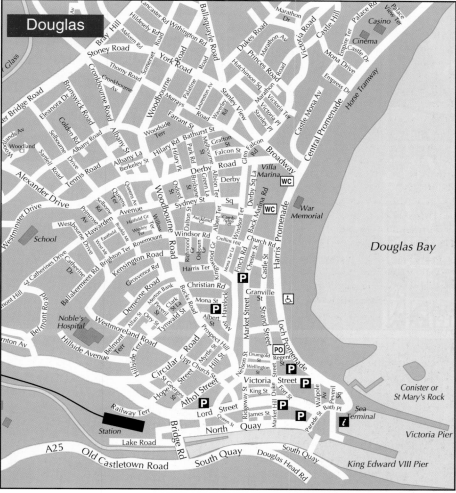

Douglas

In the decades since, the twin piers of
Douglas have welcomed the arrival of
millions of holidaymakers, and today cruise
ships are regular visitors too. There are two
interesting anecdotes relating to the piers:
King Edward Pier is the only public work
named after the uncrowned sovereign, and at
Victoria Pier the 'Dawsey' memorial
commemorates David 'Dawsey' Kewley, a
ropeman with the Isle of Man Steam Packet
Company, who is reputed to have saved 24
men from drowning.

Laxey harbour and the pleasure cruiser *Karina*

great Isle of Man railway journey to experience yet another – by disembarking for the 5-mile ascent to the Island's highest point on the Snaefell Mountain Railway.

LAXEY

Laxey translates in old Norse as 'Salmon River'. Built up over the centuries, Laxey sprawls along the sides of a deep glen, running down from the mine workings in its upper reaches to the tiny harbour at the north end of a wide bay.

Old papers of village life record that in the 18th century large shipments of fish were sent from the port to Sicily. The main products today are flour (still produced on the site of the 1513 mill) woollen goods and Meerschaum and Briar pipes. The factory shop of Laxey Pipes on the quay offers an astonishing choice of fifteen styles and six finishes in the Meerschaum range.

The biggest industry Laxey ever had was mining – for lead, copper, zinc and silver.

Highly profitable in their heyday, the Great Laxey Mines paid out the highest total in dividends of all the lead mines in the British Isles between 1876 and 1882. Earnings of this magnitude ensured a reasonable standard of living for the people of the village.

One unmissable feature of Laxey, if not of the Isle of Man, is *Lady Isabella* – one of the biggest waterwheels ever built in the world. Set to work in 1854 to pump water from depths of up to 2,000 feet below ground, and named after the wife of the then governor, it is an awesome testimony to the sheer hard graft and craft that went into winning Laxey's wealth. The dimensions of the wheel, which still turns in summer months and is a great visitor attraction, are highly impressive: 72 feet in diameter, with 95 steps leading to the viewing platform 75 feet above the ground. Little wonder the views from up here are breathtaking in every sense.

The Laxey Wheel & Mines Trail represents an important chapter in the Manx National

Groudle Glen Cottages ★★★

Onchan, Isle of Man IM3 2JP   T: 01624 623075. F: 01624 621732
W: www.groudleglencottages.co.im   E: groudlecottages@manx.net

Self catering accommodation

The cottages are set on a hillside above Groudle Glen and the beach, with panoramic views inland and out to sea.

All cottages are fully furnished, plus colour TV and DVD player, double glazing, central heating and equipped for up to six people.

- Open all year - midweek bookings accepted.
- Long lets - reduced terms.
- Washer/dryers
- Microwaves
- Individual deck area
- Travel by air or sea can be arranged.

Heritage presentation of *Story of Mann*. This tells of how life was in the mines, and the voluntary organisation Lonan Heritage Trust, located in the old fire station on the road just before the wheel, has a wealth of other information about the village and the local area.

Lower down the glen there are gardens, the beach and a small folk museum near the station. From the station itself you can embark on a 5-mile trip up Snaefell on the exciting electric mountain railway.

ONCHAN

This ancient parish immediately north of Douglas has grown rapidly since the Second World War, becoming something of an overspill for the capital although under the separate administration of the Onchan District Commissioners.

The patron saint of the parish was St Christopher, better known by his Gaelic name of Conchenn, meaning dog-head or wolf-head. In the porch of the present parish church, built in 1833, there are Norse carvings which depict dog-like monsters set on Christian crosses.

The church register dates back to 1627 although the first vicar was appointed in 1408. Interestingly, the church features some modern stained glass and in the churchyard there are headstones designed by Archibald Knox and the grave of Lieutenant Edward Reeves RN, the last surviving officer to fight with Nelson at Trafalgar. An earlier church on the site witnessed the marriage of Captain Bligh of *Bounty* fame to Elizabeth Betham, daughter of the Collector of Customs, who lived in Onchan and also lies buried in the churchyard. Beneath the churchyard wall stand two electric lamp standards, originally erected in 1897 to commemorate Queen Victoria's Diamond Jubilee and now the Island's oldest street lamps.

Close by is chapel-like Welch House, a former infant school and Sunday school now used as an office. Above that is Molly Carrooin's Cottage. It is 300 years old and up to 100 years ago had a thatched roof. The recently-created village green connects with the Onchan Wetlands, an urban nature reserve on the site of an old mill dam.

The old part of the village grew up around the church – a process repeated with Onchan's rapid expansion, the old village now fringed by a large number of estates and a modern shopping precinct, as befits the second most populated area of the Island.

Onchan, very close to Douglas and easily reached, is of interest to visitors for its country walks, King Edward Bay Golf Club, horseriding establishments, and Onchan Park and Stadium – a big magnet for all ages in summer months for activities such as boating, tennis, bowls, miniature golf, squash, go-karts and stock car racing.

PORT SODERICK

Popular with Victorian holidaymakers for its beach, bathing huts, refreshments and walks, Port Soderick lies only three miles south of Douglas on the east coast. This small resort and the capital were connected by road with the construction of Marine Drive, on the headland above Douglas harbour, but separated again when a landslide cut the road in two, as is still the case today. They were also once connected by the Douglas Southern Electric Tramway – the only railway on the Isle of Man ever to use the standard British gauge of track. Despite its demise, Marine Drive still provides an appreciation of the spectacular coastal views the tramway's passengers were treated to.

Port Soderick and Port Soderick Glen are still accessible by road, using the A6 and A37.

25

Port Soldrick, south of Douglas

TOWNS
AND VILLAGES
IN THE SOUTH

BALLASALLA

Just north of Castletown and Ronaldsway Airport, on the A5 – the main road south out of Douglas – is the village of Ballasalla. Within its boundaries are the ruins of Rushen Abbey, and following extensive restoration a new interpretive centre opened here in 2000, giving information about the site's history and significance.

It is believed that the abbey was founded in 1098 by Magnus, King of Norway, and construction commenced in 1134. As with many ancient sites, over the centuries it provided a ready-made source of building materials, but fortunately much of the fabric of the original buildings has survived.

The abbey's Cistercian monks engaged in all sorts of work – draining the land, straightening the course of local rivers and streams, and generally influencing the way of life here. Close to the abbey is an example of their achievements – Monks Bridge, dating from the 14th century. With three arches but a width of just four feet, it crosses the Silverburn River and is one of only a few

Port Erin and Bradda Head

packhorse bridges still standing anywhere in the British Isles. It is also referred to as the Crossag, a Gaelic word meaning little cross or crossing.

Records prove that a number of kings and abbots lie buried within the abbey's precincts. Excavation in the early 20th century unearthed a skeleton of a man buried with a bronze figure representing the Egyptian god Osiris, pointing to him having been a Crusader. *Chronicon Mannia* (*Chronicles of Mann*), a valuable reference work of the Island's early history, was written at Rushen Abbey. It contains an account of the murder of Reginald II, King of Mann, by a knight called Ivar.

A little further upstream from the bridge, the Silverburn is joined by the Awin Ruy, or Red River. It flows down from Rozefel – Granite Mountain, or Stoney Mountain as it is called today – and its bed is strewn with boulders. The mountain was the source of much of the building material used in the

construction of the new Douglas Breakwater in 1979. Norse settlers who recognised the colouring of the granite, exposed as it was to the elements, named the mountain Rjoofjall – Ruddy Mountain.

In summer months Silverdale Glen is one of the most frequented glens on the Isle of Man, and with good reason. It was originally the site of the Creg Mill and its dam is now used as a boating lake, very popular with children. There is also an unusual water-powered carousel here, along with a craft centre, café and wildlife and nature trails.

Ronaldsway Airport, close to Ballasalla, is easily reached from the village by bus or taxi. Ronaldsway, meaning Reginald's Ford to the Norse, is reputedly the site of King Orry's castle and has been the scene of many battles.

CASTLETOWN

It may seem a little surprising to visitors now, but until the role passed to Douglas in the 1860s this was the capital of the Isle of

Man, and had been for many centuries. Sited at the edge of a long extinct and almost untraceable volcano, the town was guardian for the Manx in times of war and peace, its medieval limestone castle a symbol of strength, power and authority.

The Castletown of today has a quiet but distinctive charm. Not only is the fortress which gave the stronghold its name still standing: it is in remarkably good nick – one of the most complete castles in the British Isles – and well worth seeing for its period recreations, fine views and deep sense of history. Castle Rushen dominates the southern lowlands and is visible for miles around. As well as being an impressive historical attraction it is also a working castle, its courthouse and precincts still in traditional use. A point of early military interest is that the staircases spiral to the right, obliging any uninvited swordsmen with hostile intent to grip their weapons in their left hand as they

ascended so that right-handed defenders had an obvious advantage.

The castle overlooks the harbour, which is built on a shelf of lava, clearly visible at low water. The virtual end to commercial seaborne traffic into and out of Castletown came in the 1970s. Since then companies engaged in banking and finance – an increasingly important sector in the Isle of Man's economy – have located in the town and stimulated a revival in business. The former capital is bustling when it plays host to one of the Island's two major agricultural shows, and draws big crowds for events such as the slightly more eccentric World Tin Bath Championships.

A walk along the shoreline from the harbour towards Scarlett Point will show you signs of past volcanic activity. Wind, tide and rain over the aeons have exposed the volcano's surviving plug, and the Scarlett Visitor Centre and nature trail make for a very informative excursion.

Practically all of the ancient buildings in the town are grouped around the harbour and to the seaward side of the castle. Among them is a cluster of small but fascinating museums – the Nautical Museum, Old House of Keys and Old Grammar School – which are significant in the telling of the Island's *Story of Mann*.

The Nautical Museum's main exhibit is the remarkable 18th-century armed sailing schooner *Peggy*, built in 1789 but rediscovered by chance in 1935, walled up in her original harbourside boathouse (now the museum) a hundred years after the death of her owner Captain George Quayle. *Peggy* was involved in local smuggling and trade, and has now been officially recognised as being 'of extraordinary maritime importance' by Britain's National Historic Ships Committee – a distinction she shares with Henry VIII's *Mary Rose* and more than fifty other historic vessels – and therefore merits long-term preservation.

The Old Grammar School, built in

Bradda Glen, Port Erin

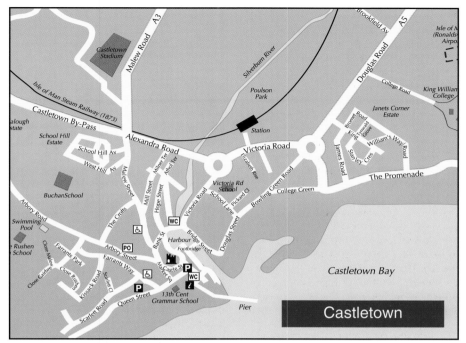

Castletown

approximately 1200, was originally the ancient capital's first church. Nearby is the old garrison church of St Mary's, built in 1826 to replace Bishop Wilson's church of 1698 and saved in recent times from dereliction. On his first visit to the Isle of Man in 1777, founder of Methodism John Wesley preached in front of the castle and noted in his journal of the 30th June, that "A more loving, simple-hearted people than this I never saw".

The Old House of Keys building was the seat of the Manx government from 1709 until 1869, when population and commercial pressures forced the move to the new capital of Douglas. The builder's receipt shows that the building was constructed for the princely sum of £83-5s-6½d (£83.28)!

Castletown's market square is little changed since the 1800s. In the centre stands Smelt's Memorial, erected in 1838 to honour Governor Cornelius Smelt (1805 to 1832) – and to this day still incomplete. The people of Castletown refused to contribute for a statue

to grace the column and for the first few years after it was erected it became known as the 'Castletown Candlestick'.

Across from the Smelt Memorial and close to the George Hotel is the former home of Captain John Quilliam RN, who fought at the Battle of Trafalgar and at the height of the fighting saved *HMS Victory* from destruction by rigging a jury (temporary) rudder.

Looking down on the square is a clock presented to the Island by Queen Elizabeth I. Curiously, it has only ever had one finger but is still going strong after 400 years!

Both anglicised and Norse names are much in evidence in the town and surrounding area – the legacy of Castletown's long association with the seat of government and early colonisation by Viking settlers. Look out for Bowling Green, Great Meadow, Paradise, Red Gap, Witches Mill and the Rope Walk, and homestead names such as Grenaby, Tosaby and Orrisdale.

Indeed, the outskirts of Castletown have

almost as much history as the town itself. Lying to the east is King William's College, a long-time site of public school education, its great central tower dominating the landscape. Facing the school is Hango Hill, where the Manx patriot William Christian was shot for leading a revolt against the Countess of Derby when Charles II was on the English throne. The Norse name for the hill was Hangaholl, or Hill of Hanging, and Christian was the last person to be executed here. It is also a very important archaeological site, with ruins of a blockhouse built by the seventh Earl of Derby at the time of the unrest in England.

To the west of the town is the Balladoole estate, centred on Balladoole House – the home of the Stevensons for many hundreds of years. There is evidence in the Manx Museum in Douglas that at least six generations of the family lived on the estate prior to a mention in the manorial records of 1511.

John Stevenson was the Speaker of the House of Keys from 1704 to 1738 and he is remembered by the Manx nation for the manner in which he led the Keys in their patriotic struggle against the tenth Earl of Derby. Bishop Wilson called him 'the father of his country' and at one time he was imprisoned in Castle Rushen for championing the rights of his fellow countrymen.

To the west of Balladoole, where the coastal footpath Raad ny Foillan (Road of the Gull) joins the main A5 road, is the area known as Poyll Vaaish – easily reached by car or on foot from Castletown. There are superb views of the surrounding countryside, especially the panorama northwards as the low hills of the coastal areas roll ever upwards to the central mountain range, with Snaefell visible in the far distance.

Poyll Vaaish in English means Death Pool or Bay of Death. There are legends galore about this corner of the Island – stories of shipwrecks, pirates and looters. In fact, the name probably derives from the black marble which comprises the sea bed in the vicinity, the ripples of lava evident at low water. Just after dropping down from the basaltic rock stack of Scarlett, you will come upon a small quarry where the black marble is worked. This was the source from which the steps of London's St Paul's Cathedral were made – a gift from Bishop Wilson – and in recent years replaced due to wear.

Close by the Stevensons' ancestral home is the site of a Viking ship burial mound. Together with a number of other important ancient historical sites, it makes this an area well worth seeing.

Also of interest in the area is Strandhall, where a spring flows down to the shore. Legend has it that although the source of the spring lies many feet above sea level, it is a salt water spring with petrifying powers. No doubt the story has taken credence from the fact that at exceptionally low tides – and particularly after a storm has moved the sands – the remains of a large petrified forest can sometimes be seen.

Visiting Castletown and all that the immediate area has to offer is easy, particularly if travelling from Douglas. There is a regular year-round bus service and the revitalised Isle of Man Steam Railway operates in both directions several times a day from early to late summer. Driving is very easy too, although the narrow streets of Castletown itself are not exactly ideal for cars and a much better option is to park and walk.

COLBY AND BALLABEG

To the east of Port Erin (and north-west of Castletown) in the flat lands of the parish of Arbory are the villages of Colby and Ballabeg. Colby (Kolli's Farm) stands at the entrance to the delightful Colby Glen.

A walk up the glen takes you alongside a brook which runs its lower course through wooded glades and higher up where the gorse is a blaze of yellow. Further up the glen again there are the remains of Keeill

The Herring Tower, Langness: a landmark built in 1811 to help prevent shipwrecks on the peninsula

Catreeney (keeill meaning church or chapel) and a burial ground. The ancient St Catherine's or Colby Fair used to be held here. Nearby is Chibbyrt Catreeney (Catherine's Well), and it was said that anyone who drank from it would forever be afflicted with an unquenchable thirst.

Another fair, which still survives, is Laa Columb Killey (St Columba's Day Fair). Held in a field in either Colby or Ballabeg at the end of June each year, it attracts people from all over the Island and gives a glimpse of Manx country life as it used to be.

Ballabeg is on the ancient quarterland and the village is named in the Manorial Roll of 1511 as Begson's Farm. The area is very rural and foxgloves and wild fuchsia line the quiet sheltered lanes. Weedkillers and pesticides are not used on Manx hedgerows and it is still possible to see wild flowers which have disappeared from other parts of the British Isles. The lanes of Arbory and the neighbouring parishes of Malew and Rushen

display excellent examples. In fact, Manx Wildlife Trust in partnership with other bodies has introduced an initiative known as the Wild Flower Project to both conserve Manx native wild flowers and encourage the planting of them wherever possible.

Churches have always played an important part in the life of the south of the Island and none more so than Kirk Arbory. Built in 1757, the present church has an oak beam supporting the roof, the beam having belonged to two previous churches. An inscription on it mentions Thomas Radcliffe, Abbot of Rushen, and appears to refer to the influential Stanley family crest of an eagle and child. The grave of Captain Quilliam of *HMS Victory* and Trafalgar fame (see under Castletown) is in the churchyard.

Along the road from the church towards Castletown is Friary Farm, and clearly visible from the road are the remains of the Friary of Bemaken, founded by the Grey Friars in 1373. The friars were assisted in its

33

Harry Kelly's cottage, Cregneash Folk Museum

completion by stonemasons who were on the Island working on Castle Rushen. Employed by William de Montacute and later by his son, the masons were on the move around Britain strengthening castles and fortifications between 1368 and 1374. Two Ogham stones were found on the site and are now in the Manx Museum, Douglas. They are inscribed in the ancient Ogham script which was used in much of western Britain from the 4th to early 7th century.

CREGNEASH

Tucked away on a hillside of the Mull peninsula, in the Isle of Man's south-west corner, is the lovely village of Cregneash – referred to on some maps in its Gaelic spelling of Cregneish, meaning Rock of Ages. You can get to it very easily by road from Port St Mary, the A31 climbing Mull Hill and giving excellent views of the uplands rising to the north. The village is the oldest in the Isle of Man and its 19th-century thatched

crofters' cottages are a folk museum representing yet another story in the Manx National Heritage *Story of Mann*.

The museum has a working farm and in summer there are authentic demonstrations of how life was for the Island's crofters in the 1800s. The cottages nestle in and around a sleepy hollow. Views over the coastline and the nearby Calf of Man and Sound are stunning. Close by this 'modern' village are the remains of an older one. The Mull Circle (Meayll in Manx, meaning Bald or Bare Hill) dates back to the late Neolithic or early Bronze Age. Used primarily as a prehistoric burial place, it is unique in archaeological terms, combining the circle form with six pairs of cists (stone coffins), each pair having a passage between which radiates outwards. The prehistoric village was below the circle, and hut foundations and other relics were discovered on the site.

On the hilltop above the village is a radio beacon used by transatlantic airliners. The huddle of buildings nearby house a similar system for Irish Sea shipping. Walking on past the beacons brings you to Spanish Head, so called because a galleon of the Spanish Armada was reputedly wrecked here. Also here is an area of land known as the Chasms – huge fissures, some a hundred feet deep, covered by gorse and heather and very dangerous for those foolish enough to ignore the warning signs and stray from the footpath.

From the village of Cregneash the road drops down to the Sound Visitor Centre, with its cafe and panoramic window overlooking the swirling tidal waters of the Sound and the Calf of Man beyond. This is one of the most scenic spots on the Island and a haven for birds and wildlife. With binoculars you may be lucky enough to spot grey seals sunbathing on the rocks of Kitterland – another small island not far from the shoreline – or even basking sharks, feeding on microscopic plants and animals just below the surface.

Walking from the Sound – the Land's End of the Isle of Man – to Port St Mary or Port Erin is also a pleasure not to be missed.

Derbyhaven, near Castletown

DERBYHAVEN AND LANGNESS

A close neighbour of both Castletown and the extremities of Ronaldsway Airport is the picturesque hamlet of Derbyhaven, and stretching south behind its sheltered bay into the Irish Sea is the narrow finger of the Langness peninsula.

Ideal for windsurfers and small boats, Derbyhaven was a thriving port in the days of the Vikings and their medieval successors. It was here that blacksmith John Wilks, from whom two former Governors of the Bank of England are directly descended, made the Island's first penny coins, an action which Tynwald authenticated by declaring them legal tender. The remains of the old smelthouse, probably dating from around 1711, are still visible. There is also evidence that Manx coinage was minted here by one

John Murrey, a merchant of Douglas in 1668 and the probable owner of the Derbyhaven Mint.

The sandy turf of the Langness peninsula is home to the Castletown Golf Links. Close to the ruins of John Wilks' smelthouse is the 10th hole and it was here, 153 years before it was transferred to Epsom Downs in 1780, that the famous Derby horse race originated. It seems that the seventh Earl of Derby wished to encourage the breeding of Manx horses and as an incentive presented a cup to be won in open competition. One stipulation he put on the race was that only those horses that had been foaled within the Island or on the Calf of Man could be entered. The Manx horses of that period were small and very hardy, renowned for their speed, surefootedness and stamina. It may well be that prior to the Derby the only time horses were in competition was after a wedding when the guests raced back to the bridegroom's home to claim the honour of

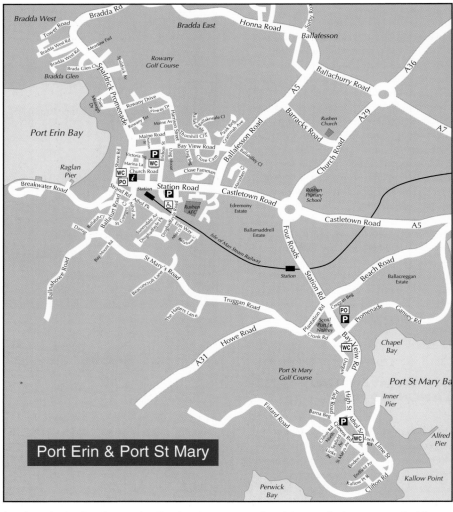

Port Erin & Port St Mary

breaking the bride cake over her head as she entered her new home!

Langness is very well known for its wildlife, especially birds – skylarks in particular - and it's often possible to see seals at Dreswick Point, the southernmost tip of the peninsula and indeed of the Isle of Man.

The waters here conceal a reef called the Skerranes which has claimed many lives. In 1853 the crew of the Plymouth schooner *Provider* perished and their bodies were buried in sight of the wreck, the grave marked by a nearby natural tombstone of rock carved with the vessel's name and the date of her loss.

The Langness lighthouse was built in 1880. It became fully automated in 1996, but prior to its construction another landmark was erected on the peninsula and is still here – the cylindrical structure known as the Herring Tower, built in 1811.

PORT ERIN

Sitting close together but on opposite shoulders of the Mull peninsula – that is to say on its west side and its east side – are the popular summer seaside resorts of Port Erin and Port St Mary.

Whether you approach Port Erin by land or by sea the views are impressive. Port Erin translated means either Lord's Port or Iron Port and in Manx Gaelic is written as Purt Chiarn. Latter-day smugglers came to know Port Erin very well, using the solitude of the bay to mask their activities and hidden from observation by the steep hills and perpendicular cliffs surrounding the village. In the 19th century the village became the playground of the Lancashire mill owners and their employees.

Situated at the head of an almost landlocked bay, which is guarded to the north by lofty Bradda Head and to the south by Castle Rocks and the peninsula, Port Erin offers shelter in most weathers. Pretty white-painted cottages trim the inner edge of the bay, bordered by grassy banks, rising up to a more formal promenade fronting a traditional line of seaside hotels.

The combination of sea, sand, cliffs, hills and heather makes Port Erin very photogenic. Add the appeal of cloud shadows, and brilliant sunsets often framed by Ireland's Mountains of Mourne, and you have some idea of the area's great visual attraction.

Port Erin is also popular for its fine 18-hole Rowany golf course and the Erin Arts Centre, a venue for regular events, exhibitions and the performing and visual arts.

More than a century ago the quality of the waters offshore from Port Erin motivated the establishment of the Marine Biological Station at the seaward end of the bay. Still operating, now as an annex to Liverpool University, it is well respected and often consulted by marine experts worldwide. Among them was the late Emperor of Japan, a renowned marine life specialist who frequently made contact with the station – a

Port Erin, with Bradda Head and Milner's Tower in the foreground

tradition maintained by the present emperor, who has visited the station.

Directly opposite are the remains of a breakwater started in 1864 and which was meant to turn the bay into the national harbour of refuge. William Milner of Bradda Head was a staunch supporter of the breakwater and he along with everyone else on the Island must have felt a great sense of loss when one night in January 1884 it was destroyed in a storm.

A notable son of Port Erin was William Kermode, born in 1775. Seeking fame and fortune, he crossed the world to take up a grant of land in Van Diemen's Land – now known as Tasmania – and did indeed amass a fortune and contributed valuable service to the Tasmanian Legislative Council. Ambushed in his coach by two bush rangers demanding his money or his life, he smacked their heads together, bound them up and drove to Hobart where they were arrested.

PORT ST MARY

Only a few miles from Port Erin across the neck of the Mull peninsula is the attractive fishing village of Port St Mary. The peninsula forms an impressive backdrop, its steep slopes and fields rolling right down into the village. The golf course here is the only 9-hole course on the Island, but no less challenging for that, designed by the 1920 British Open Champion George Duncan. And the views from the sixth tee are spectacular.

Once a thriving fishing port and home to both Manx and Scottish vessels, Port St Mary has a factory which processes the delicious local shellfish delicacy known as queenies – a variety of small scallop. The harbour is full of pleasure boats of all types. The breakwater gives good shelter and its deepwater berths are popular with visiting sailors and the few remaining fishing vessels. The inner Alfred Pier, named after a previous Duke of Edinburgh who laid the foundation stone in 1882, shelters the smaller craft and is a very picturesque part of the port.

Port St Mary, a centre for sailing

Clustered round the harbour are old Manx cottages, their original thatched roofs having long ago given way to Manx slate. The newer part of Port St Mary lies above the sandy beach of Chapel Bay. Linking the harbour and the bay is a fine walkway winding its way close to the water's edge.

Across the headland from Port St Mary Bay, on the southern side of Kallow Point, is Perwick Bay. This owes its name to the old Scandinavian word for Harbour Creek. In very recent times the hotel that once stood at the edge of the cliff has been developed for private housing but the beach is still worth a visit, particularly if you have more than a passing interest in geology: there is a noticeable fault on the bay's south-east side. The rocky pools and small caves at the foot of the cliffs make a good play area for children. Sitting high on the hillside above Perwick Bay is the village of Fistard.

Niarbyl, on the wild and beautiful west coast

TOWNS
AND VILLAGES
IN THE WEST

GLEN MAYE, DALBY AND NIARBYL

Glion Muigh (Glen Maye) means Yellow Glen, and this is a village sitting on steep hillsides at the bottom end of the mining glens of Glen Mooar and Glen Rushen. It is easy to see that the village owes its existence to the farming and mining industries, and much of its original character has been retained.

Beyond the village the river plunges over a series of waterfalls, before finishing its dash to the sea between cliffs which are 200 feet high and clad in gorse and heather.

Niarbyl (or to give it its Manx name Yn Arbyl, meaning The Tail, on account of the long reef jutting out from the shoreline) is an ideal place for picnics, with superb views to the north and south, and now boasting an attractive new cafe and visitor centre on the approach road down to the sea. The grandeur of the west and south-west coast is probably best experienced from this isolated but marvellously relaxing spot – a favourite location for film and TV productions. Massive

Picturesque village of St John's, east of Peel

cliffs stretch away southward in a series of
giant headlands and bays before Bradda Head,
at Port Erin, briefly interrupts the flow. The
Mull Hills continue the vista and from this
angle it almost seems as if the Calf of Man is
joined to the main Island. You'd also be hard
pushed to find better walking country than
this.

FOXDALE

Foxdale is a cunningly misleading name,
because it actually translates as Waterfall Dale
– very apt in view of the area's abundance of
streams. The village was once a centre for lead
mining and from the 300 or so tons of ore
mined each month, some 15 to 20 ounces of
silver per ton were extracted. When the
industry ceased in the early part of the 20th
century, many of the miners emigrated to the
colonies, and it has taken a long time for the
village to begin to recover some of its lost
prosperity.

PEEL

Draw a straight line from west to east approximately half way down a map of the Isle of Man and you will see that Peel and Laxey are exactly opposite each other on their respective coastlines, separated by a distance of about 13 miles. But while Laxey is relatively close to both Douglas and Ramsey, Peel is the west coast's only sizeable town – and the only one on the Isle of Man to have a cathedral.

In fact, Peel has two cathedrals. One is the medieval ruin of St German's, located on St Patrick's Isle within the walls of Peel Castle. The other, the present Pro-Cathedral in the centre of the town, is a fine building which technically speaking gives this ancient fishing port the status of a city.

Peel takes its name from an abbreviated form of St Patrick's Isle and has only been known as this since the name came into regular use in the 19th century. The town has

played a significant role in the development of the Island's nationhood, and excavations of the area's Viking settlement have uncovered important burial sites.

One site revealed the remains of a female subsequently known as 'The Pagan Lady'. The grave was unusual in that it was a curious mixture of Christian and Pagan rituals, and a very fine bead necklace was recovered and can be seen in the Manx Museum in Douglas.

Celebrated prisoners have been incarcerated in Peel Castle over the ages. Shakespeare makes mention in *Henry VI* of one such famous detainee – Eleanor, Duchess of Gloucester, who for 14 years was imprisoned in the cathedral crypt, accused of treason and sorcery against Henry VI as she sought to advance her husband's claim to the English throne. Her fellow plotters were not so fortunate: Roger Bolingbroke was executed and Margery Joudemain, the Witch of Eye, was burnt to death. History records

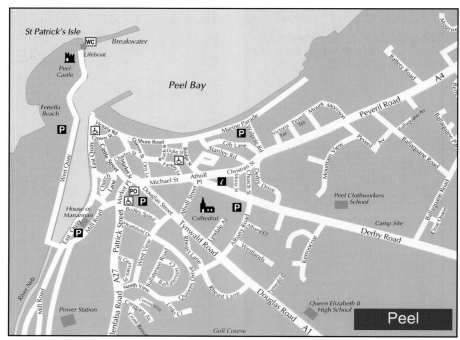

that the duchess was a difficult prisoner, capable of escape or even suicide and in need of careful guarding. Her ghost is said to haunt the cathedral's crypt.

For a long time Peel was the centre of the Isle of Man's once-thriving fishing industry, boasting a great maritime tradition and a considerable fleet of boats. Even today it is known for its oak-smoked Manx kippers, the quayside factory and museum open to visitors in summer months.

The story of Peel's long and distinguished history is told in another waterside attraction. House of Manannan, built in the late 1990s at considerable cost, is an interactive heritage centre presenting Peel's role in the *Story of Mann* in a very entertaining and engaging fashion. There is a great deal for kids to see and do here and it has become one of the Island's major visitor attractions, as well as a vital tool in the education of Manx school children.

Peel is also a magnet for its sands, ice

Peel, nicknamed Sunset City

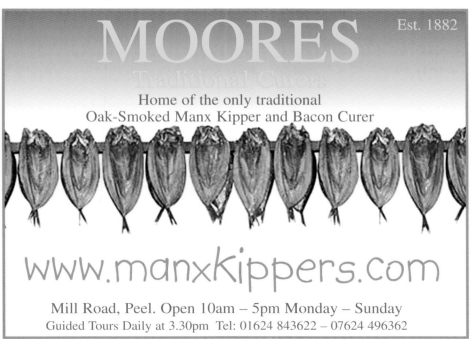

The Royal Chapel, St John's

and others. On occasions, as in 2003, Her Majesty the Queen or other member of the British royal family is guest of honour.

But it's not all pomp – many of the spectators are here to enjoy all the fun of the fair which is an important element of the day's celebrations.

St John's has other attractions too. One is Tynwald Mills Centre, on the site of the old woollen mills. You can shop here for an interesting variety of merchandise, from clothes to pictures to Manx wild flower seeds. Close by are St John's Arboretum and the nursery gardens of the Manx Forestry Department.

cream, kart racing grand prix, 18-hole golf course and fabulous sunsets.

ST JOHN'S

Inland, 5 miles to the east of Peel, you will find the attractive village of St John's. Every year in early July (normally on 5th) this pleasant and quiet community is completely transformed by the colour, splendour and ceremony of Tynwald Day – the Island's national celebration of more than 1,000 years of unbroken self-government.

Thousands of people crowd around Tynwald Hill to witness an ancient tradition which includes the proclamation, in both Manx and English but in summarised form, of Island laws enacted during the last year. These are read out by the Deemsters – the Manx equivalent of British High Court Judges – and also in attendance are the Lieutenant Governor of the Island and a whole assembly of dignitaries, civil servants

The relaxing north-west coast, near Kirk Michael

TOWNS
AND VILLAGES
IN THE NORTH

BALLAUGH

The comparatively modern north-west village of Ballaugh is within easy reach of the west coast and straddles the A3 between Kirk Michael and Ramsey. It marks the beginning of the scenery that is so typical of this corner of the Island: remote glens running down to low sandy cliffs and shoreline against the hills of the northern uplands. The new church, built in 1832, is clearly visible from a distance. Approximately a mile and a half nearer to the sea is old Kirk Ballaugh

Church, with its very distinctive 'leaning' gate posts. Ballaugh has the oldest parish register in the Island, dating from 1598.

JURBY, ANDREAS AND BRIDE

The three most northerly parishes of the Island – to the west, centre and east respectively – share virtually the same scenery, the Bride Hills providing the only high ground in the area.

This is very much farming country. The relatively flat northern plain, easy for walking and cycling, is a maze of roads and lanes zigzagging between the villages.

Jurby in more recent times grew up around the old Royal Air Force base, which since closing for military purposes has been put to good use by a variety of small businesses, the airstrip ideal for the local gliding club and motor racing events.

The old garrison church merits a visit. The porch has a fine collection of stone crosses, and wandering through the churchyard and reading the inscriptions on the old headstones evokes many images of local history. In the new part of the churchyard, the well-kept graves of Polish, Canadian, Anzac and British airmen are laid out in neat rows. On a clear day, from the back of the church, you can see Scotland's Mull of Galloway and its lighthouse.

Andreas has always been a pleasant village with a peaceful rural existence, largely uninterrupted since the end of the Viking era. In the 1940s, the land to the north and east of the village served as a base for the R.A.F. Roads and lanes accustomed to carrying

nothing bigger than a horse and cart were widened, and it was not unusual to see large aircraft being manoeuvred on the roads skirting the edge of this ancient village. In 1995 the old airfields of Andreas and Jurby were used as locations for the film *The Brylcreem Boys*.

The parish church of Kirk Andreas with its Lombardic campanile is unexpected, but the Italian style sits well with the Manx countryside. It was built in 1802 to replace a parish church from the 13th century, the time when parishes were first formed on the Island. In 1869 Anglo-Saxon coins were discovered during the building of the bell tower. Dedicated to St Andrew, probably during the period of Scottish rule (circa 1275 to 1334), there are indications that a much earlier church, whose name has been lost, occupied the site. During the Second World War the spire was removed from the church to give a clear flight path for the planes using R.A.F. Jurby and R.A.F. Andreas.

The Andreas carved stones are very fine examples of Dark Age craftsmanship and one,

The Sulby, the Island's longest river

a pillar, is particularly interesting with an inscription in Roman capitals and letters from the Ogham alphabet. Such carvings are seldom found outside Wales.

Not only the hills on whose slopes it sits but also a new rose share their name with the village of Bride. But looking at the village's past, the romance ends there. Bride was frequently raided by pirates and marauders, on clear days the smoke from the village's chimneys visible on the Galloway coast and tempting the villainous chieftain Cutlar MacCulloch and his men to set sail for a free Manx feed. On one occasion, arriving at a wedding feast just after soup had been taken, they deprived the guests of the meat by eating it all themselves.

To the west of Bride is Thurot Cottage, a private house built using timbers from the ship of a defeated French fleet led by the vessel *Bellisle*, under the command of Captain Thurot. The battle, in February 1760, was witnessed by Bishop Hildesley and probably

seen – and certainly heard – from Bride.

Bride church and its Celtic cross are interesting, and this is a very pleasant area for walking.

KIRK MICHAEL

On the west coast and a few miles south of Ballaugh, Kirk Michael (previously called Kirk Michael Towne or Michaeltown) sits at the junction of the spectacular A4 coast road to Peel and the picturesque A3 to St John's and the south.

It is also on the famous TT course, and the spotlight falls on the town in late May and early June every year when the races pass through; the inhabitants of Kirk Michael are said to have the flattest feet in the Isle of Man because their houses edge right up to the race course! A good place from which to watch the racing is the Mitre. Very close to the town is Glen Wyllin (meaning Mill Glen, and sometimes spelt without a break between the words). At one time a bridge carried a

Stunning views over the northern plain

railway line high above the glen and helped make it a very popular spot with holidaymakers. Nothing remains of the railway now except for the two redundant sandstone bridge supports, but the beauty of the glen is undiminished and still attracts many visitors, the lower section leading to the shore.

Five bishops are buried within the grounds of the local church. There is a memorial stone to the popular cleric 'The Good' Bishop Wilson, who did much for the people of the Island in his long and beneficial stewardship.

MAUGHOLD

In the north-east of the Island close to Ramsey (Maughold Head overlooks Ramsey Bay) is the village of Maughold. It enjoys stunning views of coast and countryside and was the most important centre of Celtic Christianity on the Isle of Man.

The church, Kirk Maughold, which dates from the 12th century, is dedicated to St Maughold, who is said to have been cast ashore near the headland.

The churchyard contains the remains of four ancient keeills (churches or chapels) and beautiful carved stone crosses found in the area are on display in the cross house. Of both Celtic and Norse origins, they are among the finest examples of the many carved crosses which have been discovered throughout the Island's landscape.

A path from the village takes you to the lighthouse on Maughold Head and those breathtaking views.

PORT E VULLEN

This small and attractive sheltered bay snuggles between Maughold Head and Ramsey Bay.

RAMSEY

Ramsey, the second largest town on the Isle of Man, is blessed with a wonderful setting: cradled by the 10-mile sweep of the crescent bay, whose sandy shoreline extends to the northernmost Point of Ayre, against the backdrop of the high hills of North Barrule.

Chronicles of Mann of about 1250 record this north-eastern town as Ramsa – seemingly drawn from the old Scandinavian language and meaning Wild Garlic River – yet there are no buildings of great antiquity in Ramsey other than Ballure Church. The Burial Register dates from 1611 and the building was reported in 1637 to be in a near ruinous state, but over the years at various times it has been restored.

The probable reason for Ramsey's lack of old buildings is that it suffered much turmoil throughout its early history. Olaf, King of Mann, was murdered by his nephew Reginald near the harbour in 1154. Somerled, the 12th-century Thane of Argyll, made a historic landing here, and a century later Robert the Bruce passed through on his way to besiege Castle Rushen.

Centuries on, landing in Ramsey became a lot easier when the magnificent Queen's Pier was built in 1886. Thrusting out into deep water for a distance of 2,248 feet, it

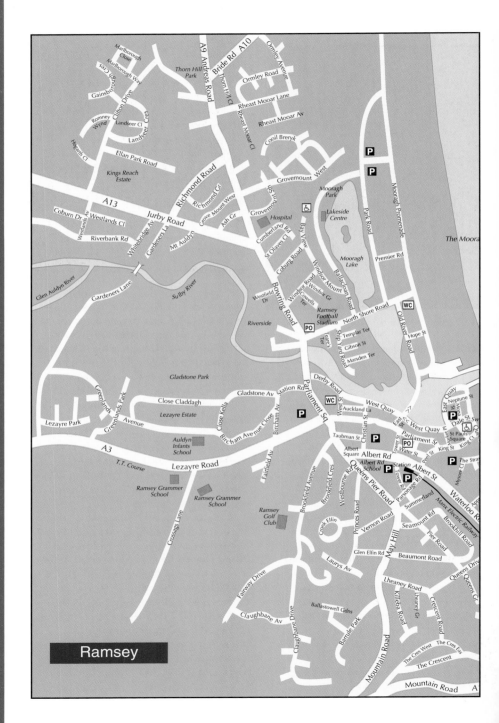

the Isle of **MAN**

Ramsey

Popular Mooragh Park, Ramsey — a centre for leisure and recreation

established Ramsey as a popular stopping-off point for steamers en route to other ports of call. Today Ramsey harbour, with its twin forcep-like breakwaters at the entrance, offers shelter to yachts, coasters and trawlers. It is the headquarters of the Manx Sailing and Cruising Club, which organises local races and is responsible for the prestigious Isle of Man Round the Island Yacht Race every summer.

Another very distinctive feature of Ramsey's harbour is the iron swingbridge, 225 feet long, which came into operation in 1892. On the landward side of the bridge is Ramsey shipyard, which constructed one of the world's first iron ships as well as *Star of India,* now displayed as an attraction in the American port of San Diego. The yard also built the world's first two ships specifically designed as oil tankers.

Flowing into the bay via the harbour is the Island's longest river, the Sulby. In fact, Ramsey was once an island. In 1630 the town was virtually destroyed by the sea, a continuous threat until the early years of the 19th century.

In 1881, Mooragh Park was created on reclaimed wasteland, protected by a new promenade and sea wall. It is a very popular spot and a great attraction for all ages, with 40 acres of gardens and a 12-acre boating lake. Canoeing, sailing and other water-based activities are part of the draw, as are the summer concerts and galas held in the park and the Lakeside Centre.

Ramsey hosts several major annual events, including Yn Chruinnaght – the Island's inter-Celtic week-long festival of music, dance, art and literature – and vintage motor rallies. The latter coincide with speed spectaculars such as the TT Festival and Manx Grand Prix, and also complement Ramsey's fun Carnival Day in July.

The town has other big sporting attractions. The summer angling festival pulls in many keen fishermen, and golfers now have a choice of two 18-hole courses in the area – Ramsey's long-established club and Glen Truan, a new course at Bride.

For visitors with a preference for history, the Grove Rural Life Museum in Ramsey – part of the *Story of Mann* – presents an interesting country house preserved as a period museum, with 19th-century furnishings and fittings.

Welcome to the most enchanting leisure centre in the British Isles

The Irish Sea is home to the Isle of Man, an island where you'll wish every moment could last a lifetime. Feel free to wander at your leisure along peaceful walkways and through stunning glens. But if you take the time to delve a little deeper, you'll encounter parts of our island that look like they're straight out of a fairytale.

Feeling adventurous? Saddle up and meander through beautiful villages and unspoilt countryside at your leisure. The quest has begun to find your special place. One you can call your own. Where time stands still and you can appreciate the things that truly matter in life.

For your free brochure go to VisitIsleofMan.com or call 08457 68 68 68 quoting AGO6.

Isle
OF
man
VisitIsleofMan.com

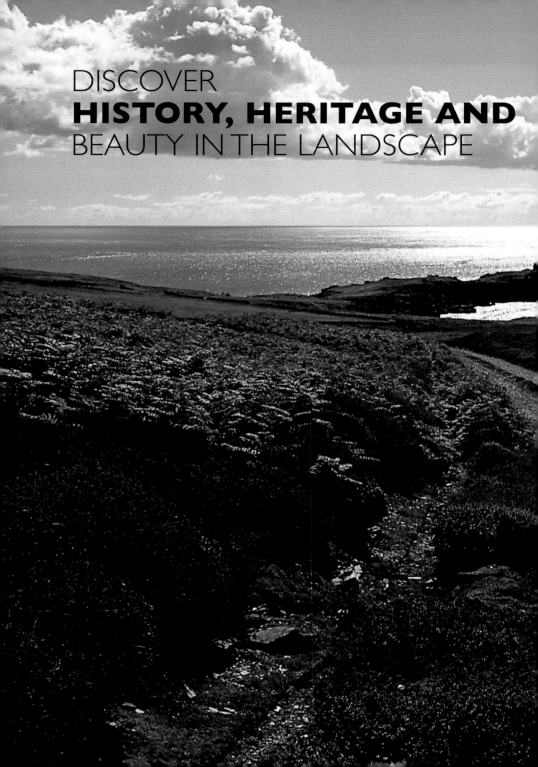

DISCOVER
HISTORY, HERITAGE AND
BEAUTY IN THE LANDSCAPE

The idyllic Calf of Man — a bird and nature reserve

THE **NATURE** OF THE LANDSCAPE

There's no better place to appreciate the topography of the Isle of Man than from the top of the Island's highest peak. At 2,036 feet Snaefell is certainly no giant, but on a clear day you can see much of the Island itself and, across the Irish Sea, the Cumbrian Mountains to the east, the purple hills of Galloway to the north, Snowdonia to the south and, to the west, Ireland's Mountains of Mourne in the north and Wicklow Mountains in the south. The view from the top of Snaefell also throws light on the fact that more than forty per cent of the Island's land area is uninhabited.

Snaefell stands in the middle of the ridge of hills which runs through the Isle of Man on a north-east to south-west axis, from Ramsey to Cronk ny Arrey Laa (thought to mean 'hill of the day watch') south of Niarbyl, where the cliffs drop steeply into the sea.

Cutting across the ridge and dividing the uplands into north and south is a central valley extending from Peel to Douglas.

The large slate massif responsible for Snaefell also produced 25 peaks exceeding 1,000 feet in height. In the process it created a very pleasurable walk; you can spend a day striding across the uplands, through gorse and heather, taking in the wonderful panoramas of the Isle of Man's east and west coasts without any great rollercoaster variations in descent and ascent.

In fact, walking in the hills will take you to some of the wildest places on the Island. The scenery is spectacular, particularly with the purple heather of late summer, and the heathland is a diverse wildlife habitat of international importance. Ling, western gorse, bell heather and bilberry are the dominant plants. Blanket bog is another globally-rare habitat found in the uplands.

Birdwatchers too will have a field day. Curlew, skylark, meadow pipit and wheatear are among the species which do well up here. The Island as a whole supports a great variety of birdlife and is recognised for its healthy populations of chough, peregrine falcon, raven and hen harrier, the latter representing somewhere in the order of ten per cent of the total hen harrier population in the British Isles. Since the 1960s the Calf of Man bird and nature reserve has been home to an officially-designated British Bird Observatory.

The hills have broad ridges with relatively smooth slopes merging into wide drainage basins. Streams cutting into the hillsides have produced the glens which collectively are one of the Isle of Man's great natural attractions.

Large areas of the uplands were once covered in forest. Tree loss in Neolithic times probably resulted in waterlogging and the formation of the peat on which the Manx people relied for fuel until relatively recently. In Viking times, many people lived on the uplands in summer, grazing livestock on the common pasture. The remains of their settlements, called 'sheilings', can still be seen.

GLENS

Though there are few valleys of significance, the Isle of Man is known for its glens, many of which have been purchased by the Manx Government as national treasures. There are 17 of these national glens – and others besides – and broadly speaking each is categorised as either mountain or coastal in nature. They vary in physical length, breadth and isolation but each is beautiful in its own way.

The national glens are also the largest areas of established broad-leafed woodland. Many are characterised by tumbling waterfalls, and the rushing waters of the steep glens were once put to good use for milling, mineral extraction and to drive turbines in the manufacture of paper. Relics of such enterprise can be found in the shape of disused mine shafts and buildings.

When Victorian holidaymakers started coming to the Island in large numbers, pleasure gardens, railways, follies and other attractions were created to further romanticise and popularise the glens.

A fine example of a mountain glen is Sulby (also known as Tholt-e-Will Glen). It starts from a spring in peat moss on the west slopes of Snaefell and runs down to Sulby. It is river-worn (the Sulby River is the Island's longest), deep and bold and represents an image of the grandest of Manx scenery in miniature. One of the glen's most charming attractions is the Tholton craft studio and shop. This produces only genuine Manx crafts, including the Isle of Man's only handmade teddy bears.

Glen Auldyn is perhaps the gentlest of Manx mountain glens and starts on the north of Snaefell as a trickling rill, then runs down through forest and a couple of hamlets to Milntown on the B17. The views at the top end are splendid.

One of the loveliest of the short coastal glens is Ballaglass, near Maughold Head in the north. It is easily accessible by Manx Electric Railway. You can walk its total length or just a section of it nearer the sea. The lower wooded part is wonderful in spring when coloured by bluebells, and the area is rich in folklore. Here you might just encounter the spectre of the giant Irish deer, the 'Londhoo'.

Dhoon Glen, a little further south and also on the route of the Manx Electric Railway, is typical of the quaint coastal glens. From the car park the walk down to the beach takes about half an hour.

West Baldwin reservoir

PARKS AND GARDENS

The Victorian tourist boom spawned a good number of parks. Many have lost their grandeur but are still very pleasant and relaxing, most with free access.

The Arboretum at St John's is a fine spot for a picnic. The park's abundant trees and shrubs were gifted to the Manx nation by world governments in celebration of the Tynwald Millennium, the 1,000th year of the Manx Parliament, in 1979. Nearby are the Manx Wild Flower Garden and the nursery gardens of the Forestry Department.

Douglas has many parks and gardens, tended with great pride. Best known are undoubtedly the sunken gardens on the promenade. Noble's Park, with its sporting and leisure facilities, and the original colonnaded Villa Marina gardens – retained as part of the all-new Villa Marina complex – were donated to the town by Henry Bloom Noble. From July to October, Summerhill Glen is a joy for children, the evenings brightened by fairy lights and illuminated animal displays. Douglas even has its own special rose – the Douglas Centenary – which celebrated the capital's 100th year as a borough in 1996. To the north end of Douglas Bay, and within walking distance of most of the Douglas hotels, is Onchan Park, which offers a great variety of family entertainment through to late summer.

Laxey has fine natural gardens. The sheltered site of the old mine washing floors has been turned into a garden to blend in with the surrounding landscape.

The biggest park in Ramsey is Mooragh. There are rowing boats, canoes, pedaloes and sailing dinghies for hire and you can learn to sail, canoe or windsurf. There are also a bowling green, crazy golf and putting green, and along the banks of the Sulby River you can enjoy the nature trails of the Poyll Dooey (Pool of the Black Ford) wetlands.

ONSHORE AND OFFSHORE

The best way to appreciate the breathtaking beauty of the Isle of Man's 100-mile coastline

'monuments' in the form of Ogham stones, and there are four fine examples in the Isle of Man dating from the 4th century.

The Romans certainly knew of the Isle of Man, but they never came as settlers and their influence, though profound on mainland Britain, was negligible here.

The Norsemen were a different proposition altogether. Essentially a maritime people, they found fame and plunder on the high seas. They harried Scotland and established colonies in the Orkneys, the Inner and Outer Hebrides and Northern Ireland. It was inevitable that they would eventually land on the Isle of Man and disrupt its peace.

What is thought to be the earliest recorded attack on the Island occurred in 798 when the Vikings landed on what is now St Patrick's Isle, off Peel. By the end of the 9th century there were Viking settlers and the Island became a pawn in the fight between Ireland and the Kings of Scandinavia.

Understandably, historical evidence is obscure, but a character from this period has formed a great part of early Manx history. Though his identity is disputed, 'King Orry' is attributed with establishing three important bulwarks of Manx society – the State, a legislative body and a standing army. The chronicles of the monks of Rushen Abbey favour the Viking King Godred Crovan, son of Harald the Black of Iceland, as the real 'King Orry'. He reached Mann in 1075 but was heavily defeated by the inhabitants. He returned with a strengthened army and landed in Ramsey Bay. Legend has it that on landing he looked up at the clear night sky and the Milky Way and declared, "There is my path, running from my country to this place", or words to that effect.

Ever since, the Manx have called the Milky Way 'Yn Rad Mooar Ree Goree' (the great track of King Orry). King Orry was sufficiently fortified to defeat the Manx on this occasion, in battle on Skyhill. He spared his vanquished opponents and ruled for 16 years. The name of King Orry is still much loved and used on the Island.

Godred Crovan established the Kingdom of Mann and the Isles and with him begins the real recorded history of the Island. There are two important 'ship burial' excavations on the Island, at Knock-y-Dooney, near Kirk Andreas, and at Balladoole, in Kirk Arbory, which date from this time. Chiefs were buried in this way. Their ship was drawn ashore and equipped with everything they might need for the 'journey to Odin', including a sword, spear, fishing gear, a bowl and a sacrificial knife.

The second Scandinavian period, started by Godred Crovan, lasted from 1079 to 1266. It is a period of great importance for the development of the Manx system of government. Godred ruled the British islands, from Dublin and Leinster to the Isle of Lewis. His descendants were to rule Mann for nearly two hundred years. At various times, the kings lived in Dublin, Northumbria and Mann. During the transition period from warriors of the seas to landowners and farmers, the Vikings left the Celts to run the farms and harvest the crops while they traded with the adjacent islands, Iceland and southern Europe.

The Cistercian Abbey of St Mary was built and constituted at Rushen Abbey during this period. It quickly became a source of great power in the Island and was a huge influence on the lives of the islanders. Another important development near the end of this period was the tying of the Island's fortunes to the English crown. Reginald, a tough Viking who reputedly spent three long years at sea, was desperate to hold on to Mann as part of his kingdom. In his anxiety, he swore to be a liegeman to Henry III of England, in return for two hogs' heads of wine and 120 crannocks of corn.

The Scandinavian influences have stood the test of time and still appear in a multitude of ways in everyday life in the Island. The most marked features are the land tenure system, the legislature and the Diocese of

Mull Circle, a Neolithic tomb overlooking Port Erin

Sodor and Mann, all of which differ greatly from their counterparts in Great Britain. There are many words of Scandinavian extraction including Snaefell, the Island's highest peak, which means 'Snow Mountain'. The Norse settlers used 'by' as the ending to many of their words and this remains a feature in many place names. Kirby meaning church farm, Colby meaning Kolli's farm, Jurby as Ivar's farm, and Sulby are a few examples.

Although the Vikings eventually became Christians, it was not before they had extinguished the light of Christianity, which had burned brightly on Mann from the 4th century onwards. Around the beginning of the 11th century the Manx began, once again, to embrace Christianity. From the time of the founding of Rushen Abbey by the Cistercians of Furness Abbey in Barrow, it is possible to get a clearer picture of developments from the writings of the monks.

The Manx bishops are known as the Bishops of Sodor and Man, and the earliest reference to the Diocese of Sodor and Man seems to be in 1154. Consisting of the southern islands of Scotland, it extended from the Hebrides to Arran and the Isle of Man itself. Sodor owes its derivation from two Norse words meaning southern isles, so in fact Sodor and Man means 'the southern Isles and Man'.

Bishops have always played an important role in the history of the Island, sometimes leading the people by good example, at other times abusing their power and privileged position. In 1266 the connection between the Isles and Sodor came to an end, although the diocese continued to be under the rule of a distant Norwegian Archbishop until the 15th century. It was during this period the Island was divided into parishes.

After Norse rule had come to an end, the Isle of Man was the subject of many struggles, which saw its ownership passing between the Scots and the English. It was not until 1346 that the Island came firmly and finally under English rule. During this period, immediately before the long reign of the

Sulby Glen

Sunset over Peel Castle and St Patrick's Isle

Stanleys, the Island's people suffered grievously. Contemporary writings of the time report that the Island was 'desolate and full of wretchedness'. In another report the writer told of a great battle on the slopes of South Barrule, in which Irish freebooters who plundered everything of value heavily defeated the Manx. Only the purchase of corn from Ireland saved the people from starvation. So poor were the Islanders that they could no longer afford to make any more of the magnificent crosses for which they had been renowned in earlier times.

The Stanley dynasty ruled the Isle of Man from 1405 to 1736. The first King of Man, Sir John Stanley I, never came to the Island and was succeeded by his son Sir John Stanley II, a wise but somewhat despotic ruler, who at least conferred some benefits on the people. It is recorded that there were two revolts against his authority. To prevent a repetition, he increased the power of the governors and substituted trial by battle with trial by jury as a means of settling disputes. Many of his successors did not visit their kingdom, and those who did come often paid only a fleeting visit.

The next major turning point in the story of Man came with the arrival of James Stanley, the 7th Earl of Derby, referred to by the Manx as 'Yn Stanlagh Mooar' ('The Great Stanley'). In 1643 he was ordered to the Isle of Man by Charles I of England to put down a threatened revolt by the Manx. Hiding an iron hand in a velvet glove, he soon made himself popular. Although the people of this period enjoyed the peace, they had less liberty.

With Charles II on the English throne, Yn Stanlagh Mooar proved his loyalty once more to the Crown. Leading his troops, 300 of them Manxmen, he set off in support of the King but was defeated and executed.

At this time, the great Manx patriot William Christian ('Illiam Dhone' to the Manx) anticipated punitive action against the Islanders and ordered the militia to take all

military installations. Everything was captured, including Peel and Rushen castles – soon given up by Stanley's widow – and the Island eventually surrendered to the Parliamentarians.

William Christian paid a terrible price for his actions. After the Restoration, some ten years after leading the revolt against the Countess of Derby, he was executed by shooting on Hango Hill at Castletown.

The 18th century was a turbulent period for the Manx. The end of rule by the Stanleys, serious disputes with the English Parliament, and the destruction of the smuggling trade (the only way the Island had been kept afloat financially) all caused unrest. The period also saw the passing of The Act of Settlement in 1704, effectively the Island's Magna Carta, and in 1736 under the rule of the 2nd Duke of Atholl, the Manx Bill of Rights was introduced. This Act in effect did away with despotic government and replaced it with an oligarchic government – the Keys or the Lower House of Tynwald. Constitutional Government was just around the corner.

Working hard for the people for more than half a century during this era was the much-loved Bishop Thomas Wilson, Bishop of Sodor and Man for 58 years. He fed the populace in times of crop failure, promoted education, established schools and libraries, and laboured long on behalf of the Manx State.

On 11th July 1765 the Island passed into the ownership of the British Crown. As the Manx standard was lowered at Castle Rushen and the Union Jack raised, George III was proclaimed King of Man. John the 3rd Duke of Atholl had sold the Island to the Imperial Parliament for £70,000. The prosperity of the Island, such as it was, disappeared overnight with the demise of the smuggling trade and London appeared well satisfied. This was not to be the end of the Atholl connections with the Isle of Man.

As the Island fell into decay and its people

into despair, the government in London felt obliged to try and rectify this state of affairs and in 1793 appointed the 4th Duke of Atholl to be Governor. This appointment was not a success and in 1829 he severed his relationship with the Island for the sum of £417,000 and left.

George IV, King of Great Britain and Ireland, became Lord of Man. The period immediately after the Duke's departure saw little change. London continued to control the Island's revenue, and the House of Keys still largely ignored the peoples' wishes by electing one of their 'own' whenever a vacancy in the House occurred. Help was at hand though, in the name of Mr Henry Loch, later to be Lord Loch and after whom part of Douglas promenade is named.

Appointed as Governor in 1863, Henry Loch brought energy and a real sense of purpose to the position. Working closely with Tynwald Court, lengthy negotiations with Her Britannic Majesty's Government were eventually concluded in 1866 to ensure that after the running expenses of the Manx Government were met, any surpluses could

be retained on the Isle of Man for improvements to a fledgling infrastructure. Part of the agreement called for the House of Keys to be popularly elected and for the English Government to receive a sum of £10,000 annually from insular revenue as a contribution towards the defence of the Realm, a payment that, although much increased, continues today.

Even before the arrival of Governor Loch, the Island had achieved popularity as a holiday destination. Certainly with more and more of the revenue being retained locally and spent on improving the infrastructure, it was not too long before the population increased and communications to and from the Island vastly improved. Towards the end of the 1800s, as the railways and their associated shipping companies opened up the adjacent islands to travel for all, a whole new industry mushroomed in the Isle of Man – tourism.

Much of the infrastructure that exists today owes its initial development to this period. Hotels, railways, piers, theatres, reservoirs, steamships and roads all played their part in thrusting the Island to the forefront of the domestic British leisure market, such as it was.

As the new post-Victorian era arrived, the Island rose to the challenge of mass tourism and for decades happily served the Lancashire cotton workers, the Yorkshire miners, Scottish engineers, Geordie shipbuilders and a whole host of other folk and their families as they sought their annual escape from a life of hard work. During the 20th century the Isle of Man, like every other place around the world, witnessed huge changes to its economy with the decline of traditional industries and the lightning march of technology. It has been a period to challenge even the very cornerstone of Manx character and philosophy. As the inscription with the ancient Three Legs of Man symbol so proudly declares, 'Quocunque Jeceris Stabit' – Whichever Way You Throw Me I Stand.

Rushen Abbey, Ballasalla

WALLABIES **AND** OTHER WILDLIFE

So wild and wonderful is the nature of the Isle of Man that the ancient gods who supervised its construction must surely have been great lovers of the countryside.

With its central mountainous uplands capped in heather moorland, rolling lower slopes of characteristic small fields and high stone-built hedges, and wide open coastal areas, the Island's dramatic and varied landscape is a vision of breathtaking beauty.

The Island's relatively modest size means that within the space of a few miles or a short drive you can experience the rolling surf of the Irish Sea pounding the coastline and the semi-alpine conditions of the mountain tops.

The isolation of the Island from its mainland neighbours has resulted in a distinct ecology. There are no native large mammals to be found here: deer, badger, fox and otter are all absent from these shores, and as in Ireland there are no snakes either. As a result, many other species do very well. Both brown and mountain hares, which are increasingly scarce in the British Isles, are relatively

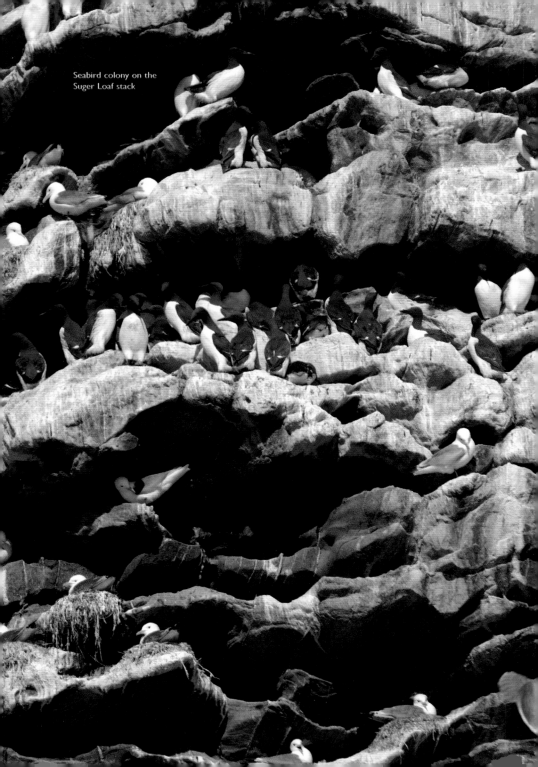
Seabird colony on the
Suger Loaf stack

common, and polecats can still be found by careful observers in some of the many conifer plantations. Feral populations of goats, ferrets and even wallabies have become established, particularly in the north of the Island, while around the shores there is a strong population of both Atlantic and grey seals. Good places to observe seals are the Sound in the south, around Peel Castle in the west and in the vicinity of the Ayres in the north. The Island's isolation also protected the seal populations from the ravages of the two outbreaks of phocine distemper – the disease which killed so many of these wonderful animals along the eastern shores of the UK.

For birdwatchers, a visit to the Isle of Man promises to be a very special treat. Currently there is a healthy and expanding population of choughs throughout the Island, though particularly localised in the south, in the Port Erin region. In the uplands you are likely to find wild red grouse and peregrines which nest in some of the more remote cliff locations, while along the rocky coastline puffins, Manx shearwaters, gannets, cormorants and shags are all to be seen in good numbers.

The sight of hen harriers is another reward for visitors to the Island. Their population on the Isle of Man is currently about 60 breeding pairs, with many adolescent birds in addition. A walk during summer in an upland valley or glen is almost certain to show you at least one of these magnificent raptors hunting along the lines of the old walls, while in spring a courting pair engaged in their aerial dance over the heather moor is a sight and sound to remember. However, for a really unique view of these birds, you shouldn't miss going to the Ballaugh Curraghs in late autumn and winter. Stand on the rooftop platform of the hide at the Manx Wildlife Trust's Close Sartfield reserve in early evening and you'll witness large groups of these birds flying in to congregate at one of the biggest winter hen harrier roosts in Europe. During 2000, the highest count for

the number of these rare birds seen in just one short evening was 110.

Another rarity which visiting ornithologists may have the good fortune to encounter is the corncrake. Now absent from almost all of mainland Britain, this species is pretty much restricted to the Scottish isles and Northern Ireland. But small numbers continue to breed on the Isle of Man and it always pays to keep an ear out for the strange 'crek-crek' call of the males in spring, especially when near hay meadows. To actually see a corncrake now is a truly unusual event.

Particularly good places for bird lovers and wildlife enthusiasts are Langness, where many migrant visitors make their landfall, and the Ayres. The Ayres is of particular note as it is one of those strange contrasts found on an island of this size. The northern plain is a post-glacial till and as a result has a low-lying rolling landscape not found anywhere else on the Island. The strong coastal currents and substrata of soft rocks and glacial sands have formed the huge shingle dune formation that is the Ayres. Looking like a piece of the north Norfolk coastline that's been tacked on to the rocky shores of the Isle of Man is a wide, open beach, 4 miles long, backed by dunes, slacks, lowland heath and an almost unique lichen heath ecology. As well as the sight of hundreds of orchids and nesting little terns in spring, you can enjoy watching seals, basking sharks, porpoises and whales passing through the fast tidal channel that lies just a stone's throw from the beach.

Another good location at which to see the rich coastal wildlife is the Sound, at the south-west tip of the Island. Here you can sit and look across another fast-flowing – and deep – tidal channel towards the Calf of Man and listen to the call of adult male seals as they bask on the rocks. Harbour porpoise, dolphins, minke whales and basking sharks are all regular visitors, and the views of the Sugar Loaf rock and its seabird colony are just a short stroll away. For the best view of the marine life you need to take a boat trip. Only

Snowdrops, one of many species of wild flower which thrive on the Isle of Man

then can you really appreciate the sheer size and magnificence of a basking shark at close quarters.

Away from the coast there is an abundance of other wildlife to see. The Island is ringed with numerous rain-fed rivers tumbling down from the uplands, many of them cutting steep winding gorges as they pass. Apart from the Sulby they are modest in size compared with rivers of mainland Britain, but most support trout, salmon and a range of aquatic life that is mostly free of pollution due to the lack of intensive industry. Many of these valleys have been planted by the Victorians and are now classed as National Glens, freely accessible and open at all times. Awash with bluebells, violets and primroses in spring, these wooded valleys hold a special place in Manx natural history.

For botanists too there are treasures to be found throughout the Isle of Man. Atop Snaefell you may be lucky in finding the small colony of alpine least willow, a last survivor of the ice ages, while lower down

the mountain sides are cotton grass, bilberry, sundew and a variety of other upland species, sometimes in abundance. The dominant purple of the heathers in summer is characteristic of these habitats, but look closer below the heather's protecting arms and you'll find a miniature garden alive with mosses.

Also characteristic of the Island's lowlands are the areas known as Curraghs (pronounced khur-uck). These low-lying wetlands are a combination of small scrub woodlands dominated by willows and alder, with wet grassland, sedges and rushes often mixed in. Important for a variety of wildlife, they are particularly critical for plants, including the royal fern, and for many species of orchid such as the heath-spotted, northern marsh, butterfly, twayblade and others. The jewel in the crown of these sites is the Close Sartfield reserve in the northern Ballaugh Curragh area. Here in late May and June you can walk amongst a colony of over 100,000 orchids growing together. Curragh habitat also occurs at the bottom end of valleys throughout the Island, and little gems can be seen just a stone's throw from the centre of Douglas and Ramsey, as well as tucked away at the head of many river valleys and glens.

Out on the coastal cliffs and shores you can discover another range of wild flowers. The often steep rocky coastline is sometimes alive with the colours of a rock garden, decorated by a mosaic patchwork of thrift, spring squill, sea campion, harebells, maidenhair ferns and stonecrops formed around the exposed rocks and soil. Areas such as Scarlett outside Castletown, Marine Drive and the slopes around Niarbyl, to name just a few, can hold great swathes of these natural rock gardens in spring and summer.

Away from the steep rocky shores, out on the open sand or shingle beaches, look for the yellow-horned poppy as well as the scarce Isle of Man cabbage – a plant restricted to the Island and other shores fringing the Irish Sea.

And as you drive, walk or ride around the Island's roads, take a moment to look at the verges you pass. Traditional Manx sod hedges are solid, built of earth and stone, and home to a wide variety of plants and animals, typically orchids, foxgloves, lizards and butterflies.

Some hedges show handsome displays of bluebells, primroses and valerian, while others such as those around Archallegan present an orchid show to shame many a nature reserve. Others hold good populations of elm, a tree that has all but disappeared from much of England due to the ravages of Dutch elm disease, and the powerful scent of abundant wild garlic in spring can seal the picture of these green roadsides in the memory for life.

The Curraghs wetlands attract abundant insects and butterflies

wallabies **and**other **WILDLIFE**

MANX **HERITAGE** AND THE STORY OF MANN

Manx National Heritage is one organisation but responsible for six distinctly different and wide-ranging functions. It is at once the Isle of Man's Museum Service, Art Gallery, National Library & Archives, Ancient Monuments Service, National Trust and National History Recording Service. The purpose of these varied roles is to care for and to tell the history of the Island and to provide research facilities for students.

The Island's history is presented by Manx National Heritage through the innovative and award-winning *Story of Mann*. From the hub – the Manx Museum ('Thie Tashtee Vannin', the Treasure House) in Douglas – the story radiates out to other Manx National Heritage sites across the Island, encouraging you to interact with the story in the most interesting way possible and to see these attractions first hand.

Ideally, your starting point is to take a seat in the Manx Museum lecture theatre to view *The Story of Mann* – a 20-minute film normally shown every half an hour during the day. It gives you an overview of the

Island's history and landscape. The idea then is to proceed through the different areas of the museum, starting with the art gallery, where all the pictures are either of the Isle of Man or are by Manx artists – a policy common to all of the Museum's collections.

Art is followed by maps and geology and a never-ending argument about whether lead or slate is the most important. Prehistory, Celts and Vikings lead through to later history, tourism and war-time internment, with side paths of literature and home design.

Model boats and typical buildings take you to the exhibition gallery, which regularly hosts temporary displays of art or history. A small exhibition links the entrance to the reading room for the library and archives, and nearby are the Bay Room Restaurant and museum shop.

Throughout the museum trail there is generous use of videos and other electronic displays, with links to the other relevant sites, monuments and landscape which are under the protection of Manx National Heritage.

Peel's interactive and ingenious House of Manannan may well be your next turn of the page in following the *Story of Mann*. It is very entertaining in bringing the Island's Celtic and Viking past to life, using a combination of video, audio and authentic recreations such as a Celtic roundhouse centred around an imaginary family of the time. The magic and wizardry are led by Manannan himself, shape shifter that he is, as the video presenter of the documentary-style tale.

Moving on in time, a replica longship, two-thirds actual size, forms the link between the Vikings and maritime history. The ship, *Odin's Raven*, was built in Norway in 1979 and in that year sailed to the Island to mark the Manx Millennium.

The House of Manannan also uses a dozen or so other characters from differing periods of the past to tell their stories. Other devices and subjects include a busy quayside scene, the natural history of the coasts, kippers and the Steam Packet, all bringing you to a final

section which introduces Peel Castle and urges you to make the short journey along the waterfront to visit it. When you do, Manannan's voice takes you wherever you want to go and explains the fortifications and buildings including the old cathedral.

More aspects of the *Story of Mann* are revealed at Rushen Abbey, Ballasalla. Founded in 1134 as a daughter house of Furness in Cumbria, it gives the opportunity to explore the remains of a small but important Cistercian abbey. Introductory displays give the history of the site and explain the background of 'the Church' then and now. At certain times of the year an archaeological dig is likely to be in progress with the possibility of being able to talk to those involved, either direct or via a video link. There are child-friendly areas where to a limited extent you can enjoy experiences such as an archaeological dig, identification of finds, building a Gothic arch and trying to produce your own version of the *Chronicles of Mann* as written by the monks.

Replica longship in the House of Manannan

Castle Rushen stands sentinel over the harbour

Not far away from the abbey is Castle Rushen – in centuries gone the main Island home of the kings and lords and today one of the best-preserved medieval castles in Britain. Authentically-furnished rooms show how they and the garrison would have lived. The spiral staircases may prove difficult for some visitors, but there is a shortened tour using normal staircases if you require it.

The castle dominates the town which with its narrow streets and medieval layout is a joy to explore. Almost opposite the castle entrance is the Old House of Keys, where on the hour for about 50 minutes you can become a member of the (now) elected house of the Island's parliament and vote on subjects debated over the years as well as one yet to come! Tickets for these sessions have to be obtained from the Old Grammar School nearby, originally built as the town chapel of St Mary's in the first half of the 13th century and worth seeing for its *Story of Mann* displays. Across the harbour, the Nautical Museum has its own fascinating piece of the

tale to relate in the shape of the historic open cutter *Peggy*, berthed in her boathouse with the club room above. The building is full of secret cupboards and exciting stories from 200 years ago – yarns the staff are usually only too happy to tell you!

Still in the south, within easy reach of both Rushen Abbey and Castletown, is Cregneash. This was the first open-air museum in the British Isles and is very much a living village with a resident community. Certain of the buildings are kept for display purposes and those not needed for display are maintained in their traditional form externally whilst being brought up to modern standards internally. The farm is part of the complex and is in general worked in the old ways and has period animals and crops, though if modern equipment is needed for a specific task it is used. The aim of this Manx National Heritage site is to show the village and its surrounds as they were about 100 years ago.

Industry rather than agriculture is the theme of the Great Laxey Wheel. The wheel, and the mines for which it was built, show the way of life of a different part of the community – men toiling far underground but joined by women and children in the surface tasks.

Different again in the *Story of Mann* is the Grove Rural Life Museum on the northern outskirts of Ramsey. In the 19th century this house was the home of the Gibb family and it retains all of their furniture and belongings. It opened as an attraction in 1979. The Gibb sisters who lived here latterly were keen bee keepers and there are displays reflecting this.

Back in the south, the Sound Visitor Centre and cafe close to Cregneash has been created to blend into the landscape and give magnificent views and good facilities. Displays and toilets are available without necessarily patronising the cafe, although the scenery and the wildlife, especially the seals, are likely to tempt you into staying longer than you originally intended.

Manx National Heritage is the Island's National Trust, and access to all National Trust land is free and usually without

restriction (except for dogs and shooting). Some ancient monument sites are available for public viewing but many are on private property and therefore prior permission is required. In recent years access to the important Braaid complex has been acquired and you can visit the remains of the Celtic and Viking homes which stood here.

The northern part of King Orry's grave at Laxey has long been readily accessible from the Ballaragh road, and more recently the purchase of the southern part of the burial site means that this too can be seen. Another area of coast with access and parking is Fort Island on St Michael's Isle, Langness. The 16th-century artillery fort and the 11th-century chapel can be freely seen but not entered.

Recently acquired National Trust lands are at Niarbyl, whilst the lands at Spanish Head and the Maughold Brooghs have the coast path running through them and are relatively well known. Killabrega on the slopes of the Sulby Valley is perhaps less familiar to many. Eary Cushlin in the south-west contains

Nautical Museum, Castletown, and the historic open cutter *Peggy*

some of the most spectacular coastal scenery and provides access to Lag ny Keeilley, an ancient chapel, burial ground and hermitage.

There are many more sites to explore, not forgetting the Celtic and Scandinavian carved cross slabs which are in the guardianship of Manx National Heritage but in general are found at parish churches (and described where appropriate on the following pages about the Island's churches).

The Manx Museum in Douglas is open Monday to Saturday throughout the year and admission is free. The House of Manannan is open 7 days a week all year round but there is a charge, as there is for all the other sites mentioned except the Old Grammar School and the Sound Visitor Centre. The charges vary and these sites are usually open from Good Friday till the last weekend in October, 7 days a week. The Sound Visitor Centre may open at other times at the discretion of the cafe franchise holder.

Grove Museum, Ramsey

KEELS
CHAPELS
AND CHURCHES

The traditionary ballad says, "That is how the first faith came to Mann, By Holy Patrick brought to us" – which should put it into the middle years of the 5th century.

However, the earliest monastic establishment in the Irish Sea area was set up at Whithorn by St Ninian some 50 years earlier. It is unlikely that such a community within sight of the Island did not have an effect here and indeed in the 12th and 13th centuries Whithorn was the major pilgrimage destination for the Island's religious. Some of the early church dedications and people mentioned in surviving stories also suggest a connection with South Wales. Other dedications show links with Iona and St Columba and his followers. At a later date Iona was part of the Kingdom of Mann and the Isles and some of the Norse Manx kings are buried there.

The Isle of Man was very firmly part of what is known as the Celtic Church which although its ritual differed from that of Rome had no central organisation of any kind and indeed looked to the Pope as universal leader. There appear to have been perhaps as many as four or five monasteries on the Island in this early period but the only one to leave any recognisable physical trace is Maughold.

A very early Christian site pre-dating chapels is St Patrick's Chair, which is a preaching site marked by a raised rectangle of stone surmounted by three standing stones, two of which are marked with simple line crosses.

A surprising proportion of the small earth-and-stone chapels (keeils) which served the community have however left some physical remains to see and visit. Most would have been surrounded by a small circular burial ground (rhullick) contained within an earth bank. Evidence for the burial grounds survives in a number of instances and in a very few cases the remains of a small hut for the visiting priest (or resident hermit) can also be seen.

Cabbal Pherick (Pherick means Patrick) has remains of a keeil, burial ground and priest's house, but also shows the way that Celtic Christianity took over former pagan sites with its relationship to the waterfall of Spooyt Vane in Glen Mooar. Another showing this take-over is the keeil at Corrody, literally built into the centre of a Bronze Age burial mound.

A remote keeil with burial ground is keeil Vreeshey (Mary's Chapel) in the Corrany valley, where an inscribed stone was found linking it with Juan the Priest and the monastic/church site at Maughold. Another with good but very difficult access and set in the most magnificent coastal scenery is Lag ny Keeilley. This has a priest's house in addition to the burial ground, whilst the access path takes you past Chibbyr Vashtey (the Well of Baptism).

The rulings of the Synod of Whitby in 664 which should have marked the end of the Celtic Church seems to have had little effect. But in the Isle of Man reform came in the 12th century with influences both from Ireland and the monks of Furness who founded Rushen Abbey.

The main visible change even then was the setting up of the parish structure and the building of parish churches. A number of parish churches still contain work of this period but all have been altered many times. They came in a variety of sizes but one basic style – long and thin.

The original churches have a simple rectangular plan without change, other than a step in floor level, to mark the sanctuary and there are no aisles. Extra space was created later by constructing a gallery at the west end – used by the choir and the church band to provide what is now known as West Gallery Music. In the early to middle years of the 19th century the band was replaced by the organ. The access is normally from an external staircase.

These churches continued to be altered throughout the centuries. Old Kirk Braddan is a good example, while the roofless St Trinian's is perhaps the least changed, built in the 12th century and altered in the 14th. By the time Bishop Wilson arrived in 1698 most of the churches were in a bad state of repair or too small for the Island's increasing population, especially in the fast-developing towns. Bishop Wilson, like certain of the bishops who came later, instigated a major building programme.

A particularly strong programme was mounted in the 1830s by Bishop William Ward, who encouraged the use of 'named' architects from outside the Island. The most prolific of these was the Hansom and Welch partnership in its various forms. Joseph Hansom was the man who designed and gave his name to the Hansom cab. They came to the Island in connection with King William's College but were responsible for rebuilding Onchan, Kirk Michael and Ballaugh, although the old church here was not demolished. John Welch, the successor to the partnership, was also responsible for 'the triplets', the three multi-purpose churches of St Luke, St James (at Dalby) and St Stephen (at Sulby), although this last has been greatly altered since.

In 1844 the newly-appointed archdeacon, Joseph Christian Moore, had his cousin Ewan Christian alter his church at Andreas. Christian

Onchan Church

FAIRIES
AND
OTHER FOLKLORE

If the British Isles is considered to be one of the most haunted and supernatural places in the world, then the Isle of Man can probably be thought of as the centre of this supernatural activity. Virtually every square mile of the Island lays claim to its own tales of fairies and other unearthly creatures.

The Isle of Man has a wide and varied folklore tradition but the most famous and well-known aspect of Manx folklore is its fairy belief. Manx fairies, or Themselves as they are called by the Manx, are not the small pretty creatures with gossamer wings illustrated in children's fairy tale books. Instead, Themselves are described as small human-like creatures, often three or four feet in height and dressed in blue or green with red peaked caps, who most definitely do not have wings.

Traditionally they are neither good nor bad and can be quite helpful or spiteful depending on how the mood takes them. They also take offence easily, which is why you should never talk about them directly or call them by name but only use terms such as Themselves or Mooiney Veggey (Manx Gaelic for the Little Folk). Therefore, when crossing the Fairy

Bridge on the main Douglas to Castletown road en route to and from the airport, it is always important to be extra polite and say hello to Themselves. It is uncertain how old this tradition actually is, but for several years locals and visitors alike have been very careful to observe it, and many have cautionary tales of what happens when you forget to say hello!

Tradition also has it that Themselves were particularly fond of hunting, feasting and fighting, with pitch battles between different bands of fairies. There are several sites on the Island specifically identified with such fairy activity.

The Fairy Mound in Rushen, next to Rowany Golf Course, was considered to be the home of one of these fairy bands. A young man walking home late one night was 'took' by Themselves into the Fairy Mound where he witnessed a great fairy banquet. He managed to escape to tell his tale, taking with him a fairy cup as evidence of his adventures. Most are not so lucky and are doomed to stay permanently in the Fairy Kingdom or to escape decades later, Rip Van Winkle style.

Another story of such a rare trophy relates to the Ballafletcher fairy cup given to the Fletcher family by the Lhiannan Shee (the 'peaceful spirit') of Ballafletcher. The Lhiannan Shee promised to protect the family and ensure no harm came to them as long as the cup remained unbroken and stayed within the family. The Fletcher family no longer lives at Ballafletcher, now known as Kirby, but the cup traditionally known as the Ballafletcher Fairy Cup still exists and can be seen on display at the Manx Museum in Douglas.

Fairy Hunts were considered to be a popular pursuit by Themselves, with various popular fairy hunting grounds being found around Douglas. A more physical relic of these nocturnal hunting parties is the 'Saddlestone' on the Saddlestone Road just outside Douglas. Here an apparently nondescript large stone protruding from a field wall is identified as being a saddle magically turned to stone.

The story is that the vicar of the parish

Fairy Bridge at Santon

found his horse tired and sweating every morning although it appeared that no one had ridden it. Very early one morning, as he returned home from a late-night visit to a sick parishioner, he saw the reason why his horse was always exhausted. A group of fairies was taking the saddle off his horse, which they had just ridden all night. When the fairies saw the vicar, they vanished in panic and horror and the saddle, which they had put on the wall, turned to stone! Maybe a more plausible explanation is that the stone was built into the wall to help people to mount their horses at the roadside – but the Fairy Saddlestone is the more popular and favoured version.

Another great fear and concern for the Island's people was that Themselves took human babies and exchanged them for fairy changelings. As a result there were several ways to protect babies from being 'took'. The most powerful form of protection was to have a child baptised as soon as possible. Another was to sew vervain, the potent and powerful Manx herb, into the baby's clothes. If all else failed, it was critical to always put the iron tongs across the cradle if the child had to be left alone for even a moment – iron was considered a great

Winter snow, Snaefell

defence against Themselves.

Fairies were believed to be particularly powerful and active at certain times of the year, one of the most dangerous being the end of winter and beginning of summer, May Eve. This was the time when the cattle, who had been kept inside all winter, were put back out on to summer pastures. It was also when cows began to produce milk again. Milk was an important part of the Manx rural economy because of its versatility – used as a drink and for making butter and bonnag (Manx soda bread). So for a subsistence crofting community, the difference between a cow producing milk and not producing milk could be the difference between respectable poverty and borderline starvation – and there was understandable anxiety that Themselves could stop the cows from milking or stop the butter from being made by tainting the milk.

Therefore every possible precaution was taken on May Eve when Themselves were abroad. There were two main lines of defence. One was to spread primroses or other yellow flowers such as kingcups (the more powerful and effective Manx blutyn) on doorsteps and thresholds to stop evil spirits from crossing over; and the other was to make and put up over the doorway a crosh cuirn or rowan/mountain ash cross. The small crosh cuirn was made from two Rowan twigs formed into a cross shape and tied together with a length of handtwisted sheep's wool.

To make sure the cross was effective as a protective charm, no iron could be used in making it. Therefore the twigs should be broken by hand and not cut with a knife. To be extra sure of protection, the crosh cuirns would be put up over the entrance to the cowshed and even tied to the cows' tails. People may not be so concerned now about protecting their cows from Themselves but many people on the Island still put up crosh cuirns on May Eve. When visiting Cregneash Village Folk Museum, have a look inside the doorway of Harry Kelly's cottage and see a crosh cuirn already positioned to do its work!

Hunt the Wren, a Boxing Day tradition

The Isle of Man has more than one type of fairy. A solitary and hardworking but potentially bad-tempered Manx fairy is the Phynodderree – a large hairy shaggy house elf. The Phynodderree is renowned for being a good worker and helper to any Manx farmer lucky enough to have one. The only problem is that if the Phynodderree is offered a new set of clothes by a farmer as thanks and payment for all his hard work, he will be mortally offended by the gift and instantly disappear.

Another potential problem is that sometimes he takes his work far too seriously. Visitors to the Island can see the mountain railway climbing to the top of Snaefell, but folklore tells of something far more alarming rushing around the mountain top. The Phynodderree was rounding up a flock of Manx Loaghtan sheep and, having easily caught 99 of them, proceeded to spend the rest of the long night on the slopes looking for the missing one. It took several hours but he finally made it, placing the last small Loaghtan back in the pen

A sure sign that it's Christmas!

with the rest of the flock. Proud that he now had them all, the poor Phynodderree was dismayed to discover from the farmer that he only had 99 sheep and he had spent several hours trying to catch a mountain hare!

Not all Manx fairies are so hardworking or even mischievous, and one stands out as the most dangerous and terrifying of all – the buggane. This is the evil hobgoblin of the Manx fairy kingdom. Although there are various tales of bugganes around the Island, the most famous is the tale associated with the roofless church of St Trinian's on the main road between Douglas and Peel.

The tale is told that several attempts were made to complete the church but that each time it neared the final stage, the buggane would appear and tear off the roof. As the fearsome reputation of the buggane grew and a new roof was put on the church, a bet was made by the local tailor, Timothy, that he would stay in the church and make a pair of trousers regardless of what the buggane may or

may not do.

The tailor promptly undertook the wager and sat in the newly-completed church making a pair of trousers. But as he sewed away, the buggane slowly emerged up through the church floor uttering fearsome oaths. The tailor, undaunted, kept on sewing as the buggane continued to threaten him. When the last stitch was sewn the tailor fled from the church. The buggane tore the roof off, leaving behind the ruin you see today, and chased the tailor all the way to St Ruinius (Old Marown) Church, where the tailor dived over the churchyard wall for safety. In his fury at being outsmarted, the buggane tore off his own head and threw it in vain at the tailor. Although the tailor was safe and the tale has a happy ending, St Trinian's Church is still roofless.

In addition to fairies and hobgoblins, the Island has its own Black Dog – the Moddey Dhoo of Peel Castle. This is one of the oldest folk tales on the Isle of Man and was first published in 1732. The tale though is said to be older still and relates to a period in the 1600s when Peel Castle was a fortress with its own garrison of soldiers.

By all accounts, the soldiers on night guard duty had become accustomed to the fact that they were not alone and that they shared their guardroom with a spectral hound. One of them, under the influence of too much drink, announced that he was not afraid of the black dog. So when the castle keys needed to be returned to the Captain of the Guard, he was happy to do it on his own although his friends warned him strongly against it. Off he went, alone, followed by the Moddey Dhoo, which had left its usual resting place by the fireside.

Shortly afterwards, the guard's screams were heard echoing through the castle. Although he lived for three more days, the guard could not utter a single word or in any way describe what had frightened him, and the Moddey Dhoo was never seen again in Peel Castle.

Castle Rushen too has its supernatural side. There are stories of miles of underground passages, chambers and even magnificent

Native Manx Loaghtan sheep

mansions. The entrance to this mysterious underworld was apparently sealed up because all those who ventured down into the tunnels never returned, except for one brave soul who took the precaution of leaving behind him a trail of thread to lead him back out. This intrepid explorer, although courageous enough to travel through the underground passages, couldn't quite conjure up the nerve to enter the last mansion, where a great giant was asleep on a massive table. After making his retreat he was informed that his act of discretion rather than bravery had saved him – and so he lived to tell his tale.

Manx folklore can be witnessed as a living tradition, both on Tynwald Day (Old Midsummer's Day, July 5th) at St John's and when White Boys perform the traditional Christmas mummers' play around the streets of Peel.

Tynwald Day is the Island's national day, when the Island's Parliament, Tynwald, holds an annual open-air sitting on Tynwald Hill for the reading aloud of all new laws. Part of this tradition is that rushes are strewn along the processional way as a symbolic tribute to Manannan, the mythical sea god and shape-shifting magician king who is brought vividly to life in the House of Manannan heritage centre in Peel.

Christmas of course has its own special magic, and a variety of Manx festive customs are still practised on the Island. Traditionally, Christmas on the Isle of Man was never a single day's celebrations but rather twelve whole days (and nights) of festivities and merrymaking and was appropriately called 'Foolish Fortnight' (or Y Kegeesh Ommydagh in Manx).

The Christmas period would begin on Christmas Eve with the Oie'l Voirrey service, held in local parish churches decorated with seasonal hibbin as hullin (festoons of ivy and large branches of holly). After a short service, the clergymen would leave and the Oie'l Voirrey would begin in earnest with the

Mill at Douglas is now converted into offices. Only Laxey flour mill continues in use as a mill.

The real growth industry in the latter part of the 17th and early part of the 18th century was what has become known as 'the trade' – a euphemism for the noble art of smuggling. Fortunes were won and lost smuggling 'duty free' French wine and brandy into England. Lucrative profit was also to be had importing salt and goods from East India and China. The end for such activities came with the 'Mischief Act' of 1765.

By the start of the 19th century, woollen and cotton milling had found a small following in the Island, the principle establishments being at Sulby, Laxey, St John's and the Douglas area. Traces of the buildings remain and place names such as Union Mills and Tynwald Mills give big clues as to their location. Remnants of the industry can be seen at St George's woollen mills at Laxey.

By far the most important of the mills in this particular line of business was Moore's mill at Cronkbourne on the outskirts of Douglas. The mill was the first truly mechanised factory and provided industrial workers' cottages nearby, along with electric light from the factory. The mill produced sailcloth of excellent quality and at one time held a contract to supply the British Admiralty and a suit of sails for *SS Great Britain*. However, the factory's eventual fate was that it became the Island's largest laundry works.

From the 13th century fishing had existed as an industry alongside farming, reaching its height at the turn of the 19th century and encouraging other trades in its wake. Boatbuilding became a major industry in the principal towns and Peel was the fishing capital of the Island, its boats produced by several local shipyards.

Qualtroughs of Castletown and Port St Mary built top-sail schooners which not only traded in the Irish Sea but also as far as the Baltic. At Ramsey the shipyard produced

A monument to Foxdale's 19th-century Beckwiths mine

similar vessels, including some of the earliest iron-hulled square-rigged ships. The best known was *Euterpe*, launched in 1863 and later named *Star of India*.

It is claimed to be the world's oldest active ship and is preserved at the Maritime Museum of San Diego in California.

There were shipyards in Douglas both at the inner harbour and at Bath Place opposite the present Sea Terminal. John Winram's yard built the third vessel for the Isle of Man Steam Packet Company in 1842. It was named *King Orry* and although only 140 feet in length with a displacement of 433 tons, it operated winter and summer on the Liverpool route for 16 years.

Sail and rope makers started businesses in Douglas in support of this new industry. Messrs Quiggin and Co had a ropewalk at their yard in Lake Road, roughly located where the rear aisle of the Tesco supermarket is at present; their rope was much in demand in the port of Liverpool because of its excellent quality. There were ropewalks in the most unusual places, for example in Woodbourne Lane which at the time was beyond the upper limits of the town. There were also net makers at Peel and numerous chandleries in all the major ports.

During the same period mining on the Island became a force to be reckoned with. It had been known since the 13th century that lead and silver deposits existed on the Island, but it wasn't until the middle of the 19th century that mining became a serious industry – and the dominant one at that. Trial shafts and exploration for lode-bearing veins were enthusiastically pursued, eventually centring on Laxey, Foxdale and to a lesser extent Port Erin where ore had been extracted through addits and shallow shafts for many years.

The mineral wealth of the Island in relation to its size was outstanding during the latter half of the 19th century. Between 1845 and 1900 no less than 233,292 tons of lead ore, 215,397 tons of zinc ore and 150 tons of silver were produced with smaller amounts of iron and copper. The value of the ore shipped from Laxey Mines in 1876 reached £90,000, with the value of ore produced from the Foxdale group of mines regularly reaching half that figure.

Foxdale had the most extensive workings with at one time up to twelve shafts involved. The three main shafts were Bawdens Shaft, Potts Shaft and Beckwiths Shaft, the latter being the deepest and reaching 320 fathoms. Some surface remains can still be seen at Foxdale.

Just to the west of the Shoulder Road leading to the Round Table Cross Roads there are visible remains of three more mines – Cross Vein, Dixons and Beckwiths, the latter being the most westerly of the mines in the Foxdale group and easily distinguished by the leaning brick chimney which forms a familiar landmark. At its peak 350 people were employed at Foxdale including women and children. All of the mines were hard rock mines, the upper levels in slate, the lower sections in granite and the main problem being water.

Conditions were much the same at Laxey, where the problems with water became much greater as the mines were driven deeper underground. The earliest records of mining at Laxey date from 1781. By the time the mine reached its zenith there were seven main shafts, all of which were connected underground and by 1854 were all operated by the Great Laxey Mining Company.

This was the same year in which the Great Laxey Wheel was built to pump water from the mines, from a depth of 200 fathoms. The wheel, designed by engineer Robert Casement, is now the focal point in the telling of the *Story of Mann*. The Laxey mines produced significant quantities of zinc blende and although production of lead ore was less than at Foxdale, the quality was exceptional and contributed to some of the finest silver in the British Isles.

The oldest group of mines was at Port Erin and operated latterly by the Bradda Mining Company. Although it is believed that these veins were worked in the 13th century, it wasn't until 1869 that the enterprise was significant. Shafts were sunk to a depth of 72 fathoms but their location, so close to the sea, meant that flooding was a constant problem, leading eventually to an early demise. Surface remains can be seen almost at sea level at Bradda Head.

By 1929 the mining industry of the Isle of Man had ceased due to world competition and other factors which made it no longer profitable to extract the ore.

One other extractive industry involved quarrying for building stone. There are many scars around the Island which hold testimony to this activity. In Douglas there are two large industrial sites built in what remains of two quarries from which most of the stone was won for the building of lower Douglas and the older houses on the promenade.

Summerhill Quarry nestles behind the horse tramway stables and was the source for most of the houses on the nearby sections of the promenade. At the other end of town the Douglas Head Quarries, long since defunct, form the backdrop to the inner harbour.

There were many similar quarries near to the other towns, still easily discernable. At Peel some attempt was made to obtain roofing slate but the poor quality of the country rock meant that the slates were both large and very coarse. Some better slate for

roofing was won in the Sulby Valley and at Glen Rushen where levels and inclines are visible on the hillside. Large slate lintels were obtained from the cliffs at Spanish Head near Port Erin from what can only be described as a most dangerous location.

At Billown, in the south of the Island, limestone has been worked for many years and still is to a limited degree. Remains of some of the oldest limekilns can be found here.

In 1713 the first highway act was

introduced, putting the onus on landowners to repair highways. This saw the start of many small parish quarries for the purpose of winning roadstone. As traffic increased and the horse and cart eventually gave way to the motor vehicle, the need for a harder stone became apparent and after 1923 the production of roadstone in the form of granite was concentrated on four main quarries in the Island – Oatland in Santon, Glenduff in Lezayre, The Dhoon in Maughold and Poortown near Peel. The latter is still the main source of roadstone in the Island, supplemented by production from South Barrule at the site of an earlier spar and mica quarry.

The majority of these industries fell into decline and their workers sought employment elsewhere. In the case of the miners many took their skills across the Atlantic to the New World but for many others unemployment became the stark reality.

The saviour was the tourism industry, already established in 1850 but at its climax at the start of the 20th century. It generated many small tourism-related businesses, notably manufacturers of seaside rock, confectionery, beer and mineral water. The brewing industry also blossomed. Two breweries survived into the 20th century, one at Castletown and the other in Douglas. Okells brewery is a thriving business today, producing several types of beer but in new premises on the outskirts of Douglas.

Tourism was a huge employer, but when the Depression struck a severe blow to the north of England, from where the majority of the Island's visitors came, the shockwaves were felt on the Isle of Man. Two world wars followed. Later came the advent of package holidays to the sun and suddenly there was another cloud over traditional British seaside destinations.

The Manx Government responded by attracting light industry to the Island and the manufacture of high-precision parts for the aeronautical industry resulted in significant

Travelling back in time at the Manx Museum, Douglas

new employment. But something more was needed to fill the gap – and the answer was a long-term plan to capitalise on the Isle of Man's advantageous tax laws. As a result, offshore banking, finance and insurance have presented an attractive proposition to investors and a profitable business for the Manx economy. The strategy has worked and today the Isle of Man enjoys virtually full employment.

NORTHERN
LIGHTS

Lighthouses were born out of the need to protect the lives of those in peril on the sea – yet the great fascination of these often brilliant feats of engineering goes far deeper than the vital function they perform.

Towering above treacherous shorelines and from remote rocks far out in the ocean, these beacons of reassurance inhabit some of the least hospitable places on earth and stand up against the most hostile conditions nature can contrive. Even in the 21st century, this triumph over the elements appeals greatly to our imaginations and sense of wonder. Tales of the men who built them and those who served in them until the switch to automatic operation are woven into the very fabric of Britain's rich maritime heritage.

Today there is more interest in lighthouses than there has ever been, with many groups dedicated to researching and preserving this heritage for younger and future generations. The first lighthouses of the Isle of Man were built in the early 19th century and their history, and that of subsequent Island lights, is very well recorded.

Weather vane, Ramsey harbour light

wasted no time in bringing about. Fortunately, despite the appalling conditions, the crew of ten were able to take to the ship's lifeboat and make the beach safely at Port Moar, just to the south of the lighthouse.

A more bizarre incident in lighthouse history occurred on 20th March 1947. An R.A.F. Spitfire returning to the nearby airfield at Jurby in bad fog hit the keepers' houses, causing extensive damage. The pilot was killed but nobody at the station was injured. Records show that the property repairs cost £711.11s.6d.

Maughold Lighthouse, automated in the early 1990s, still uses its original lens and equipment. The huge lens revolves 24 hours a day and the light gives three white flashes every thirty seconds. To get the best view from land you need to travel into Maughold village centre and take the narrow track around the edge of the graveyard and continue up the hill for a further 300 yards or so. The lighthouse is well hidden until you take the left turning, up the rise, immediately before the lighthouse gates, but there is no

access to the grounds as the keepers' quarters are now private houses.

Moving south down the east coast brings you to Douglas Head Lighthouse, which is not easily accessed. There are no roads leading to the light and only two steep paths take you directly to it. Originally all its supplies were delivered by boat from the harbour to Port Skillion, a short journey. The lighthouse grounds included keeper accommodation but no gardens because of the difficult terrain.

Today you can walk to Port Skillion and on to the lighthouse along South Quay and up the track past the gas works by the Battery Pier. The lighthouse isn't open to visitors and the houses are in private ownership, but steps lead up to the top of Douglas Head and give you magnificent views over the bay and beyond.

The long history of a lighthouse guiding seafarers into Douglas goes back to 1671. Records show that various lights and beacons were erected at the harbour entrance, an early one of which is described as a great lantern displaying two lights.

Throughout the 18th century, as Douglas developed, the Harbour Commissioners built a pier with a brick lighthouse at the entrance to the port. In the summer of 1787 fierce easterly gales swept away part of the pier and the lighthouse with it. In 1793 a sum of £24,000 was provided from public funds to build a new stone pier. Called the Red Pier, it was well over 500 feet long and extended into the bay to provide much-needed shelter. It was completed in 1801, but three years into its construction a 34-foot tower was erected at its end, the light visible six miles out to sea and greatly increasing safety for ships heading into Douglas.

In 1826 Sir William Hillary, resident of Douglas and founder of the Royal National Lifeboat Institution, proposed the building of a 'Great Central Harbour' with a lighthouse. Although this never materialised, the current Battery Pier and its lighthouse, completed in 1879, is based on Hillary's original idea but to

Winkie — the small secondary lighthouse at Point of Ayre

Langness lighthouse, operational since 1880 and automated in 1996

a smaller design, and is now protected from the seaward side by a larger breakwater built in the 1980s.

In 1832, six years after Hillary's proposal, the Isle of Man Harbour Commissioners built Douglas Head Lighthouse. In 1857 they handed over control of it to the Commissioners of Northern Lighthouses, to whom the annual running costs of £200 were insignificant in comparison with the 1845 surplus of £4,000 they had accrued from dues collected in respect of Manx lights under their control. Following the take-over it was proposed to extend the station's living quarters to accommodate two resident keepers and their families, but by the late 1880s the buildings were reported to be in need of a great deal of repair and engineer Stevenson advised that the old buildings, including the tower, should be removed and rebuilt to a more convenient plan.

This task was duly completed in October 1892. The new Douglas Head Lighthouse became a very popular tourist attraction and in the summer of 1895 an average of 74 people every day paid to see it.

Throughout the 20th century the station

changed little in outward appearance. The revolving light has a candle power of 738,461, one white light flashing every ten seconds. It was automated in 1986.

Next stop on this clockwise tour of the Isle of Man coastline is Langness in the extreme south-east. This low-lying two-mile peninsula forms natural havens in the shape of Castletown and Derbyhaven bays, and the lighthouse stands at the peninsula's southern tip.

Despite its wildlife and tranquil scenic beauty, Langness has claimed the lives and vessels of many unsuspecting mariners over the centuries. In 1811 the British Government built the unlit Herring Tower to the seaward side in the centre of the peninsula, but it was of limited help to shipping, and wrecks continued to pile up.

In 1850 the Harbour Commissioners used the old 13th-century fort of Fort Island to place a beacon at the northern end of Langness. Initially it was lit only during the herring season to guide the fishing fleet safely back into Castletown, but pressure from the local community soon saw the light operating during hours of darkness all year round. As a result, the number of shipping casualties fell considerably and demonstrated the need for a lighthouse.

But it was not until 1st December 1880 that the Langness Lighthouse was finally built and operational. The layout remains much as it was then: the 50-foot tower in the centre of a courtyard with three keepers' houses, workshops and gas plant room (for the foghorn) surrounding it in the two-and-a-half-acre complex. The light had a power of 9,000 candles with a sequence of one flashing white light every five seconds. The light at Fort Island was discontinued in 1883.

On 12th December 1933 a fire broke out in the Langness light room, destroying the lamps. Gilmour, the keeper on duty at the time, claimed he was in the toilet when the fire broke out.

In 1937 new apparatus was installed, boosting the light power to 200,000 candles and its character changing from a one-second flash every five seconds to a one-third second flash every ten seconds. In more recent times the configuration has been changed to two flashes every thirty seconds.

In the summer of 1996, Langness became the last of the Island's lighthouses maintained by the Northern Lighthouse Board to turn to automatic operation.

On the opposite end of the south coast, off the south-west tip of the Island, is the Calf of Man, where the rewards for lighthouse historians are probably unsurpassed anywhere. The modern lighthouse of 1968, originally occupied by three resident keepers, sits neatly between its 19th-century predecessors and is the most powerful light in the Irish Sea area.

The building of Robert Stevenson's two lighthouses, unique examples of great construction engineering, began in 1817, at one time employing more than 300 men who toiled in all weathers without adequate shelter. By 1st February 1819 the lights were illuminated for the first time, the higher tower standing at 375 feet above high water and the lower tower at 282 feet. The lights

could be seen from 24 and 22 miles' distance respectively.

The two lights were built in line, one above the other, on high cliffs overlooking Chicken Rock, which is one and half miles out to sea. The light tower on Chicken Rock itself was not built until 1875.

Stevenson incorporated many unusual architectural features which are unaltered today. Close by the lower light are the remains of the smithy, a stable and an assortment of other buildings used for stores.

Originally, four light keepers and their families lived on the Calf of Man. Life was pretty basic — no shops, school, church or doctor — but they made this their home. Census information suggests that the Calf's total resident population in 1820 was fifteen people. And then, an unforeseen problem: the higher of the two lights was all too frequently rendered useless by the constant menace of fog. In 1866 the Commissioners for Northern Lighthouses recommended a new

Point of Ayre — the most northerly building on the Island

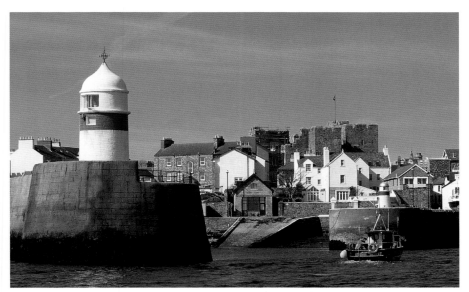

Castletown harbour entrance

tower should be built on Chicken Rock as a matter of urgency.

Thus began the process of replacing the lighthouses on the Calf of Man. But it was seven years before David and Thomas Stevenson had their light built on Chicken Rock – a granite tower 150 feet high, built on a pinnacle of rock with only 4,000 square feet exposed at low water, and located in extreme isolation. The cost of building it soared £20,000 over the £46,000 estimate. Tide and weather conditions created enormous difficulties in landing on the rock and construction work could only be carried out on site during calm summer months. And even then it was restricted to five-hour periods between tides before the rock was underwater again.

Thirty-five skilled artisans toiled on Chicken Rock during the construction. Granite stone was imported from Dalbeatie in Scotland, dressed and shaped into dovetail blocks, assembled together course by course at the Port St Mary workyard, and shipped out to Chicken Rock for construction. This method of building was developed by Robert Stevenson at the Bell Rock off the east coast of Scotland in the 1830s.

The first 32 feet of the tower were built of solid granite masonry. A bronze access ladder climbs up the outside of the tower, leading to the entrance door. From the entrance there are seven storeys to the lantern machinery room and then to the lantern itself..

On 1st January 1875 the new light on Chicken Rock was exhibited for the first time and the two lights on the Calf of Man extinguished.

Three keepers lived on the rock at all times – a principal and two assistants – with one relief keeper living ashore on rotation. Life on the rock was barely comfortable, let alone luxurious. The duty keepers' accommodation consisted of two rooms with twin bunks, a kitchen and living room. Naturally, all the rooms were circular and no more than ten feet in diameter. So much for the romantic notion of the adventurous lot of a lighthouse keeper!

The most traumatic event at Chicken

ENJOY
PLACES TO SEE AND
THINGS TO DO

Powerboats at Douglas in 2005

WHERE
TO GO AND
WHAT TO SEE

The following alphabetical listing gives a broad but by no means exhaustive survey of the Isle of Man's natural and man-made attractions.

ANCIENT SITES & MONUMENTS

Many of the Island's ancient monuments stand on privately-owned ground and can only be viewed with prior permission, but among the freely-accessible sites are Balladoole (remains dating from prehistoric to Viking times) near Castletown, Cronk ny Merriu (Iron Age promontory fort) at Port Grenaugh between Douglas and Derbyhaven, The Braaid (Iron Age and Norse settlement) west of Douglas, St Michael's Isle (12th-century chapel and 16th-century fort) at Langness, Mull Hill (a circle of Neolithic burial chambers) near Cregneash, King Orry's Grave at Laxey, 14th-century Monks Bridge at Ballasalla and the well-preserved Neolithic chambered tomb of Cashtal yn Ard near Glen Mona, overlooking the parish of Maughold.

Throughout the Island there are more than 200 decorated stone crosses of the type which have served as grave markers and memorial stones on the Isle of Man since the 5th century. Most of them remain in the churches and the churchyard cross shelters of their parish of origin, but cast copies of all the stones are housed in the Manx Museum in Douglas as a permanent record.

ALL ABOARD!

One of the great joys of exploring the Isle of Man – particularly for children and families – is to experience the extraordinary network of Victorian railways and trams which is still so vital to the Island's public transport system.

You can travel all the way from Port Erin in the south-west to Ramsey in the north-east – a journey of about 33 miles – by a combination of steam and electric railways which meet roughly halfway at Douglas. You also have the option to stop off en route at Laxey and take the 5-mile electric mountain railway to the top of Snaefell. Not forgetting a 2-mile canter along Douglas promenade by horsedrawn tram!

It was the tourist boom of the latter half of the 19th century which inspired the creation of this surviving rail network, which is now well into its second century of operation and,

amazingly, still using much of the original equipment, rolling stock and motive power.

At one time both Douglas and Ramsey were connected by rail to Peel on the west coast, as described in the walks section of this guide. For more information about railways and trams, see their individual headings and the separate chapter describing a journey on the coast-hugging Manx Electric Railway.

The Isle of Man's public transport system is not served exclusively by rail, of course. In fact, there are many more parts of the Island accessible by bus than there are by train or tram.

BASKING SHARKS

The world's second biggest fish, sometimes exceeding 35 feet in length, these giants of the ocean have been regular annual visitors to Isle of Man waters in recent years. For more information see under *Wildlife & Nature Reserves*.

CAMERA OBSCURA

Acquired by the Isle of Man government in the 1990s and reopened in 2005 after major restoration, the Great Union Camera Obscura on Douglas Head, overlooking the harbour, was built for the Victorian tourism

Basking sharks are regular summer visitors to Isle of Man waters

boom and is one of only four now remaining in the British Isles. Through a series of mirrors and lenses it gives spectacular views over Douglas.

CASTLES

The Isle of Man has two historic castles – one a ruin and the other in remarkably good state of preservation.

The latter is Castle Rushen, which gave its name to Castletown. It is one of Europe's best-preserved medieval castles, its origins dating from the 12th century with the fortification of a strategic site to guard the entrance to the Silverburn River. The oldest part of the castle, believed to have been built during the time of Magnus, the last Viking King of Mann, who died here in 1265, is the keep – a central stone tower standing in an inner courtyard. The castle was developed by successive rulers for a further 300 years, being surrendered to Parliamentary forces during the English Civil War. In more recent times

the castle has served as a centre of administration, a mint, a law court and a prison, and today it is a major visitor attraction, showing detailed displays which authentically recreate castle life as it was for the kings and lords of Mann.

Peel Castle stands on St Patrick's Isle, which in the 6th century was established as a centre of Manx Christianity and survived in this role until the arrival of the pagan Norse Vikings at the end of the 8th century. In the 11th century it became the ruling seat of the Norse Kingdom of Mann and the Isles. A major programme of excavation conducted in the 1980s revealed much about the site's prime importance, and Viking jewellery and other finds are on display in the Manx Museum in Douglas. The story of St Patrick's Isle is introduced in the nearby House of Manannan, Peel's other great heritage attraction, and by means of an electronic aid Manannan himself will give you an exciting personal tour of the castle.

The renovated Camera Obscura, a Victorian attraction on Douglas Head

CHURCHES

From the cathedral in Peel to the Royal Chapel in St John's, the Isle of Man is richly endowed with ancient and modern sites to visit, as detailed in the chapter *Keeils, Chapels and Churches.*

COACH TOURS

In summer months you can take your seat for a round-Island excursion and other coach tours.

ELECTRIC RAILWAY

The Manx Electric Railway runs for almost 18 miles between Douglas and Ramsey, much of the route giving magnificent views along the east coast. At Laxey, roughly mid-way, you can transfer to the Snaefell Mountain Railway.

In operation since 1893, the Manx Electric Railway has the two oldest working tramcars in the world. With a 3-feet gauge double track, it is also the longest vintage narrow-gauge line in the British Isles.

A journey from Douglas to Ramsey and the sights and places of interest en route are described in detail in *All Aboard the Manx Electric Railway.*

ENTERTAINMENT

Douglas is undoubtedly the focus of Island entertainment, boasting as it does the wonderful Gaiety Theatre and new Villa Marina complex.

The latter incorporates the Royal Concert Hall, cinema, Dragon's Castle children's adventure play centre and the Promenade Suite, where live family shows are presented throughout August. The Gaiety is a venue for year-round entertainment and offers a great variety of drama, musicals, comedy, opera, music and dance to maintain its broad audience appeal.

Douglas also has its lively pubs, clubs, discos, tenpin bowling and other popular nightspots, including a casino.

Away from the capital, in the south at Port Erin, you'll find plenty of entertainment on offer at Erin Arts Centre – a venue which hosts many of the Island's major annual music festivals and also has a film club. In the west, the grounds of Peel Castle often provide an open-air stage in summer, with more entertainment on offer at Peel's Centenary Centre. And in Ramsey, in the north, Mooragh Park hosts a variety of summer concerts and colourful special events.

See also the separate chapter *Arts and Entertainment.*

EVENTS

See the separate chapter for information about major annual Isle of Man events such as the TT Festival and Tynwald Day.

FARM & ANIMAL ATTRACTIONS

One of the biggest attractions for children of all ages is Curraghs Wildlife Park in the north. Within its 26 acres are more than 100 species of birds and animals from wetland areas around the world, along with nature and butterfly trails and the Island's smallest passenger-carrying railway – the very popular Orchid Line.

Another welcoming family attraction is Moaney Mooar Open Farm & Tea Room, where kids can make friends with farm animals and small pets. The Mann Cat Sanctuary at Santon, in the south, and the Home of Rest for Old Horses near Douglas – the retirement destination for the tram-pulling shires – are pleased to welcome visitors.

FILM & TV LOCATIONS

In the last decade, the Isle of Man's magnificent scenery and great natural environment have been a magnet to film and television producers from around the world. The number of feature films and TV drama series shot on location here currently exceeds 80 and continues to increase at a pace.

Traditional ploughing matches at Cregneash

Big screen productions such as *Waking Ned, The Brylcreem Boys, The Tichborne Claimant, Treasure Island, Alice Through the Looking Glass* and *I Capture the Castle* have brought a host of famous actors to Niarbyl, Laxey, Sulby Glen and other delightful locations. The Isle of Man's fledgling but rapidly-growing film industry has also created new studio and production facilities at Ramsey.

The Island's screen locations are included in the programme of summer coach tours.

FUN & FROLICS

When it comes to keeping kids amused, what the Isle of Man lacks in Orlando-style theme parks it more than makes up for with the sheer variety of other possibilities.

Water, of course, is one of the big attractions – beaches at Peel, Port Erin and Port St Mary, the pools complex at the National Sports Centre, the boating pool and water-driven carousel at Silverdale, the lake at Mooragh Park in Ramsey, and a variety of swimming pools such as that at Castletown.

Just north of Douglas is Onchan Park & Stadium, overlooking Douglas Bay. There's great fun to be had here – motorboats, karting, squash, tennis, stock car racing, mini golf, flat and crown green bowling and more besides. Another park with lots of facilities and attractions is Noble's Park in Douglas, and for younger kids the Dragon's Castle in the new Villa Marina provides a mix of play and adventure.

Also in the capital is Superbowl – a big hit with youngsters - and around the Island there is interactive entertainment at the Manx Museum and House of Manannan (steer a Steam Packet ferry into harbour!), the animals and birds and miniature railway at Curraghs Wildlife Park, activities such as cycling and pony trekking, and colourful and exciting summer events which include street kart racing in Peel, an international soccer festival, and the ever so slightly potty World Tin Bath Championships.

GLENS

These havens of peace and tranquillity are among the Isle of Man's greatest charms, much favoured by the Victorians and generations of holidaymakers ever since.

The 17 glens which are now owned by the Manx Government and designated as protected national glens are Summerhill, Groudle, Molly Quirk's, Laxey, Port Soderick and Ballaglass in the east; Colby and Silverdale in the south; Elfin, Ballaglass, Dhoon, Tholt-y-Will (Sulby), Bishopscourt and Glen Wyllin in the north; and Glen Maye, Glen Helen and Glen Mooar in the west.

You can read more about them in the chapter *The Nature of the Landscape*.

HORSE TRAMS

Horsepower has been keeping trams on the move along Douglas promenade since 1876. The horses are specially bred for the task and

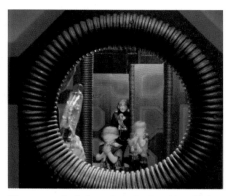

There s great family fun to be had at Laserblast, Onchan

their working conditions are enviable: a two-hour shift per day in the summer season, the rest of the year off to enjoy the grazing, and a Douglas Corporation pension scheme which on retirement guarantees permanent residence at the Home of Rest for Old Horses. This is on Richmond Hill, on the bus route to Castletown. With ample car parking,

The Tynwald National Park & Arboretum is in a beautiful setting

and facilities for the disabled, it offers a warm welcome to visitors.

A compliment of 42 horses and 23 tramcars operates the service, the route running for nearly 2 miles between the depot at Derby Castle and the Sea Terminal at the other (southern) end of Douglas promenade. The trams are the oldest in the world. On display in the depot is a restored Douglas electric bogie tramcar – the only one outside San Francisco still in existence.

MINIATURE RAILWAYS

Unlike the Island's other railways, the Groudle Glen and the Orchid Line were created purely as leisure attractions and are not part of the public transport system.

Lovingly restored to its former glory by the volunteers and supporters who run it, the Groudle Glen Railway is a marvellous little reminder of the feats achieved by Britain's great railway builders. The 2-feet gauge line just to the north of Douglas climbs up out of the glen's lower reaches and winds along the very edge of the hillside through trees, gorse, bracken and heather to the clifftop terminus – a distance of about three quarters of a mile. The views are fabulous. The railway celebrated its centenary in 1996, and the meticulously-restored carriages are still pulled by *Sea Lion* – the original 1896 steam engine. Opening hours are limited to certain times in summer and at Christmas only – you'll need to check with the Tourist Information Centre in Douglas.

On a smaller scale still – and great fun for children of all ages – is the Orchid Line in Curraghs Wildlife Park. The track gauge is just three and a half inches! This has to be one of the tiniest passenger–carrying railways anywhere in the world.

MINING HERITAGE

In the 19th century, the lead mines at Laxey and Foxdale were highly productive and their rich mineral deposits continued to

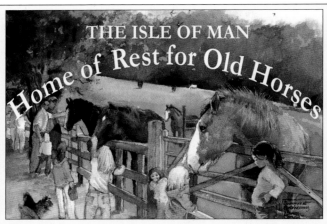

THE ISLE OF MAN
Home of Rest for Old Horses

PARKS & GARDENS

Children love parks for the opportunity to let off steam while adults are often content to enjoy the peace and quiet of a relaxing location and appreciate the colourful creations of expert gardeners. Based on these criteria, the Isle of Man has parks and gardens to keep everyone happy.

For fun and activities, the pleasure parks of Noble's (Douglas) and Onchan certainly hit the mark. As does Silverdale Glen near Ballasalla: boating pool, water-driven carousel, picnic area, nature trails and the very popular Craftworks, where kids can create their own prized piece of art or craftwork based on local Manx designs.

Even bigger on activities is Ramsey's Mooragh Park. It boasts a 12-acre boating lake – ideal for beginners to learn the ropes in canoeing and sailing – and 40 acres of parkland. Bowling and crazy golf are other attractions here.

As for gardens of the horticultural variety,

The joys of spring at the Arboretum

it's hard to beat those at Laxey, laid out on the old washing floors of the mines, or the beautiful setting of historic St John's. The village's Tynwald National Park & Arboretum contains many species of exotic trees, and the ducks and pond make this an ideal picnic spot in summer. Close by, at Tynwald Mills Centre, you can also enjoy the Manx Wild Flower Garden.

Lining the promenade in Douglas are the

A scene fom *The Railway Children?* No — Douglas station

where **to** go and what **TO SEE**

capital's famous sunken gardens. A riot of colour in spring and summer, the gardens often reflect the theme of notable anniversaries and other important occasions and are designed and planted accordingly.

PLEASURE CRUISES

What's an island holiday without venturing out on to the sea?

At harbours all round the Isle of Man coastline you can board a fishing or pleasure boat for a bit of sporting action or a very leisurely cruise.

Karina, a distinctive sight in the summer season, will take you from Douglas to a choice of destinations – Laxey, Port Soderick, Derbyhaven and around Douglas Bay.

If your holiday base is at Ramsey in the north or Peel in the west, good news – pleasure cruises operate from both. And in the south you can join a boat trip at Port St Mary or Port Erin, where your options (conditions and visitor numbers permitting) include dropping anchor at the Calf of Man island nature reserve.

SEALS

These appealing marine mammals are resident in Island waters and are frequently seen on rocks close to shore, as described under *Wildlife & Nature Reserves*.

SHOPPING

If shopping is one of your holiday treats, the Isle of Man has plenty to show you. The redevelopment of Douglas as an important offshore banking and commercial centre has seen a proportionate emphasis on designer shopping, with some swish new outlets. Trusted High Street names such as M&S and Next can be found in Strand Street, and there are two excellent shopping centres – the spacious Strand and the more recent Tower House galleria in Castle Street, built round a large central atrium.

And if you're self-catering in Douglas, you'll be pleased to know that there are three supermarkets – Tesco and the Island's own Shoprite, which also has stores in Onchan, Ramsey, Peel, Port Erin and Castletown.

Tynwald Mills Centre at St John's will satisfy your appetite for shopping and good food

Away from the capital, each of the Island's towns is well served by local shops and the Isle of Man is developing something of a reputation for its number and variety of antique shops.

The same applies to specialist arts and crafts studios and outlets. Some of the best examples are Tholtan in Sulby Glen, Ballabrara Arts and Gansey Pottery (both in Port St Mary), Courtyard Crafts (Port Erin) and the Fabric Centre in Peel. Also in Peel is Celtic Gold, which specialises in Celtic Manx and Archibald Knox jewellery, as well as producing Manx, Scottish and Irish kilts for sale or hire. And don't forget that Peel is the place to buy your Manx kippers, or mail a pair or two to a friend!

If auctions are your cup of tea, there's one every Friday in Ramsey. At the other end of the Island, in the south, Castletown has an interesting 'old world' health foods shop, highly distinctive for its enticing array of aromas, flavours, colours and containers. Not far away, in Silverdale Glen at Ballasalla, there's another unusual attraction. The

Celtic Gold

Craftworks Studio, much loved by children, gives you the opportunity to create and paint your own unique piece of Manx pottery.

Laxey is very well known for the genuine Manx tweeds produced at St George's Woollen Mills. But perhaps the biggest shopping surprise of all is to be found at the Tynwald Mills Centre – an attractive selection of shops sharing the old mill buildings in the very pleasant setting of St John's, a few miles inland from Peel. Food, fashions, furniture, housewares, gifts, garden products and pet products are all on sale here in a very cosy and relaxed environment. Manx Wildlife Trust has a shop here too, close to Courtyard Gallery.

STEAM RAILWAY

It's timeless and hypnotic: the sense of wonder evoked by the sight of a living, breathing, hissing, fire-eating steam locomotive.

You have only to stand on the station platform in Douglas or Port Erin to sense the magic of the Isle of Man Steam Railway. The unique cocktail of sights, sounds and smells is as exciting to today's kids as it has been to any generation before them. *Thomas and the Magic Railroad* was filmed on the Island – and the title and the location were made for each other.

Lynx at Curraghs Wildlife Park

A walk on the wildside

Over 100 species of wetland wildlife - in the spacious surroundings of the Ballaugh Curraghs, the Island's premier wildlife conservation site.

View the local wildlife - birds, butterflies and rare plants of the curraghs along the unique nature trails. Life on Islands - new walkthrough aviaries exhibit endangered species from islands around the world, showing evolution in action.

Around the World in 80 Minutes - endangered species from wetland habitats around the world are arranged in walkthrough enclosures and aviaries on a geographic theme and many rare species are part of international breeding programmes.

Find the Wildlife Park - halfway round the TT course, between Ballaugh Bridge and Sulby Straight.

Explore the wonderful world of wildlife

The Orchid Line Miniature Railway runs on summer Sundays & Bank Holidays.

OPEN DAILY
10am-6pm.
Weekends only during winter 10am-4pm

curraghs
wildlife park

Picnic Area • Lakeside Café • Adventure Playground **Tel: 01624 897323 Web: www.gov.im/wildlife**

Opened in 1874, this is the oldest of the Isle of Man's surviving railways and the longest narrow-gauge (3 feet) steam line in the British Isles. The restored Beyer-Peacock 2-4-0 locomotives date back to this time. But far from nearing the end of the line, the railway has been given a brand new lease of life. A recent two-year programme of renewal, improvement and maintenance represented the biggest reinvestment in the railway since it was built, and it returned to full service in May 2004.

In July and August, the peak months of the holiday season, there are 7 return trains a day, each leisurely one-way journey snaking through some of the Island's prettiest countryside in about an hour. The station at Port Erin has a cafe and a museum of railway memorabilia. The Douglas terminus also has a cafe.

VISITOR CENTRES

There are five dedicated visitor centres on the Isle of Man, each concerned with aspects of Manx natural beauty, wildlife or geology.

Scarlett Visitor Centre near Castletown explains how volcanic activity created the spectacular rock formations at Scarlett about 250 million years ago. Along with a nature trail, the refurbished centre gives an insight into the area's local flora and dramatic old limestone workings.

The focus of the Marine Interpretation Centre at the Marine Laboratory in Port Erin is the Island's marine life, and particularly that of the Calf of Man.

Also in the south is the Sound Visitor Centre and cafe near Cregneash, which opened in 2002. A panoramic window looks out across the tidal waters of the Sound to the Calf. Niarbyl in the west also has a new visitor centre and cafe.

At the opposite end of the Isle of Man, near the most northerly point, is the Ayres Visitor Centre. Run by Manx Wildlife Trust, it tells you about the Ayres National Nature Reserve and its unique variety of habitats and special ecosystem, comprising shingle beach,

The Manx Wild Flower Garden at St John's is an inspiration to all keen gardeners

A picture-postcard moment at Kewaigue in spring

dunes, lichen heath, dune slacks, conifer plantation and gorse scrub.

WILDLIFE & NATURE RESERVES

Basking sharks, seals, hen harriers, choughs, gannets, mountain hares, wallabies – on the Isle of Man you can see them all, and in the wild at that. Then there are the more exotic bird and animal inhabitants of Curraghs Wildlife Park and the rare flora to be found in the Island's many and varied nature reserves.

Basking sharks are attracted to the waters of the south and west coasts from about mid-summer onwards and have been regular visitors since 1988. They feed just below the surface on microscopic plants and animals and are not difficult to spot – particularly if you take a boat trip to observe them at close quarters.

There are several places where you're likely to spot seals, notably the Sound in the south and the Ayres in the north.

Manx Wildlife Trust has 20 nature reserves, including Close Sartfield in the north – the largest winter hen harrier roost in Western Europe. Details of the reserves are available at the Trust shop in Tynwald Mills Centre, St John's, as are the seeds of native Manx wild flowers to grow in your own garden.

The Calf of Man is also a nature reserve and bird sanctuary but is under the protection of Manx National Heritage. A little over 600 acres in size, the island has been an official British Bird Observatory since 1962. A small flock of Manx Loaghtan sheep is kept here. This rare native breed is distinctive for its rams, which have four or even six horns. Grey seals can be seen all year round in the surrounding waters. Summer boat trips run to the Calf from Port St Mary and Port Erin, but visitor numbers have to be limited because of the island's sensitive environment.

THINGS TO DO
AND
WHERE TO FIND THEM

Whether you want to participate or spectate, the Isle of Man's combination of first-class facilities and idyllic surroundings gives you many ways to pursue your sporting and leisure interests and activities.

BOWLS

Bowling of all kinds is very well catered for, including annual festivals. There are venues in Douglas (crown green and ten-pin), Onchan Park (crown and flat green), the National Sports Centre (indoor flat green and

short mat), and crown greens in Port Erin, Port St Mary, Castletown, Peel and Ramsey .

CYCLING & MOUNTAIN BIKING

From family groups to committed cyclists and mountain bikers, the Isle of Man's beautiful coast and countryside and varied terrain are a sheer delight for everyone on two wheels. To help you explore the Island there are six designated cycle trails, described and shown in detail on pages 244-252.

139

The Venture Centre near Maughold offers expert instruction for all ages

DIVING

Based at Port St Mary, Isle of Man Diving Holidays promise you some of the best diving in the British Isles – a combination of great natural beauty, diverse marine life and a fascinating variety of wrecks. The weekly and long-weekend packages includes 4-star accommodation, and a wide choice of courses is available.

Experienced divers making their own arrangements to visit the Isle of Man should note that many of the wrecks are protected by the wreck laws and some are owned by local people or sub-aqua clubs and should not be dived without permission.

FESTIVALS OF SPORT

The Isle of Man's action-packed calendar of annual events is never short of exciting sporting festivals and tournaments (as well as less serious competitive events such as tin bath and Viking longship racing) and typically includes yacht racing, soccer, rugby, table tennis, walking, marathon and fell running, darts, motorsport, motorcycle racing, angling, hockey, crown green and flat green bowling, drag racing and street kart racing.

FISHING

No wonder anglers are hooked on the Isle of Man: two annual festivals, more than

twenty great locations for sea angling (conger eel, wrasse, ray, tope, cod and mackerel), a dozen rivers and streams (rainbow and brown trout and migratory sea trout and salmon), and five reservoirs (rainbow and brown trout). Rivers and reservoirs, good until the end of September and October respectively, require licences but these are widely available on the Island. Late summer and autumn are the ideal time to land salmon and sea trout.

A challenge for experienced sea anglers is the Point of Ayre, where fast-flowing tides and the Gulf Stream call for every ounce of strength and concentration, though the rewards can be fabulous. For details of boat hire and offshore fishing grounds, contact the Tourist Information Centre in Douglas.

GOLF

The Isle of Man is something of a golfers' paradise. In a week you could play all nine courses, particularly as each is open to visiting players, and the game is very much part of the Manx way of life. Queues are rarely a problem here and the mild climate makes it a year-round sport.

The links course at Castletown was used for the 1979 PGA cup matches against the USA. It was laid out by golfing legend Mackenzie Ross in the late 1920s and early 1930s and provides some of the best links golf anywhere in the British Isles. The infamous 17th calls for a 185-yard drive across a gaping sea gully. King Edward Bay at Onchan has magnificent views across Douglas Bay, although the 6th tee at Port St Mary (the Island's only 9-hole course, designed by 1920 British Open Champion George Duncan) boasts one of the finest views of all.

HEALTH, BEAUTY & FITNESS

If you want to address mind, body and spirit, and engage in personal luxuries which hectic lifestyles too often forbid, the Isle of Man is the perfect place to indulge yourself. Opportunities include beauty salons, stylists, well-equipped venues such as the National

Abseiling with the Venture Centre

Sports Centre, Mount Murray's total Fitness Club and the Hilton Health Club. A new experience for many people awaits you at Brightlife – a leading centre for holistic learning, stress therapy, yoga, reflexology and other aspects of personal care and development.

KAYAKING

A sea kayak is unbeatable for exploring the Island's coastline and taking you into otherwise inaccessible coves and bays and close to grey seals, dolphins, basking sharks and other marine wildlife. Tuition is available from Adventurous Experiences and the Venture Centre.

NATIONAL SPORTS CENTRE

This is the flagship of the Island's sports and leisure facilities, incorporating a first-class watersports complex. You can make quite a splash here: as well as the 25-metre competition pool, there are leisure pools and fun features such as bubble tub, flow pool, jets

Sea kayaking off St Patrick's Isle, Peel

and geysers, water cannon, mushroom sprays and a toddlers' slide.

There's also a fitness zone and health suite, a 5-rink indoor flat green bowling hall, a secondary sports hall, 6 competition-standard squash courts, an athletics stadium and astroturf pitch, and a licensed cafe.

Other sports and leisure facilities can be found at two large municipal parks and at Onchan Park & Stadium.

Noble's Park in Douglas has an 18-hole mini golf course, tennis courts, bowling greens and a children's play area, while Mooragh Park in Ramsey is best known for its 12-acre boating lake – ideal for beginners to learn the ropes in canoeing and sailing – and also has a bowling green, mini golf, tennis courts, BMX track and children's playground. Onchan Park, just north of Douglas, has tennis courts, a bowling green, pitch'n'putt and a children's playground.

OUTDOOR PURSUITS

There's probably no better way to appreciate the Isle of Man's natural attributes than through its great outdoors. Maughold's multi-activity Venture Centre on the north-east coast offers an impressive range of activities and professional tuition starting, alphabetically speaking, with abseiling, archery and the assault course and going right through to raft building, rock climbing and supervised activity days for children – with lots more in between.

The Island's other dedicated centre for outdoor pursuits and extreme sports is Adventurous Experiences, specialising in sea kayaking and offering British Canoe Union courses for absolute beginners and upwards. Other activities include coasteering.

PONY TREKKING & RIDING

Whether you're new to the saddle or an experienced rider, seeing the world from horseback gives you a unique perspective. Isle of Man establishments such as Abbeylands Equestrian Centre and GGH Equestrian

Equestrian centres cater for all ages

Centre cater for all abilities and take you from the quiet lanes of Manx coast and countryside to the Island's more challenging and expansive open moorlands and high hills.

QUAD BIKING

Quad Bike Trail Rides are a fabulous and fun way to enjoy the great outdoors. Full instruction, protective clothing and home-made cakes and tea are all part of the deal.

SAILING & WATERSPORTS

One of the big attractions for sailing enthusiasts is the Isle of Man's varied conditions – the relative calm of Ramsey and Douglas bays for novices, and the more rugged north and south coasts for those sailors who relish a challenge and the chance to put their experience to the test.

Cruising, racing and dinghy sailing are all very popular and the Island has six sailing clubs. Port St Mary is home to the Isle of Man Yacht Club and is the main sailing centre. The star event of the sailing calendar is

Reservoir fishing at West Baldwin

the Round the Island Yacht Race, supported by numerous competitions throughout the year.

The abundance of safe harbours also makes the Isle of Man a regular stopping-off point for vessels crossing the Irish Sea. Harbours information and telephone numbers are included at the back of this guide.

As for watersports, surfing in Gansey Bay is really taking off in a big way and Derbyhaven on the Langness peninsula is an ideal spot for windsurfing.

TT & MOTORCYCLE RACING

The Isle of Man is famous around the world for its annual Tourist Trophy races. For more information see *Wheels, Wigs and Other Events.*

WALKING

The Isle of Man Walking Festival was introduced in 2004 and was so successful that there are now two festivals a year - in summer and autumn. This guide details 14

Island walks including the 95-mile coast path (broken down into seven sections) and a selection of easy but interesting town walks. If you really want to discover the Isle of Man, on foot is the perfect way to do it.

See the Manx countryside with Quad Bike Trail Rides

ARTS **AND** ENTERTAINMENT

As the statistics show, the arts are very much at the heart of Manx life. The Island has nine brass bands, a wind orchestra, a chamber and youth orchestra, dozens of Celtic music groups (jazz, blues and pop), organists, pianists, five drama groups, two musical theatre groups, seven choirs, and hundreds of visual artists, embroiders, spinners, weavers, woodworkers, poets, novelists and sculptors – and all this with a population of only 76,000!

Not surprisingly, so much creativity produces many arts events. There are also lots of ways to find out what's on, and where, as detailed in full on page 149.

It also follows that the Isle of Man has no shortage of excellent venues for the performing arts. The Gaiety Theatre in Douglas, renowned the world over, was designed by the great British theatre architect Frank Matcham and opened in 1900. The theatre has been painstakingly restored to its former glory over a 10-year period, a story told in the wonderfully illustrated book *A Full Circle*, available at the Manx Museum and Island bookstores. You can also enjoy a fascinating Saturday morning behind-the-scenes guided tour of the Gaiety.

Linked to the Gaiety, via the Colonnade Walkway and the Villa Gardens, is the impressive new Villa Marina, the centrepiece of which is the magnificent Royal Concert Hall. Together, the Villa Marina & Gaiety Theatre complex present a great variety of entertainment – from orchestral music, dance and theatre to comedy, light entertainment, film, pop concerts and ballroom dancing..

In addition to its professional programme of events, the Gaiety Theatre provides a stage for local amateur groups such as the Manx Operatic Society, Douglas Choral Union and the Gilbert & Sullivan Society. These musical groups produce popular shows such as *Hot Mikado*, *Guys & Dolls* and *The Witches of Eastwick*, achieving exceptional production standards and performing in front of large and appreciative audiences.

In the south of the Island, the Erin Arts Centre – a converted church in Port Erin – is the home of the Mananan International Festival of Music & the Arts, the international Lionel Tertis Viola Competition and an Opera Festival, and is hired by many local organisations. A centre of excellence for over thirty years, it is well worth a visit. There is usually an exhibition to see, and don't miss *The Viking*, a stunning sculpture by Michael Sandle which is sited in the arched doorway of the original church.

The Centenary Centre in Peel is also a place meriting a visit. Its varied programme of events includes the annual pantomime by Peel Pantaloons, concerts with young Manx bands of the calibre of King Chaillee, and international stars such as blues musician Eric Bibb.

For lovers of fine art, the National Art Gallery at the Manx Museum houses a wonderful collection of Archibald Knox watercolours and a wealth of paintings and sculptures. The Courtyard Gallery at Tynwald Mills Centre in St John's stages exhibitions by contemporary Manx artists, and the work of many Island artists and craftspeople is displayed and available at local shops and studios. In July 2006 an Open Studio Tour will make it possible to see artists at work as many open their studios for public viewing. Details are available from the Courtyard Gallery and the Arts Council.

Beach bonfire at Port Erin at the end of '*Wire & Wool: Life in the Women's Internment Camp* — a 2005 project

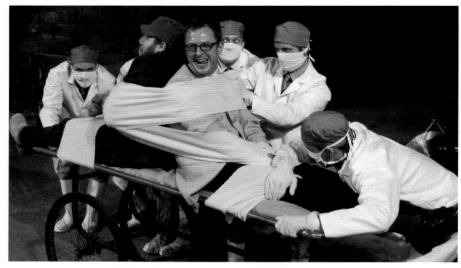

Northern Broadsides Theatre Company performing at the Gaiety Theatre

THE WORK OF THE ISLE OF MAN ARTS COUNCIL

The Isle of Man Arts Council was set up 30 years ago to support the work of local amateurs, professionals and visiting artists. It funds many organisations and offers advice and information to hundreds of people every year, encouraging and enabling participation and development in all aspects of the arts.

The Arts Council promotes visits by major companies and orchestras. In July 2006 the Island is hosting the BBC Philharmonic Orchestra, starting with a week's residency for youth orchestra coaching and community events, and culminating with two major concerts in the Villa Marina. The programme will feature singers from the Island's many choirs, performing together as a massed choir on Sunday July 9th to sing Carl Orff's *Carmina Burana*.

Arts in Education is a key element of the Arts Council's work. Many school-based workshops encourage dance, drama, creative writing and crafts, with free tickets for school children to attend matinee performances by visiting companies.

Major public artworks commissioned by the Arts Council include *The Viking* at Erin Arts Centre and the RNLI Memorial in the sunken gardens on Douglas promenade (both by Michael Sandle), and Bryan Kneale's plaque of Henry Bloom Noble – one of the Island's greatest benefactors – on the Villa Marina. Other examples of Bryan Kneale's work are *The Three Legs of Mann* at the Ronaldsway Airport, the bust of Victorian writer Hall Caine in the Summerhill Gardens, *The Watcher* outside the Manx Museum, and Captain Quilliam (who steered *HMS Victory* at Trafalgar) at Castle Rushen. Stunning examples of stained glass include windows designed by James Hogan in The Church of Our Lady Star of the Sea and St Maughold in Ramsey (a church designed by Sir Giles Gilbert Scott), and windows by Harry Clarke at St Mary's Catholic Church in Castletown.

The Arts Council's work in Community Arts in 2005 included a major project based in Port Erin entitled *Wire & Wool: Life in the Women's Internment Camp*. Stories were gathered from many people who remembered the World War Two women's camp in Port Erin and Port St Mary, and these were woven into a promenade play. Over 40 local adults and children were in the cast, performing to an audience of more than 350 on two separate evenings in August. Exhibitions of the research and artefacts were held in Erin Arts Centre and the Manx Museum. All the research for this project is now archived in the Manx Museum, and many of the stories can be seen on *The People's War* BBC Website.

In 1993, for modern art, the Arts Council started the Contemporary Art Loan Collection – a superb collection of contemporary prints – as a way to bring contemporary art into the everyday lives of the Island's schoolchildren. Now one of the foremost loan collections in the British Isles, it comprises 305 prints by artists as varied as Anthony Gormley, Patrick Heron, Gordon House, Pablo Picasso, Elisabeth Frink, Terry Frost, Graham Sutherland and David Hockney, as well as many Manx artists. Displayed in virtually all of the Island's schools, and in many public buildings, these prints act as a catalyst for discussion and discovery.

For film the Arts Council runs a Film Season in conjunction with the Palace Cinema in Douglas. This presents a fortnightly programme of international films that would not normally be seen on the Island. In addition, there are film clubs at both Erin Arts Centre and the Centenary Centre in Peel. These initiatives have broadened the choice of films available on the Isle of Man – a choice that has included productions such as *Goodbye Lenin* and *Whale Rider*. Details of films being shown are available at the Palace Cinema and the Arts Council's office and website.

The Noble Arts Programme at the new Noble's Hospital is another initiative from the Arts Council, achieved in partnership with the Department of Health & Social Security. This 'arts in healthcare' concept has already provided the hospital with a rolling programme of exhibitions, musical events and a major new sculpture commission.

The Island has a strong tradition of creative writing, and this is nurtured by the Isle of Man Poetry Society and various writers groups. Support from the Arts Council has enabled the Poetry Society to publish an anthology of local poets entitled *This Island Now* edited by Jeff Garland. The Council also supported local writer Denys Drower's first novel, *Amaryllis Tontine*, published by Lily Publications and available in local bookstores.

The Arts Council is the lead agency in the National Arts Development Strategy 2005–2014, which has two aims: to provide an overview of all the artistic and cultural activities on the Island, and to identify how the arts can further contribute to the quality of life in the Isle of Man. Copies of the Strategy, and the Review of its first year, are available from the Arts Council at 10, Villa Marina Arcade, Douglas (tel: 01624 611316).

WHAT'S ON?

There are several easy ways in which you can acquire up-to-date details of what's on, and where:

Contact the Tourism Information Centre at the Sea Terminal in Douglas, or the Villa Marina and Gaiety Theatre Complex Box Office.

Listen to Manx Radio.

Visit any of these websites:

www.gov.im

www.isleofman.com (events listings)

www.manxradio.com

www.gov.im/artscouncil (which has many links to other sites)

THE
GRAND OLD HOUSE
AND THE STYLISH NEW VILLA

S ince the curtain went up in 1900, the Gaiety Theatre and Opera House in Douglas has been playing out its own dramatic story.

From a great beginning, to a tragic and premature ending avoided at the eleventh hour, it's the stuff that theatre is made of: amazing characters, twists and turns, heroes and villains, highs and lows, tears and laughter, love and heartbreak, and triumph over adversity.

And more than a century after it began, the story which has already engaged a

multitudinous cast and audience is still being written, with the hope and promise of much more to come.

The great beginning was assured when the Palace and Derby Castle Company Limited decided to entrust the creation of their new theatre and opera house to Frank Matcham (1854-1920). He was the man who in the late Victorian and early Edwardian era set the standards in theatre design. His reputation for architectural and engineering ingenuity was without equal, and over a 34-year period he worked his magic on at least 150 theatres throughout England and Wales, including the London Palladium and the Coliseum.

Today, only about 25 Matchams survive in the British Isles – and of these, the magnificent, restored Gaiety is universally acknowledged as one of the most outstanding examples.

The Gaiety opened on 16th July 1900 to cater for the boom in tourism which was bringing summer holidaymakers to the Isle of Man in their droves. For decades the Gaiety's popularity was assured by the kind of light entertainment they craved – comedies, musicals, revues and variety – and in winter the theatre provided an important stage for local companies and locally-produced shows.

Even though the programme was interrupted by two world wars, an item of note from 1942 is that actor Jon Pertwee, later of *Navy Lark*, *Doctor Who* and *Worzel Gummidge* fame, established the Service Players – a company which has endured and still performs at the Gaiety today.

It was in the years following this war that the already-waning fortunes of both the Gaiety and the Isle of Man became all too apparent. Live entertainment had long been threatened by the growing popularity of cinema, and by the late 1950s the big screen was providing the Gaiety's main source of income. The building itself was badly in need of care and attention, the lack of investment by its owners in maintenance and general upkeep inevitably taking its toll.

As for the Island, major economic and social challenges had to be faced. Significant declines in tourism, traditional Manx industries and even the population demanded deep thought and positive action to steer the course for a much more secure and sustainable future.

In the late 1960s, with the Gaiety losing money, the Palace and Derby Castle Company Limited decided first to sell it and then to demolish it. The order for the latter came from the top – but the man whose signature was required to execute the

demolition bravely defied his boss. Arthur Corkhill, the company's secretary and accountant, opted instead to make an impassioned plea to the Manx Government to prevent the loss of the Island's only remaining playhouse.

Result: in 1971 Tynwald approved the purchase of the Gaiety Theatre and Opera House, the £50,000 expenditure including £9,000 for essential repairs. Even so, the theatre's fate was still uncertain until, in the face of vigorous campaigning by local amateur dramatic societies for the need for a national theatre, the decision was taken to keep it. Despite the Gaiety's shamefully run-down state, the cost of building a replacement was prohibitive.

Amazingly (or so it appears in hindsight) at this time the significance, prestige and historical value of the theatre was not realised. In the 1970s the name Frank Matcham meant very little to anyone other than a minority of academics working in a highly specialised field. Many Matcham creations in Britain's towns and cities had already suffered the ignominy of conversion into bingo halls, much of their original fabric destroyed in the process.

In fact, it was not until Mervin Russell Stokes began delving into the records of the Manx Museum in the mid 1980s that the Isle of Man became aware that it possessed such a rare national treasure.

Mervin started working at the Gaiety in 1970 on a part-time basis, rising to become house manager in 1980 and general manager in 1984 – a vocation he still performs with great pride, energy and enthusiasm. It was his vision, backed by painstaking detective work and ceaseless fundraising which led to the astonishing and meticulous restoration of the Gaiety. The work was carried out mainly over the period 1990-2000, under the control and direction of Mervin and theatre expert Dr David Gilmore.

The complete story is told in Roy MacMillan's excellent book *A Full Circle: 100*

Elkie Brooks in concert at the Royal Hall in the Villa Marina

Years of the Gaiety Theatre, which contains many fascinating photographs and other records.

But to truly appreciate the experience of Victorian theatre-going at its best, there is simply no substitute for taking your seat in the grandest of grand auditoria, whatever the show and whatever the occasion.

From the astounding house-size act drop to the incredible craftsmanship of the ceiling, prepare to be amazed – and you won't be disappointed.

THIS WAY TO THE NEXT STAGE...

As you come out of the Gaiety Theatre, turn left and you'll come to the Colonnade Walk. Follow this and another first-class Douglas entertainment venue soon looms up in front of you – the highly impressive new Villa Marina.

Opened in 2004, the new Villa is linked to

the Gaiety not only by the walkway at the front and the gardens at the rear, but also in marketing terms, under the umbrella of the Villa Marina and Gaiety Theatre Complex.

Both share the same box office, located on the promenade between the two, and each complements the other for the variety of live entertainment and other attractions on offer. At the Villa Marina these attractions range from a safe indoor children's play area to outstanding new facilities for conferences, meetings, exhibitions and functions such as weddings and other special occasions.

The new Villa Marina is much more than a refurbishment of the rather tired Edwardian building which previously stood on this site at the corner of Broadway.

The impressive entrance welcomes you with a Bryan Kneale bronze of Henry Bloom Noble (1816-1903) – one of the Island's most generous benefactors, whose 8-acre estate occupied this land and was purchased by

Situated on Harris Promenade in Douglas, the Villa Marina and Gaiety Theatre Complex is the hub of live entertainment on the Isle of Man. The Complex presents an exciting year-round programme of entertainment, theatre, cinema, art and music.

Finding out what's on couldn't be simpler - details of all events can be seen on the **www.villagaiety.com** website or you can call in at the Box Office on Douglas Promenade - next to the Villa Marina Arcade - **Monday to Saturday 10 a.m. - 4.30 p.m.**

Shows • Concerts • Conferences • Cinema
Children's Play Area • Plays Pantomimes • Operas • Musicals • Ballet

Box Office: 01624 **694555** email: **tickets@villamarina.dtl.gov.im**
Website: **www.villagaiety.com**

Robert Plant — climbing the stairway to heaven in the Villa Marina

Douglas Corporation in 1909 for the purpose of creating a centre of entertainment.

At the Villa's centrepiece is the superb octagonal Royal Hall, distinctive not only for its shape but also for the traditional and elegant high ceiling which enhances the sensations of light and spaciousness. The hall, a perfect venue for major summer shows and concerts, incorporates the latest in sound and lighting technology and comprises a large dance floor, a two-level auditorium seating up to 1,500, and four separate and individual bars laid out along the wide corridors which wrap around the stalls and circle. These bars are named after showbiz legends such as Joe Loss, Ivy Benson and Florrie Forde, who for

many years were regular and popular performers on the Isle of Man.

The size and pleasing environment of the Royal Hall is undoubtedly geared to suiting the needs of large corporate or public events – conferences, meetings and the like – particularly given the Villa Marina's appealing seafront location overlooking Douglas Bay. No doubt this fact was not lost on planners and government when the project was given its seal of approval.

For summer visitors to the Isle of Man, the new Villa Marina's Promenade Suite offers further live entertainment. The family cabaret presented here from the end of July to the end of August is suitable for children too –

and it's free to everyone!

If films are more your preference, the new complex caters for you in the shape of the state-of-the-art Broadway Cinema. Although not huge – it seats just over 150 – it promises a wide and varied programme suitable for family viewing.

Families – or kids at least – are certainly the audience for the Dragon's Castle. This is the new Villa's exciting adventure play area, with a variety of safe-play equipment and a couple of larger-than-life characters to add to the fun, and facilities for parents which include seating, baby-changing rooms, refreshments and children's meals.

The multi-purpose nature of the new Villa Marina is further evident from the Colonnade Suite – a function room for up to 140 people, opening out on to its own private terrace and spectacular sea views and

It's showtime at the Gaiety Theatre

overlooking the mature Villa Marina gardens. In summer months the gardens are a very pleasant and relaxing place to while away an hour or so.

WHAT'S ON, WHEN AND WHERE

Details of how to contact the new Villa Marina and Gaiety Theatre box office, and other up-to-date sources of entertainment and events programmes, are on page 149

Katie Melua – the young Russian-born star

WHEELS
WIGS
AND OTHER EVENTS

The Isle of Man's rich Celtic and Viking heritage, and more recent traditions such as the TT Festival, have created an action-packed calendar of annual events overflowing with interest, colour and variety – particularly in the months from spring through to late summer.

From its unique and extraordinary parliament to celebrations of music, dance and culture, the road race capital of the world proudly displays its spirit of independence in a way which guarantees great entertainment for everyone, locals and visitors all.

TT RACING: HOW FOUR WHEELS BECAME TWO

To trace the beginnings of the world's most famous and enduring motorcycle races, you have to go back to the last years of the 19th century and a wealthy American living in Paris.

James Gordon Bennett, son of the owner of the *New York Herald*, had gone to the French capital to establish a continental edition of the newspaper. He quickly embraced the European way of life and particularly the passion for automobiles.

The French were already elevating the status of the horseless carriage to something far more exciting than a rich man's toy. In the summer of 1895 they staged a road race from Paris to Bordeaux and back to Paris – a distance of 727 miles. It was the first of several such contests in that decade, and Bennett wanted a piece of the action, not least to promote this thrilling new sport to his fellow countrymen back home.

In 1900 he instituted his first competitive event – the Gordon Bennett Cup Race, open to countries which had national automobile clubs. His sponsorship over the next 5-year period was to play a significant role in the development of international motor racing.

In Britain, a speed limit of 14 mph meant that such foolhardiness on public highways was a non-starter, and the Automobile Club of Great Britain and Ireland cast envious eyes across the Channel to the achievements of their continental cousins and the emerging superiority of their cars and drivers.

Undaunted, the great English racing driver and motoring entrepreneur S.F. Edge drove his much-improved Napier to victory in the 1902 race – the only starter to complete the 351-mile Paris–Innsbruck course. As it was down to the winning nation to host the following year's event, that honour fell to Ireland, the Emerald Isle seizing the opportunity and passing new legislation to permit racing on public roads.

The 1903 race duly took place in County Kildare, over a distance of 327 miles, and was won by the German driver Jenatzy. Despite the failure of the British team, and the prohibitive speed limit (by now increased to 20 mph), interest in the sport in Britain was very much on the up. For the sake of national pride and the future development of the British automobile industry, one man believed he could redress the balance. Julian Orde, cousin of Lord Raglan and later to be knighted, had an ace up his sleeve. That ace was Raglan himself – Governor of the Isle of Man.

Orde reasoned correctly that this small island nation, with its own parliament and a fledgling tourist industry, was ideally placed to host the eliminating trials to decide the British entries for the 1904 and 1905 Cup races. To permit such road racing on the Isle of Man, Tynwald passed the Road Closure Act.

On 10th May 1904, the Gordon Bennett Cup Eliminating Trials began on the Island and paved the way for a long tradition of Manx motor car and motorcycle racing. The teams competed in three separate events – a hill climb, speed trials on Douglas promenade, and a high-speed reliability trial over five laps of a 51-mile course.

This automobile spectacular was a great success and repeated a year later for the 1905 eliminating trials. But this was to be the last of the Gordon Bennett Cup Races, and the Automobile Club of Great Britain and Ireland (forerunner of the RAC) decided to fill the void by introducing its own Tourist Trophy races to aid development of touring cars for the benefit of ordinary motorists.

It was also in 1905 that the Auto Cycle Club (later to become the Auto Cycle Union) held eliminating trials on the Isle of Man for the International Cup event in France. This race event too was short lived and so the Club followed the lead of the cars and in 1907 launched its own Tourist Trophy motorcycle races. The trophy awarded to the winner – a silver statuette of Mercury poised on a winged wheel – is the same in every detail as the trophy awarded today to the winner of the Senior TT Race.

Almost 100 years later, the Isle of Man's two-week summer TT Festival has long acquired cult status and is now an even bigger spectacle of speed and colour than ever, attracting spectators and riders from all over the world.

Many regular spectators have their own favourite vantage points, the best being those that enable you to move around during the races. For a lot of competitors it is the

Tynwald Day 2003 and some very special guests of honour

■ Manx motorsport also includes all the thrills and spills of Jurby Drag Racing, the Roush-Manx and Manx International car rallies, and the Peel Kart Racing Grand Prix.

A PROUD NATION'S VERY SPECIAL DAY

Change – and very rapid change at that – is the way of the world in the 21st century, bringing with it the fears of instability, insecurity and uncertainty as well as all the challenges of new opportunity.

All the more remarkable then that an island nation of just 76,000 population and 227 square miles, located within the British Isles, has managed to sustain the longest continuous parliament in the world.

Tynwald is a form of government which was established on the Isle of Man by Norse rulers more than 1,000 years ago and survives intact to the present day. It is very much a government for and by the people, proudly expressed in the national open-air celebration of Tynwald Day in the village of St John's every July.

It is a great festive public occasion; not

only for the traditional proceedings, pomp and ceremony conducted from Tynwald Hill but also for the colour and excitement of a fair and other entertainment which make the event so accessible to everyone, visitors included.

TYNWALD FAST FACTS

■ Tynwald is the Isle of Man Parliament. Its first meetings date back to the 10th century and probably even earlier, held at a place called Thing-vollr (Parliament field) from which the word Tynwald is derived.

■ On Tynwald Day (held on July 5th except when that date falls at the weekend), Parliament meets publicly in the open air and all the law passed during the legislative year is announced in Manx and English.

■ The traditional site at St John's is an ancient one, close to Norse burial grounds. The four-tier Tynwald Hill is artificial,

reputedly covered by sods of turf from every one of the Island's parishes.

■ Tynwald is the only parliament in the world which has 3 chambers – Tynwald Court and its branches, the House of Keys and the Legislative Council.

■ The House of Keys consists of 24 popularly elected members representing the Island's 15 constituencies. There is no parliamentary party system, the majority of the members being independent. So decision making is by consensus, which promotes political stability.

■ Each year a Junior Tynwald is held, at which sixth-form students (16-18) take the role of members of Tynwald and hold a mock sitting at the court.

■ The Tynwald Millennium was celebrated in 1979.

■ Apart from the national level of government, the Isle of Man also has a system of democratically elected local government.

■ Head of State of the Isle of Man, by virtue of the title Lord of Mann, is Her Majesty Queen Elizabeth II. She is represented in the Island by a Lieutenant Governor but in 2003 attended in person as the Tynwald Day guest of honour.

■ In 1765 the Isle of Man came under the full control of the British Crown as a Crown Dependency, the Island's current status. As such it is not part of the UK, Great Britain or EU and has its own parliament, taxation system, flag, currency and language.

■ Since 1765 the Isle of Man has gradually developed to become largely self-governing, the UK now only providing defence and foreign relations, for which the Island pays an annual fee.

■ The Isle of Man has no representations in either the UK or EU parliaments, but free movement of manufactured goods and agricultural products between the EU and the Island is conducted under a special protocol.

Tynwald Day attracts a large audience

A **TASTE**
OF MANX HOSPITALITY

Over the centuries, the Manx population has depended heavily on the fruits provided by land and sea to put food on the table. Farming and fishing were the traditional staple industries. But in a changing world which even touches these independent shores, finance and insurance now top the economic menu as the Island's main breadwinners.

Paradoxically, this shift in fortunes means that today eating out on the Isle of Man promises more choice than ever before – a veritable feast of taste sensations. Now you can enjoy the best of fresh local produce, dishes

and seafood alongside a banquet of popular international cuisine.

Although agriculture has slipped overall in the Island's income rankings, farming is still very healthy. There are around 450 commercial farms. Their meats, dairy products and cereals are much in demand, both on Island and off it,

and flower exports are blooming.

Succulent Manx lamb and Ballacushag beef have an excellent reputation for consistent quality. Meat from the native breed of Loaghtan sheep, which were probably introduced by the Vikings or descended from those bred by the Celts, is not only dark and tasty but has less fat and is low in cholesterol.

The long tradition of cheesemaking on the Island also dates back to the Viking era. The variety of mature full-flavoured cheddars includes oak smoked and black peppercorn, which are also available off Island at selected UK branches of Sainsbury's and Morrison's.

Undoubtedly, the most famous Manx offering of all – with even bigger celebrity status than the TT – is the humble but delicious kipper. Despite the decline in the Island's fishing industry, which at its height in the 1870s and 1880s provided the daily bread for one in every five of the population, Isle of Man kippers are still in great demand around the world.

The sea fisheries fleet is now less than a hundred strong, about half of which are smaller part-time vessels. Quota restrictions mean that the catch is focused mainly on shellfish, and the Island's twelve-mile territorial waters are patrolled by a fisheries boat.

Most of the shellfish is processed on the Island prior to export, but fresh crab, lobster, scallops and fish are served up in many Isle of Man restaurants. There are two varieties of scallop – small but delicious queenies in summer and larger king scallops in winter.

Manx kippers are a treat all year round. They are still prepared in the time-honoured way practised on the Island for more than two centuries. The herring is gutted, soaked in brine and smoked over oak chippings for exactly the length of time required to create that very distinctive flavour. Eating kippers with butter or marmalade, as they often are, is a delight to the taste buds.

Other food producers on the Isle of Man make heather honey, Manx preserves, chocolate, ice cream, pate (take home some kipper and crab) and mineral water. There are also three breweries and a distillery. Home-made Manx offerings you may come across on your travels round the Island are bonnag (made with soured milk and sultanas or other dried fruit) and blaeberry pie.

EATING OUT

The Food Directory – a complete guide to the Isle of Man's restaurants, pubs, wine bars, cafes and tea rooms – is available from the Tourist Information Centre in Douglas, but the following will give you a good idea of the many choices you can expect to find, essentially catering for all tastes and budgets – cafes to carveries, fast food to fine restaurants, steaks to vegetarian.

The emergence of Douglas as a major centre of international banking and commerce, and its extensive and ongoing redevelopment to reflect this status, is good news for visitors. As well as Italian, French, Spanish, Chinese, Indian and Cuban restaurants, you'll also find fashionable wine and tapas bars alongside pubs, hotels and other eating places offering a warm Manx welcome and a friendly atmosphere – something you can expect wherever you choose to eat on the Island.

Many country and village pubs such as the Highlander Inn at Greeba and The Waterfall at Glen Maye are particularly well known for their menus and hospitality. And Manx National Heritage can satisfy your hunger as well as your thirst for knowledge, with the Bay Room restaurant at the Manx Museum, tea rooms at Cregneash Village Folk Museum, the Garden Conservatory at the Grove Rural Life Museum, the cafe with spectacular views at the Sound Visitor Centre and the new cafe and visitor centre at Niarbyl.

DR OKELL AND THE SCIENCE OF BEER MAKING

Beers bearing the Okells label rank amongst the best in Britain and they've been produced on the Isle of Man since 1850.

Now owned by Heron & Brearley, the business was started by a man whose profession was more akin to scars than bars. Dr William Okell, a surgeon from Cheshire, opened his first brewery at Castle Hill in Douglas.

THIS **ISLAND'S** MADE FOR WALKING

I t doesn't matter whether you're a dedicated or an occasional walker – if you love fresh air and beautiful surroundings, the Isle of Man is a truly invigorating experience. As well as the wonderful variety and richness of the landscape, stepping out to explore offers you a rewarding choice of options. You can simply go where the fancy takes you – countryside, beaches, clifftops, glens, high hills – or use this section of the guide to help you conquer and enjoy some of the Island's designated waymarked trails.

FOURTEEN TOP WALKS

The walks described in the following pages touch each end of the spectrum – from the challenging long-distance coast path to much more leisurely circular town walks.

The first route covered, broken down into seven manageable sections, is the 95-mile coast path itself, Raad ny Foillan – the Road of the Gull.

Following this are the Heritage Trail (11.5 miles), the 26-mile Millennium Way, the Foxdale Line (just 2.5 miles along disused

The breathtaking view from the top of South Barrule

railway lines) and four town walks – in Douglas, Castletown, Peel and Ramsey.

THE COAST PATH

The Road of the Gull opened in 1986 and embraces most of the Island's dramatic coastal paths, but also takes in unusual rural walks and the vast beach walks of the northern alluvial plain. The total length of 95 miles is approximate and will vary according to the options you take along the way.

Serious walkers, using overnight accommodation at the main towns en route, can manage the coast path at a comfortable pace over a week's holiday. Purely for the purposes of this guide it is assumed that you will be (a) walking it in sections, (b) using public transport each day to get you to the start and to return from the finish of the walk, and (c) based at accommodation in Douglas (though bus and train links are good wherever you stay.)

Options (for half-day or even shorter walks) are highlighted in italics where appropriate.

MANX PLACE NAMES

Many of the Island's place names are in Manx Gaelic, or a corrupted form of it, and often describe very aptly either the shape or some other feature of the place. Others describe the origins of the place in relation to the family name of the historical owner. The remaining names have their origins in Norse and date from the Viking period. Where appropriate the English translation is given in the text to add interest and a better understanding of the Manx name.

WHAT TO WEAR

For reasons of safety and comfort you should always wear suitable shoes or, preferably, walking boots. This is particularly important on cliff paths where wet grass can be very slippery and catch out even the most experienced walkers.

As for clothing, it is sensible to bear in mind that although you will never be far from civilisation, exposed coastal areas are sometimes subject to rapid changes in the weather and if unprepared you can easily get caught out before reaching shelter.

MAPS

The Isle of Man Public Rights of Way Map, published by the Island's Department of Local Government and Environment, contains a wealth of information essential to serious walkers.

Ordnance Survey's 1:50,000 Landranger map 95 is also well worth obtaining, whether you're walking, motoring, cycling or exploring the Isle of Man by any other means.

RAAD NY FOILLAN: THE ROAD OF THE GULL

The seven sections into which this guide divides the 95-mile coast path (signposted along its route by a gull symbol) are as follows. The walk time indicated against each section is a guideline only and reflects the terrain and places and points of interest en route.

1: Peel to Port Erin (13 miles, 7 hours)

2: Port Erin to Port St Mary (6 miles, 4 hours) page 180

3: Port St Mary to Douglas (15 miles, 8 hours) page 184

4: Douglas to Laxey (9 miles, 4 hours) page 187

5: Laxey to Ramsey (12 miles, 6 hours) page 190

6: Ramsey to Ballaugh (18 miles, 8 hours) page 192

7: Ballaugh to Peel (13 miles, 5 hours) page 195

COAST PATH SECTION 1

PEEL TO PORT ERIN (13 MILES, 7 HOURS)

Take public transport to Peel and leave it at the House of Manannan. The site of the former railway station, this is a Manx National Heritage attraction, part of the *Story of Mann*.

The walk starts from here. There are options to take two half-day walks, one from Peel to Glen Maye and return, and the other from Port Erin around Bradda.

Begin by walking alongside the harbour to the bridge at its head. Cross the bridge and head towards the castle. After a short distance, follow the broad track up the hill, being careful to take the grassy track sharp left at the corner as the castle comes into view. You will soon see that there are two distinct parts to the hill which dominates Peel. The first, which you have just passed, is Peel Hill and the next part is Corrin's Hill, surmounted by Corrin's Tower.

From the saddle between the two hills you

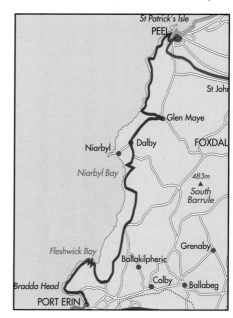

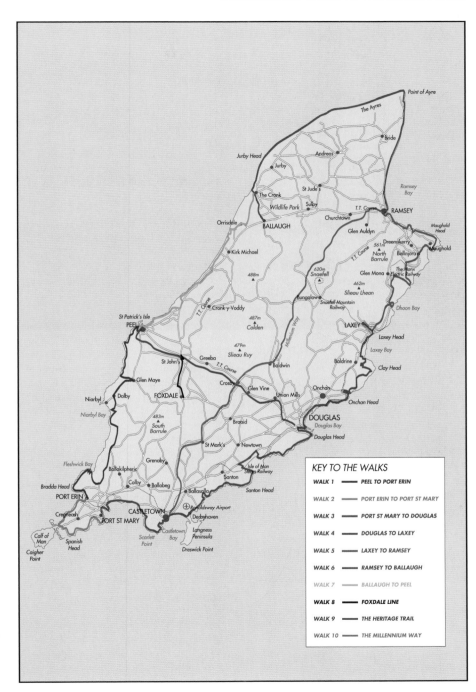

Point of Ayre

The Ayres

Bride

Jurby Head

Jurby

Andreas

Ramsey
Bay

The Cronk

St Jude's

Wildlife Park

Sulby

T.T. Course

RAMSEY

Maughold
Head

Orrisdale

BALLAUGH

Churchtown

Glen Auldyn

Maughold

Dreemskerry

561m

North

Ballajora

Kirk Michael

488m

Snaefell
620m

Barrule

T.T. Course

The Manx
Electric Railway

Glen Mona

Slieau Lhean
462m

St Patrick's Isle

T.T. Course

Cronk-y-Voddy

487m
Colden

Bungalow

Snaefell Mountain
Railway

Dhoon Bay

PEEL

LAXEY

Laxey Head

479m
Slieau Ruy

St John's

Greeba

T.T. Course

Baldwin

Baldrine

Laxey Bay

Clay Head

Glen Maye

Crosby

Glen Vine

Onchan

Niarbyl

Dalby

FOXDALE

Union Mills

Onchan Head

Niarbyl Bay

483m
South
Barrule

Braaid

DOUGLAS

Douglas Bay

St Mark's

Newtown

Douglas Head

Fleshwick Bay

Grenaby

Isle of Man
Steam Railway

Ballakilpheric

Santon

Bradda Head

Colby

Ballabeg

Ballasalla

Santon Head

PORT ERIN

Creaneash

CASTLETOWN

Ronaldsway Airport

Derbyhaven

Calf of
Man

Spanish
Head

PORT ST MARY

Scarlett
Point

Castletown
Bay

Langness
Peninsula

Caigher
Point

Dreswick Point

KEY TO THE WALKS

WALK 1	——	PEEL TO PORT ERIN
WALK 2	——	PORT ERIN TO PORT ST MARY
WALK 3	——	PORT ST MARY TO DOUGLAS
WALK 4	——	DOUGLAS TO LAXEY
WALK 5	——	LAXEY TO RAMSEY
WALK 6	——	RAMSEY TO BALLAUGH
WALK 7	——	BALLAUGH TO PEEL
WALK 8	——	FOXDALE LINE
WALK 9	——	THE HERITAGE TRAIL
WALK 10	——	THE MILLENNIUM WAY

On the coast path, en route to Port Erin

can either carry straight on to the summit of Corrin's Hill, or take the path to the right that follows the old horse tramroad to the quarry on the back of Corrin's Hill. The latter is by far the more spectacular but the path is close to the cliff edge in places so care is needed, particularly with young children – and this caution applies to many places on the walk.

Either option will bring you to the same spot, overlooking the south-west coast of the Island. Niarbyl (literally meaning the tail – from the tail of rocks stretching out to sea) is clearly visible. Cronk ny Irree Laa (hill of the dawn) dominates the skyline above and the hills stretch south to Fleshwick (green creek) and Bradda, with the Calf of Man just appearing in the far distance.

The path now becomes a real cliff path but is easy to follow as it skirts the various bays and inlets. Look for Traie Cabbag (cabbage shore – so named after the wild cabbage that grows here) and the unusual rock known as

the Bonnet Rock, which is surrounded by water at most states of the tide. You will see why it has this local name when you find it.

Now, as you approach Glen Maye (yellow glen) you have another choice. The path reverts to the coast road here for a short distance. You can follow the path down to the mouth of the glen as you round the headland and take the path up the opposite side of the glen to join the main road. Alternatively, carry on down into the glen and follow the lower path, stopping to admire the waterfall before climbing the steps to the main road.

There is an opportunity here to break for lunch at Glen Maye before returning by public transport or walking back to Peel along the main road – the first of the two half-day walk options referred to on page 175.

Turn right, follow the road down the hill and climb the other side to continue south parallel to, and in sight of, the coast all the way to Dalby (glen farm). Follow the signs through the village and start to climb. After a short distance look for the footpath signs directing you down the Dalby Laag Road.

The narrow road parallels the coast, drops down to a pond and finishes. You must look for the signs again here and follow them by crossing the pond on large stepping stones.

Continue towards the large house, looking for the signs and the stile directing you over the hedge and into the field opposite.

Follow the waymarkers and you will soon start to climb to a broad path on Manx National Heritage property that will take you south above Feustal (precipice) towards Cronk ny Irrey Laa.

Cross the stone wall over the wooden stile. The path is on the top of a cliff and should be treated with extreme care. Above Gob ny Ushtey (headland of the waterfall, although the literal translation means beak of the water; the early Manx often described headlands as looking like the bill or beak of a bird and so the description came into

common use), the path swings inland to cross a stream and wall.

From here strike uphill past the old farmhouse at Eary Cushlin (Cosnahan's shieling), now an outdoor pursuits centre. Continue uphill, following the signs all the way to the top of Cronk ny Irrey Laa. There are spectacular views all the way up the climb and when you reach the summit you will be at the highest point on the coastal path. Take time out to admire the view back over Niarbyl towards Peel with Corrin's Tower visible in the distance.

Now make your way down towards the Sloc (or Slough, meaning pit or hollow) over open moorland. Flocks of chough frequent this area and they are quite distinctive birds – very crow-like but with bright red beaks and legs contrasting sharply with black plumage.

Choughs are very rare in much of the British Isles and the Island is one of their last refuges.

Cronk ny Arrey Laa, west coast

this **island's** made **FOR WALKING**

At the Sloc you will leave the moorland very briefly to use the road, rejoining the moorland almost immediately by the picnic site on the other side of the boundary wall. Here as so often with the coastal path you are faced with a choice – the easy wide track to the left, or the path to the right which is for more experienced walkers and takes you to the summit of Lhiattee ny Bienee (literally meaning summit on the side), commanding excellent views back towards Cronk ny Irrey Laa and the big bay below.

Take the wide track and follow it to Surby (a Norse word – 'Saurbyr' meaning moorland farm) where it joins a surfaced road. At Surby turn right and follow the road to Fleshwick (green creek) down the east side of the valley. As you approach the end of the valley look for the signs on the left of the road, just after the farm, which will take you over a stile to start a really steep climb to the top of Bradda.

Take your time climbing the path and admire the views behind you of the coast all the way up to Niarbyl and across the valley to Fleshwick. Once you are over the top of this climb, the view down the coast to the Sound opens out in front of you.

The descent into Port Erin is easy and you will pass Milner's Tower on your way. Here again you are faced with a number of alternative paths. Take the one following the coast through Bradda Glen and on to the upper promenade at Port Erin. Walk into the village and follow the signs to the railway station and bus depot from where you will have a choice of transport back to Douglas.

The second optional half-day walk – from Port Erin around Bradda – starts from the railway station.

From the station cross the road into Bridson Street past the Cherry Orchard Hotel. Turn right into Bay View Road, left up Harrison Street and on to a Public Right of Way, which takes you across Rowany Golf Course. Be aware of golfers and keep an eye out for wayward golf balls! The path is clearly marked and the views are good.

Keep heading for the valley ahead, avoiding the junctions with other paths, and eventually emerge at Honna Hill, crossing through an old stone-built stile in the boundary wall.

Turn left and head up the hill to the top. Look for the sign marking the Ernie Broadbent Walk off to the right. Follow this narrow road down the west side of the Fleshwick valley until joining the surfaced road to Fleshwick beach just past the farm.

Turn left and look for the signs showing where Raad ny Foillan leaves the road a little distance further on, and where the longer walk from Peel joins.

There is time to walk down to the beach at Fleshwick and admire the views up the coast towards Niarbyl from sea level. The cliffs below the Carnanes sloping down to the sea are dramatic from here, and you can see where the high-level path from the Sloc descends to Fleshwick and why it is for more experienced walkers.

COAST PATH SECTION 2

PORT ERIN TO PORT ST MARY (6 MILES, 4 HOURS)

This is perhaps the most beautiful of all the Island walks, whatever the weather and time of year. You should allow about four hours to give yourself enough time to take in the terrific views.

The starting point for section two is Port Erin station. *An option here is to get to Port Erin by first travelling to the Sound, with its visitor centre and car park, and take in the village of Cregneash. This is a folk museum, part of the* Story of Mann *and well worth seeing. The road from the Sound leads you to the village, from where the Darragh Road (place where oak trees grow) takes you into Port Erin.*

Make your way from Station Road down to the lower promenade and follow the sweep of the bay to the Marine Biological Station. You will have to look very carefully for the start of this next section of the coast path – it begins from behind an electrical sub station!

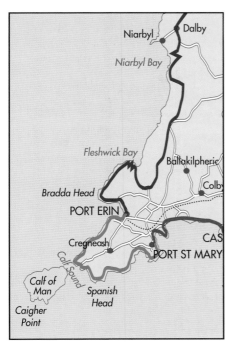

But once you've found it, the path is easy to follow.

There is a fairly stiff climb around the back of the Marine Biological Station and up above Kione ny Garee (literally meaning the end of the thicket) where fulmars nest on the north-facing shaded cliffs throughout the year.

The path levels out above Bay Fine and you have a good view back towards Port Erin and Bradda Head before descending towards Aldrick (old people's creek). On the way, look out for an unusual finger of rock known as Jacob's Rock. Ahead is the Calf of Man, the Sound, Kitterland and Thousla Rock. You can often see the tide race here and if it's at all stormy you'll be treated to spectacular seas and views.

Crossing Manx National Heritage land, the path skirts around Burroo Ned (nest hill) and you will see the back of Spanish Head above Baie ny Breechyn (bay of the breeches – so named because it resembles a pair of blue

Port St Mary's harbour is a haven for all sorts of pleasure boats

Port Erin in the winter snow

trousers laid out on the sea!).

Pass through a gate and cross a small stream to commence the very steep assault on the back of the Cronk Mooar (big hill – although it has a local name of Cronk y Feeagh, meaning hill of the raven, which is more appropriate as ravens do nest here). This is the southernmost hill in the Island – not very high but you will know it's a hill after you've made the climb!

Pause at the top and take in the views all round over the Sound and the Calf. If you're lucky and the wind's in the right direction, you may hear the baying of common seals as they bask on the Cletts (rocks) on the Calf immediately opposite this point.

The path now starts to drop, still skirting the cliff edge and then turning north to start its run up the east coast. The path is very close to the edge above Black Head, so take great care, especially if you have children with you.

The path now starts to fall quickly towards Bay Stakka (a corruption of Baie yn Stackey, referring to the stack of Sugar Loaf Rock) which it skirts and then climbs to the Chasms, which are on the right. Again the path is exposed at this point so tread carefully. Then cross the wall on the substantial stile and head towards the new Sound Cafe.

Go through the wooden gate and follow the waymarked route alongside the wall on your left. This should avoid having to cross any of the Chasms – deep clefts in the rock and quite an unusual phenomenon. Be careful to descend the path beside the wall on your left all the way to a metal kissing gate above Cashtal Kione ny Goagyn (meaning the castle of chasms' head) or Sugar Loaf Rock as it is more popularly known because of its unusual shape. It is inhabited by colonies of guillemots, kittiwakes, fulmars and the occasional razorbill and puffin, and this is perhaps the most spectacular view of the rock, providing you have a good head for heights.

The path crosses the next field diagonally, heading for a gap in the stone wall opposite. Before leaving the cliff edge you can just catch a glimpse of 'the anvil', or as it is sometimes called 'the pulpit rock', which is a rock standing clear of the cliff in the small bay behind the Sugar Loaf.

Follow the well-defined path between walls, leading eventually to a surfaced road to Glenchass (an English corruption of Glion Shast meaning sedge glen) and Port St Mary. At Glenchass take the right fork in the road and follow it downhill for a short distance, looking for a sign on the right to take you to

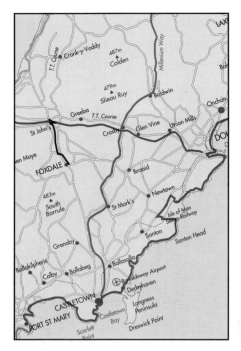

PORT ST MARY TO DOUGLAS (15 MILES, 8 HOURS)

If arriving at Port St Mary by bus, get off at the harbour. If you're travelling by train, it's only a short walk from the station to the village.

Start this section by rejoining the path along Port St Mary's lower promenade and Gansey Point to Bay ny Carrickey (bay of the rock), following the coast road to Fishers Hill for approximately one mile. You will pass the gatehouses and boundary wall to Kentraugh House, and where there's a break in the windswept trees that form the boundary you may just catch a glimpse of this fine mansion.

Continue along the sea wall and take the right fork at the bottom of the hill to follow the single-track surfaced road almost on the shoreline to Poyll Vaaish (literally meaning the pool of death; the name's origin is obscure but one likely explanation is that a slaughter house associated with the farm drained into one of the many sea pools).

The whole area teems with birdlife, particularly herons fishing patiently in the rock pools and on the edge of the water, competing with curlews and oystercatchers.

The path continues through the farm buildings at Poyll Vaaish and round the low headland beside the quarry from which the black marble for the steps of St Paul's Cathedral in London was reputedly obtained. Cross the stone stile over the wall on to the grassy headland at Scarlett (cormorant's cleft).

The path follows the edge of the fields and skirts the rocks, which change dramatically, showing their volcanic origin and culminating in Scarlett Stack – a volcanic plug to a vent long since extinct. The broken, jagged rocks are the remains of an ancient lava flow. The rock changes from basalt to limestone as you approach Castletown.

Enter the town square and turn right to skirt the castle, passing the police station. Turn

the shoreline at Perwick (harbour creek).

The route follows the beach at Perwick and Traie Coon (narrow beach) before swinging up a zigzag path from the stony shoreline to join the path beside the golf course and on to Port St Mary promenade. Walk along the sea wall, passing the disused limekiln and past the breakwater into Lime Street and the inner harbour. Port St Mary remains largely unspoilt but the harbour is now occupied by pleasure craft rather than commercial fishing boats.

Turn left at the end of Lime Street and then right to follow the lower promenade and join the Cain Karran elevated walkway, which gives an impressive entrance into Chapel Bay – without doubt one of the Island's prettiest and most sheltered bays. Walk up into the village, where you'll find a variety of places to eat and a bus to take you back to Douglas.

Above Sugar Loaf rock, a stack colonised by seabirds

immediate right again, then left over the footbridge to cross the harbour. Turn right into Douglas Street and past the Nautical Museum, which together with the castle is part of the *Story of Mann*. Continue along Douglas Street, right into College Green and follow the promenade towards King William's College and the airport.

Carry on as far as Derbyhaven, turning left along the shoreline as far as you can go. At the end look for the waymarkers which will take you around the edge of the airport boundary and under the approach lights gantry.

You will climb to an ancient raised beach, which you must follow to Cass ny Hawin (the foot of the river) where the Santon River joins the sea through a dramatic gorge. The gorge was cut by the meltwater from the retreating ice sheet during the last ice age, and you'll have a commanding view of the gorge from the site of an ancient Bronze Age fort.

The path now follows the gorge inland,

crossing the river bridge and returning to the coast down the other side of the gorge. Although signposted it is often wet and difficult underfoot, in which case it may be best to take to the fields and follow the top of the gorge until you join the coast again.

Once at the coast the path is easy to follow along the top of the cliffs. You will be rewarded with good views all the way to Douglas.

The next bay you will come to is Port Soldrick (sunny creek). Just where the path turns inland to drop down to the shoreline, you will see large caves in the opposite headland, with a view of the coast north towards Santon Head. After travelling along the beach for a short distance, climb back on to the path as it takes you higher still to continue along the cliff top.

The next inlet is Port Grenaugh. Again, after reaching the shoreline, climb up the other side of the bay. Look for the promontory fort and Viking settlement at Cronk ny Merrui (literally the hill of the

Laxey is a charming coastal village with a variety of attractions

dead people) on the right as you climb.
Continuing along the coast you will pass Purt
Veg (little port) and Santon Head before
starting the climb up to Ballanhowe, where
the path goes inland once again.

The single-track road crosses the line of
the steam railway before joining the Old
Castletown Road. Turning right, follow the
road for a little over a mile, but take care as
there is no footway.

Descending Crogga hill (from the Norse
Króká meaning winding river), you will pass
Crogga House and its decorative lake before
seeing a waymarker directing you down
towards Port Soderick (which has the same
meaning as Soldrick – sunny or south-facing
creek), this passing under the line of the
steam railway.

Keep to the road and take the left fork
along Marine Drive, where the coast path
follows the route of the former Marine Drive
tramway all the way to Douglas. Proceed

along the coast, passing the inlet at Keristal.
Note the change again in the rock
formations, the contorted strata now in
fragmented slate and clearly visible in the
cliffs all around you. Problems with sliding
cliff faces over the years mean that as a
through road Marine Drive has been closed
to traffic for quite a time, but be aware that
cars are still able to use a large section of it
from the Douglas end.

The sight of the old toll gatehouse means
that you're almost at Douglas, confirmed by
the panorama of the whole bay spread out
before you as you round the corner.

The coast path now descends the steps
between the lighthouse and the Camera
Obscura to the breakwater, passing the
Lifeboat House. The Douglas Lifeboat is
appropriately named *Sir William Hillary* in
honour of the founder of the Royal National
Lifeboat Institution, who lived in Douglas in
the early part of the 19th century.

COAST PATH SECTION 4

DOUGLAS TO LAXEY (9 MILES, 4 HOURS)

This is a good half-day walk and Laxey has a lot to show you, including a fine choice of places to lunch and the fascinating Laxey Wheel and mines area – an important part of the Island's rich industrial past.

Start at the Sea Terminal at the southern end of Douglas's impressively wide and sweeping 2-mile Loch Promenade. The prom was built in the 1870s to enclose part of the foreshore and to extend the lower part of what was then the Island's newly-appointed capital. Some of the original Victorian facade is now giving way to modern development as the changing face of Douglas continues to take shape, but enough survives to give you more than a flavour of Victorian grandeur as you make your way north along the bracing and spacious seafront.

On the opposite side of the promenade note the attractive elevations of the Sefton Hotel and the Gaiety Theatre. The church to the left and set back off the prom was completed in 1849 and dedicated to St Thomas, the patron saint of architecture. It was designed by Ewan Christian R.I.B.A., who was of Manx descent and Architect to the Church Commissioners, noted particularly for his work at Carlisle Cathedral.

The construction of the church was by local contractor Richard Cowle. It was built to serve the needs of an expanding town, and the arrival of the tourist development along Loch Promenade led to it being referred to as 'the visitors' church'.

A fire in the tower in 1912 destroyed the bells and the organ made and installed in 1886 by William Hill of London. The fire damage was repaired and a new peal of bells installed five months later. At the same time the organ was repaired and enlarged, and today recitals and concerts are a regular feature of church life.

As you continue towards the northern end of the crescent-shaped promenade, where stands the terminus of the unique Douglas Bay Horse Tramway, you'll see more evidence of redevelopment. The horse trams are a summer-only attraction and date from 1876. Here also is the southern terminus of the Manx Electric Railway, which has been running north to Ramsey since operation commenced in 1895. Both the horse trams and the railway still use original equipment and, unsurprisingly, they are a mecca for transport buffs from all over the world.

Continuing past Port Jack and around the loop of Seaview Road, you'll soon see why it is so named, overlooking Douglas Bay. Look for the coast path waymarker directing you along the cliff top and almost through the front gardens of the houses here. The path joins the road again at Lag Birragh (literally the sharp pointed hollow – referring to the rocks below) and continues along King Edward Road to Groudle (narrow glen), where you should follow the narrow road

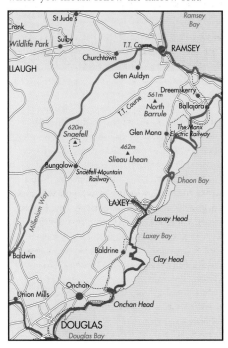

Laxey Bay, where low tide reveals a small beach and interesting rock pools

down to the shore by the holiday homes.

Cross the river by the footbridge and climb up the path to cross the Groudle Glen Railway. A popular Victorian novelty and attraction, the restored railway is now operated by enthusiasts at various though limited times during summer months and for Santa specials.

Follow the path upwards and on to a narrow surfaced single-track road. Look for the waymarker directing you across the fields to Garwick, and also for the signpost to Lonan Old Church – well worth a detour, not least to see the stone Celtic Wheel Cross in the grounds.

Walk through the fields to the point where

the path joins Clay Head Road, which you must follow towards Baldrine. Look for the waymarker directing you to Garwick, and follow the fishermen's path to the shore and climbing immediately all the way back up the other side of the glen. Follow the signs to join the main road again.

Turn right at the top and continue towards Laxey, following the tramway (there's no pavement so be careful). Reaching Fairy Cottage presents you with an option – as long as you know the state of the tide! At low water you can take another fishermen's path down to the beach and walk to Laxey harbour the very pretty way. Alternatively, stay on the coast path and continue down Old

Laxey Hill into Old Laxey and the harbour.

Follow Glen Road to Laxey village and up the hill under the church to the centre of the village. Christ Church Laxey is situated in what must be a unique setting for any church and its history is entwined with the mining history of Laxey. The village was a very busy place in the mid 1800s as a direct result of mining. The population had increased significantly, and with the temptation of public houses on the doorstep the need for a place of worship within the village was long overdue.

In fact, the Laxey Mining Company and one of its principal shareholders, G.W. Dumbell, were instrumental in promoting a

church. Built largely by the miners themselves, right in the middle of the village on land which was formerly part of the garden of the Mines Captain's House, it was designed by architect Ewan Christian. Early English in style, it has an interesting scissorbeam roof and simple internal decor and it merits spending a little time here.

Take lunch in the village and complete this leisurely day's coastal walk with a visit to the Great Laxey Wheel & Mines Trail – yet another chapter in the Manx National Heritage *Story of Mann*.

Return to the railway station and take the train back to Douglas.

COAST PATH SECTION 5

LAXEY TO RAMSEY (12 MILES, 6 HOURS)

From Douglas, travel by bus or electric railway to Laxey station and you're ready to resume your conquest of the coast path.

Start by taking the path alongside the station building and down to Captain's Hill. Turn right to join Glen Road opposite St George's Woollen Mills and make your way to the harbour. Note the large factory-type building on the opposite side of the river – built to generate the power for the Laxey section of the Manx Electric Railway.

At the junction by the harbour bridge, look to the opposite side of the road for the coast path waymarker. It directs you up an old packhorse road to Ballaragh (of doubtful origin but best seen as derived from Balley arragh, meaning farm of the spectre or apparition). Continue up through Ballaragh to the top of the hill and the views towards Maughold Head and east across the Irish Sea to Cumbria and the Lake District.

The road curves away from the coast but look for the waymarker on the corner, pointing you over the fence and diagonally down through the fields. Cross the road and the railway track and continue on the footpath until it joins the Dhoon Glen Loop Road. Cross one stile on to the road and then immediately back over the adjacent stile to follow the track down to sea level again. It is worth the effort even though this is another of those down-and-back-up-again detours.

The path skirts Dhoon Glen and you will catch a glimpse of the wheelcase of the Dhoon Rhennie Mine (Dhoon is probably derived from an Irish word meaning fort and rhenny is a ferny place), which extracted lead and zinc but was not productive and eventually abandoned. Then the mouth of the glen opens up and you will have a view of the headland of Kion e Hennin (Kione ny eaynin – headland of the cliff; Kione literally means beak or bill of a bird but by common

usage has come to mean headland). Its inclined grey slate is the native rock of the area, and immediately behind the headland was a granite boss which for years was quarried for its pink granite.

The path drops to the shore and then returns behind the picnic table. Follow the path within the glen, climbing past the Island's most spectacular waterfall, comprising three falls emptying into a pool beside the path. A further steep climb will take you back to the point where you began this detour.

Turn right back onto the Dhoon Loop Road and follow it over the railway back to the main road, where you turn right. Almost immediately turn right again and at the bottom of the hill take yet another right turn, making sure you follow the right fork by the ford and the single-track road down to Cornaa (an ancient treen, meaning land division, name).

You are now back at sea level again, but this time with a difference. Behind the

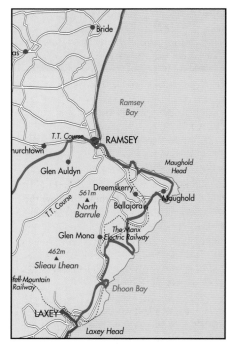

Looking south towards Laxey from Maughold Head

shingle bank is a saltmarsh with an attendant variety of birdlife.

The path crosses the river and follows an unsurfaced road known as Benussi's lane all the way up the right-hand side of the valley, heading inland. Cross the railway again, and the main road, to continue up the Raad ny Quakerin (the Quakers' road), noting the Quakers' burial ground at the summit.

Descending through Ballajora (farm of the strangers), you'll enjoy a view of Maughold Head and the lighthouse. At the bottom of the hill look for the signs taking you right to Port Mooar (the great harbour). Follow the path round the coast through the tall grass to Gob ny Rona (headland of the seals) where you may very well see some of these marine mammals. At Dhyrnane, before climbing away from the shore, you'll pass derelict workings from an iron ore mine.

Now cross fields past a lime kiln to join the road to the lighthouse, turning right for a short distance before turning left on to Maughold Brooghs. Follow the path over the

headland through more old mine workings at Gob Ago (literally edge headland) before joining the road again and turning right towards Ramsey.

Not for the first time, you have a choice of routes: carrying on into Ramsey along the main road or, if the tide is out, going down the slip at Port e Vullen (harbour of the mill) to the shore and following the cliff path around the headland at Tableland to rejoin the road again a little further on.

Either way, it is back up to the main road, passing Belle Vue railway halt and all the way down into Ramsey. At Ballure (Balley euar meaning yew tree estate or farm) you could make a detour into Ballure Glen and on to Ramsey along the beach, but this option is only possible at low water. Once in Ramsey, proceed along the promenade and the harbour. At the end of the promenade is the church of St Maughold and Our Lady Star of the Sea, built in 1900 and designed by Giles Gilbert Scott.

This marks the end of the Laxey-Ramsey

clear to see that the whole area is subject to storm erosion.

If you've taken the road to Bride and onwards, you will pick up the coast path again at the Phurt (port) north of Shellag Point. Follow the raised beach and the glacial formation of the northern plain is clearly evident. The whole of the Ayres was formed by alluvial deposit and here the terrain changes yet again with shingle underfoot all the way around the northernmost tip of the Island. The lighthouse which marks the Point of Ayre was designed by Robert Stevenson for the Commissioners of Northern Lights and built in 1818.

The shingle is constantly on the move, as can be seen by the smaller lighthouse added 72 years after the original and now automated, controlled from a remote central station.

Continuing along the coast on the shoreline is heavy going underfoot but worth it for the wild natural beauty to seaward, with

birdlife in abundance. Look for gannets, whose spectacular dive-bombing action, black-tipped vivid white wings and highly distinctive blue bills set them apart. As you make your way along the beach it's probable that you'll be followed by curious seals and constantly leapfrogged by flocks of oystercatchers – a wonderful sight in flight.

Passing Rue Point and Blue Point, where the rifle range and the old coastguard lookout are located, will put sand back underfoot. The whole of the northern plain has been drained by successive generations to reclaim many acres of fertile agricultural land. The last major undertaking was the formation of a lengthy drainage channel which discharges at the Lhen (Lhen Mooar – meaning great ditch). You'll know when you reach it, as the Lhen Trench discharges across the shore and wading is the only way to get across – so it's boots off and round the neck.

As you approach Jurby Head, the sand cliffs are back with a vengeance and continue

Jurby Church, a distinctive landmark

almost to Peel. If the tide's well out at Jurby Head look for the remains of the trawler *Passages*, which was driven ashore in 1929 in a north-west gale, the crew rescued by the rocket brigade of the day.

After passing Jurby Head you approach the Killane (from the Scandinavian kjarrland, meaning brushwood land), where another drainage ditch discharges to the sea. Shortly after this, look for the signs where the Ballaugh shore road joins the shoreline at the Cronk.

Leave the shore and walk to the village of Ballaugh, passing the old parish church of St Mary de Ballaugh. Dating from the middle of the 18th century, it is noted for its leaning gate pillars. Old photographs and other sources suggest that the pillars must have been in this condition for a hundred years or more.

Walking towards Ballaugh, you can admire the backdrop of the western hills and see the tower of the 'new' parish church. Work on the church commenced in May 1830. The

A view north along the west coast

old church was considered too small and, as the village community grew, too far from the centre of the population it was supposed to serve – even though it was no more than a mile away!

Designed by Hanson and Welch, the church is built in local stone in a style unique for the Island. The tall lancet-type windows and intervening buttresses to the nave, and the ornate pinnacles, make it quite distinctive.

You will arrive in the centre of the village opposite the public house and beside Ballaugh Bridge – a famous landmark along the TT course.

COAST PATH SECTION 7

BALLAUGH TO PEEL (13 MILES, 5 HOURS)

To complete your anti-clockwise conquest of the Isle of Man coast path, here's a walk which is easy going all the way.

It begins from the centre of the village, beside Ballaugh Bridge. Leave the village by Station Road and proceed to the Cronk, passing the two churches described in Section 6.

On the way you will pass the Dollagh (a corruption of Doufloch, meaning black lake) – a name rooted in the fact that in much earlier times, a great deal of the northern plain was flooded, the land dominated by several large lakes. No visible signs of these lakes remain, except in periods of heavy rainfall, when remnants appear here and there. Other places such as Ellan Rhenny (ferny island) and Ellan Bane (white island), and even the parish name of Ballaugh (a corruption of Balley ny Loughey – lake farm), give a clue to what this area was like in those days long gone.

At the Cronk turn left and follow the Bollyn Road (Boayl ein – spot of the birds) as far as the Orrisdale Road. There are good views of the western hills which form the backdrop to Bishopscourt, the ancient seat of the Bishop of Sodor and Mann but now a private residence. Turn right at the junction with the Orrisdale Road and follow the road through Orrisdale (from the Scandinavian Orrastaðr, meaning estate of the moorfowl).

At the corner after the farm look for the signpost leading to the shore at Glen Trunk. Go through the gate and follow the wide grassy track to the shore, past one of the Island's best-preserved lime kilns.

Once on the shore you will be able to see Peel in the distance. Turn left and walk along the shore, flanked by steep sand cliffs, and note how these are also subject to erosion. For this reason it is advisable to steer a wide berth when walking underneath them.

This is an interesting spot for bird lovers. You're likely to be in the company of oystercatchers, herring gulls and black-backed gulls. Curlews, living on the slopes of the western hills, graze the foreshore in flocks and ringed plover and the occasional chough are often seen in these parts.

As you approach Glen Wyllin (glen of the mill) you will spot sea defence works on the foreshore – an attempt to slow down the rate of erosion. Beyond these, a little further along the shoreline, look for the waymarkers directing you off the shore at Glen Mooar (the great glen).

Leave the shore here and make your way up the narrow surfaced road to the main coast road. Look across the road and you will see a waymarker directing you into the glen. Follow the path as far as the stone pier – one of two piers which once carried the railway across the glen on lattice steel girders. Climb the roughly-cut steps up the side of the embankment to join the disused railway track. This now forms part of the coast path and will take you to the old station at St Germain's Halt, 3 miles away.

Once on the track, look back and this elevated position will show you just how severe the erosion of the sand cliffs is at this point. In places it will not be long before the coast road is threatened.

There are a couple of farm crossings before you approach a rock cutting and the road

overbridge at Skerisdale (or more correctly Skeresstaðr from the Norse meaning rocky farm). The railway now runs closer to the sea than the road does and you can imagine just how dramatic a journey it must have been as the train clung to the cliffs and spanned the glens on viaducts and embankments.

Leaving the cutting, the track bed emerges on to an embankment at Glion Cam (the winding glen), opening up views of Peel and the castle on St Patrick's Isle in the distance. The coast road can be seen to the left and above, winding around the head of the glen – hence the local name of the Devil's Elbow.

Half a mile further on, in a shallow cutting which is sometimes quite wet and muddy, the path emerges into the open and really does cling to the cliff. This section, known as the 'donkey bank', suffered continuous settlement problems when the railway was operating, and these are evident as you proceed. Below, as you cross the second of the embankments,

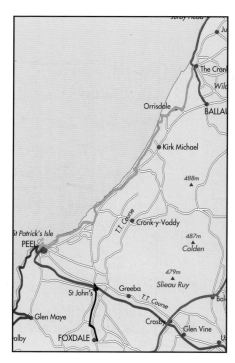

you can also see rocks on the shoreline at Gob y Deigan. From here on in the physical features of the coast change yet again – from the sand cliffs to slate and to red sandstone as you get nearer to Peel.

The path continues on the track bed for a further mile, crossing yet another glen on an embankment at Glion Booigh (the dirty glen). It's worth stopping on the embankment to look down at the trees growing in this glen. There's a great variety, with some surprises, and in many ways it is one of the most unspoilt corners of the Island and only really appreciated from this location.

The path now curves left to join the coast road at the site of the former St. Germain's Halt, the old station building and gatehouse just about recognisable as such.

Leave the track here and follow the road for a short distance downhill and round the corner at the bottom. Look for the waymarker on the right and go through the kissing gate to join the headland path. The path climbs rough-cut steps and reaches a

promontory above Cass Struan (stream end). Stop and look north back along the route you've just walked and you'll see the sand cliffs stretching all the way north to the prominent white outline of Jurby Church and Jurby Head in the distance. Now look down below where you're standing and you'll see the sandstone (referred to earlier) which outcrops here in a glorious burst of russet red.

The path continues to Peel along the headland above Traie Fogog (or more correctly Traie Feoghaig – meaning periwinkle shore), commanding probably the best views over Peel and the castle. Continue on the headland path and descend into the town and the promenade. There are several places to take refreshment and any of the roads off the prom leads to the town centre and the bus station for return to Douglas.

If you've completed all seven sections of Raad ny Foillan, you'll have to admit it's been an adventure. Congratulations – and here's to the next time!

Looking south along the west coast

THE HERITAGE TRAIL

DOUGLAS TO PEEL (10.5 MILES, 4 HOURS)

This easy and leisurely walk along a disused narrow-gauge railway follows the route of the first line which connected Douglas to Peel.

When the railway was built in 1873, the Isle of Man Railway Co. had a simple wooden building as its station. But by 1892 it had developed at such a pace that the company had built a new station to rival many of the mainline stations in the British Isles – so where better to start the walk than in the station forecourt on Railway Terrace, close to Athol Street and the heart of Douglas's business community.

Unfortunately, the first half mile or so of the original line has been extensively built over, so you have to make a detour before joining the line at the Quarterbridge. But as you leave the station, look at the impressive Victorian clock tower, which gives a good idea of the grandeur of the station architecture when it was built.

From the station turn left up Peel Road. The shops you pass on the left were also built by the enterprising railway company. Continue to the junction with Pulrose Road and turn left over the bridge – built in 1938 to replace an earlier level crossing on the line you'll be joining a little further on. Note the bridge's two arches. The intention was to construct a double track, but it was an ambition never realised. You'll also be able to make out the route of the track bed as it threads its way behind the development in this area, which has taken place over the last twenty-five years.

Continue on towards the power station and turn right immediately before the bridge over the Douglas River. Follow the pathway behind the Bowl, part of the King George V playing fields. The whole area was reclaimed using waste from the spoil heaps at the Foxdale mines. The Isle of Man Railway locomotive No.15 *Caledonia* was used almost

exclusively to haul thousands of tons of material here between 1935 and 1939.

The path takes you to the confluence of the River Dhoo (black river) and the River Glass (green river), and now you can see how the name of the town of Douglas evolved. Follow the right fork alongside the Glass and cross it by the bridge, which leads to the National Sports Centre. Follow the river for a short distance past the rear of the grandstand and join the railway track behind the office building. This is where the railway crossed the river on a skew lattice girder bridge.

Now you can start the walk in earnest. A little way along the old track bed you'll reach the site of the level crossing which took the railway over the Castletown Road. Note the crossing keeper's gatehouse on the left, but take care crossing the very busy road because visibility is restricted.

All of the Island's disused railways are now service corridors for gas, electricity, water and telephones. They are also public rights of way and over time have been improved for walkers. In 1989 this line was the most complete in terms of the overall scheme and was designated the Heritage Trail. Work to improve it continues and the ultimate aim is to create a cycle way to broaden the trail's use.

The next section of the track bed serves an access road for vehicles to the inside of the TT course when the main road is closed for racing. Continue behind Quarterbridge Lodge, climb the gate across the track and walk between the stone boundary walls. On the left you will see Kirby Estate and possibly catch sight of grey herons, which roost here and range the river. The name Kirby is Scandinavian in origin and means church farm.

As you pass under the road you're approaching the site of what was formerly Braddan Halt. This was used in connection with Open Air Sunday Services at Braddan parish church, shortly coming into view to the left. It was not uncommon to see ten-

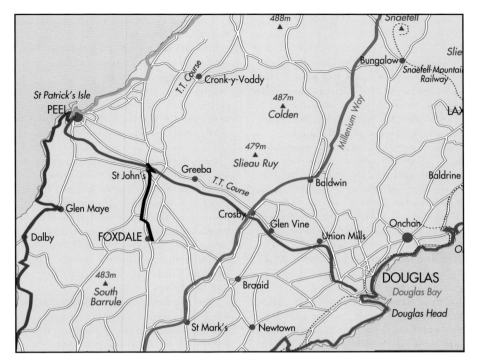

coach trains on this short special service from Douglas and hundreds of visitors getting off at the halt, which had no platform, and walking up the steps by the bridge and up Vicarage Road to the fields behind the new parish church.

Leave the surfaced roadway and carry straight on along the old track bed, at this point more recognisable as a disused railway. The River Dhoo, which has never been very far away from you, is now beside the railway. The local commissioners have provided a wooden walkway between the railway and the river as part of a conservation scheme.

At Union Mills the line curves left after crossing the river on a steel girder bridge. This replaced an earlier stone–built structure which gave rise to flooding in the early years of the railway. A small wayside halt existed here originally to serve a horseracing course at the Strang.

Now, with industry left behind, the scenery

becomes more attractive. It's hard to believe that even as late as 1960 there was little or no industrial development between Pulrose Bridge and Union Mills!

Entering Union Mills station through the tall trees which have grown with the railway, you are now 2.5 miles from Douglas. Early photographs show almost no cover at all. Successive station masters took tremendous pride in the station, which became noted for its wonderful rhododendron and floral displays.

The station was on the curve and had a very long passing loop, added some time after 1906. On the left you will see the single platform serving the station. Look for the name of the manufacturer of the non–slip paving slabs which form the edge of the platform. Also on the left, before you reach the platform, there's a roadway accessing the station area. There was a short trailing siding here serving goods traffic and a cattle dock.

Douglas Bay, with the harbour, Sea Terminal and Tower of Refuge in the foreground

The line, now 5 miles out of Douglas, swings right with Greeba and Slieau Ruy (red mountain) straight ahead. As you approach and cross the track leading to Cooilingel Farm, you are into the true remaining curragh of the central valley. This was an accommodation crossing and the gates were always open to the railway. Walk over another short bridge which crosses the Greeba river and continue close under Creg y Whallian. This is the narrowest part of the valley and very near to the summit of the line.

The next level crossing over the Rhenny road (boayl y rhennee – place of the fern) was also an accommodation crossing. The house with the unusual farm buildings on the right is Northop (another Scandinavian word meaning north village). Here is another chance to look at Greeba before the curragh closes in and you pass through a very wet area which was the site of an early settlement. You emerge approaching the Ballacurry Road, another unmanned crossing. The summit of the line, at 185 feet, was marked by the small stream after the Ballacurry Road. The Greeba sports field is on your right, just visible through the trees.

This is the site of an accident in 1909 when the locomotive *Derby* (No. 2), acting as pilot engine on a late train running to Peel, had the misfortune to hit a fallen tree. It was completely derailed and toppled on to its side – the second accident in which it was involved (but more of that shortly).

As you pass through Greeba the curragh is still visible in places, but over the years drainage work and farming activity have reclaimed a large portion of it. The wooded hill ahead is Slieau Whallian, although its true summit is further to your left. The hill dominates the village of St John's, and it is up its flank that the Foxdale Railway climbed the 1 in 49 gradient to the mines. This is the point from where the Isle of Man Railway Co. at one time proposed to build a branch line to Foxdale. It would have gone off to the left, climbing the side of the hill above Kenna (Aodha's hill – Aodha being a name of Irish descent).

Next you cross the Kenna Road, which was yet another unmanned accommodation crossing. After a shallow reverse curve under the trees, the track runs straight all the way to St John's.

Now Slieau Whallian is much closer and you can see the gatehouse for the keeper at the Curragh Road level crossing. The track bed has been surfaced here and an additional road built to serve an amenity site. Cross the road and the stile on to the right-hand track – the original route of the railway – and pass under the bridge which carried the Foxdale Railway over the Peel line. The bridge is covered with ivy but you can see the brick arch springing from the stone abutments.

You are now approaching the site of St John's station. It grew from very modest beginnings to become the 'Crewe Junction' of the Island railways. In its final form the line was single, passing under the bridge and running for a short distance parallel to a three-line steel carriage shed on the right. There was a fourth carriage siding in the open on the far side of the shed.

A small signalbox near the trees stood in the middle of the grassed area to your right. Here the line split into two, each with a passing loop and served by a single low platform, just one brick high, placed between them. This is where the Ramsey line and the Peel line divided. At each end of the central platform was a water tank supported on a brick structure. To the right, sidings served a cattle dock, the remains of which can still be seen, and there was also a head shunt to the carriage sidings.

St John's was served by a simple wooden station building situated on the left near the road (the site now part of a housing development). It had a small waiting room, ticket office and station master's office and was never developed or replaced by more impressive facilities despite the relative importance of the station.

Two lines crossed the road on a gated level crossing, the Peel line on the left and the Ramsey line on the right.

To continue the walk you have to make a slight detour from the original route, as the bridges over the Mart have been removed. Cross the road and go through the gate opposite, leading to the sewage works, and rejoin the track alongside them.

Walking down from the road you can see an interesting red brick building behind the hedge on your right. This was the terminus of the Foxdale Railway and was a grand building compared with the IMR's modest station at St John's.

Passing through the gated stile puts you back on clear track bed again. The two lines were still running parallel here, the line to Peel on the left and to Ramsey on the right. As you approach the two bridges crossing the River Neb at Ballaleece (Leece's farm), you will see the Ramsey line start to rise alongside you in order to pass over the Peel road as it swings away to the right.

The Peel line makes a gradual descent from the river crossing before levelling out on the ancient flood plain of the Neb (the meaning of the river's name is obscure). The river, having looped around to the left towards the Patrick Road and joined with the Foxdale river since the bridge at Ballaleece, is now back alongside the railway on the approach to Shenharra (meaning Old Ballaharra, possibly referring to an ancient earthwork).

The river meanders away to the left as you approach the cutting at Ballawyllin (Byllinge's farm), which was a notorious spot in winter for snow. The cutting is through the tail of what appears to be a moraine, deposited at the time of the retreating ice sheet in the last ice age.

Through the crossing at Ballawyllin you can now see the true flood plain extending out towards Patrick, and the full extent of Peel Hill and Corrin's Hill, surmounted by Corrin's tower.

Further to the left are the Creggans (literally rocky place but describing the small rocky outcrop), forming the southern boundary to Knockaloe (Caley or Allowe's hill), the site of a First World War internment camp. A branch of the railway was built to serve the camp and shortly you will see where it joined the Peel line. The line ran straight for a short distance before skirting the sand cliffs of Ballatersen (part of the old Bishop's Barony but literally meaning farm of the crozier), now the location of Peel's golf course.

You'll see that the railway passed through the last remnants of the curragh and if you're particularly observant you might spot the remains of some of the drainage channels dug in the 1940s as a winter employment scheme in a further attempt to drain this area.

The line now ran beneath the cliffs and through boggy ground again – terrain which caused big problems throughout the entire lifetime of the railway. You can get some idea of the nature of the ground as you pass close under the sand cliffs. The willow catkins are a sight to behold in spring and the area abounds with the yellow heads of wild iris.

A little further on and the river is once more back alongside the railway and slowed by a dam built for the Glenfaba Mill (a mixture of English and Manx; it should be Myllin Glenfaba, meaning Mill in the glen of the Neb). The pond is known locally as the 'red dub', and you can see where the mill race was taken off the dam and under the track on its way to the mill. The name for the area, which also gives its name to the weir, is the Congary (rabbit warren).

Before reaching the mill you'll cross a small stream by means of a footbridge. Pay particular attention to the widening of the track bed just after the bridge. This is where the branch railway to Knockaloe Internment Camp left the Peel line by means of a trailing point from this direction. You can just make out the line of the branch as it curved round to cross the river on a wooden trestle bridge to climb for a little over a mile, at a gradient of 1 in 20, to the village of Patrick and Knockaloe.

Next on the right is the Glenfaba Mill. Some indication of what it was like can be gleaned from the size and shape of the building. The waterwheels remain and the overflow from them would have discharged under the track into the river. In fact the railway occupied the original river bed here, the river re-aligned to accommodate it.

The railway passed under the Patrick Road and alongside the river, which was also diverted here to allow the line to run through this natural gorge on a gentle curve. It was here, in 1874, that the ill-fated locomotive *Derby* suffered the first of its two major accidents.

Following heavy rain, the embankment gave way and the loco tumbled into the river. It was the first train of the day and although the driver saw that the track had been washed away he was unable to stop. He and the fireman both fell with the engine but were uninjured, as was the only passenger who fortunately occupied one of the coaches which remained on the track. The railway was temporarily diverted on a reverse curve to the right, almost on the original line of the river, while the present retaining wall was built on the original alignment.

Follow the railway through the remaining fields of Glenfaba farm as you enter Peel, through the back door past the old power station on the left. On your right are the Total Oils storage depot and the new Peel power station. When the railway was running the first buildings encountered would be the brick kilns and tall chimneys of the Glenfaba Brick Company – no doubt aesthetically more pleasing than the concrete chimney now occupying the site.

Straight ahead on the left-hand side of the track is one of Peel's original kipper houses, now operated as a working museum and worth a visit. The modern kipper houses are in the fish yard on the right.

The railway finally arrived at Peel station by a level crossing over Mill Road. The station site had been reclaimed from the harbour bed. The water tank, station building and goods shed are all that remain of the station itself, the last two buildings incorporated into the House of Manannan heritage centre, which now occupies the site. Behind the water tank there was a small engine shed and on the right a cattle loading dock and the goods shed. This had a loading bay into Mill Road which can still be seen. The station, having undergone several changes throughout its life, ended with four roads and a run-around loop served by a long platform.

The Creek Hotel – originally the Railway Hotel – is a good place to stop for well-earned refreshment.

The railway ceased operation between Douglas and Peel in 1972 after five years of uncertainty. The rails had been lifted and sold for scrap before the Isle of Man Government stepped in and purchased everything, which fortunately included the now-thriving Port Erin line of the Isle of Man Steam Railway.

THE MILLENNIUM WAY

RAMSEY TO CASTLETOWN (26 MILES)

This can be undertaken as a full-day walk or as two walks breaking at Crosby.

The Millennium Way was the first long-distance path to be introduced in the Isle of Man as part of the celebrations associated with 1,000 years of independent government. Opened in Easter 1979, it is based on the ridgeway used by the Norse kings to travel from their ancient landing place on the Sulby River near Skyhill to their fortress on the southern plain. The road is recorded in the *Chronicles of Mann and the Isles* – the first written record of Island life, produced by the monks of Rushen Abbey.

NORTHERN SECTION: 14 MILES

Take a train or bus to Ramsey and make your way from the station to the harbour, which is a short distance along Parliament Street and down Post Office Lane opposite the Courthouse. Turn left at the harbour and follow it to the junction with Bowring Road. Note the shipyard on the opposite side of the harbour which was built on the site of a former salt works.

Cross the road at the top of the harbour and look for the public footpath sign leading to Pooyldhooie (pool of the black ford), where a nature reserve has been constructed on what used to be the town tip. It is now a very pleasant walk and a credit to the local commissioners and the volunteers who have carried out the work.

The path emerges by the Whitebridge, which crosses the Sulby River, and this must have been the most likely place for the Vikings to have made their safe harbour. At the time of their invasions and subsequent settlement the Island was a very different place and the Sulby was by far the biggest river. Here they could sail their longships at least a mile and a half from the open sea and moor them in a sheltered lagoon – something which was not possible anywhere else on the Island.

Walk up Gardeners Lane to the main road and turn right for a short distance, looking for the distinctive waymarkers for the Millennium Way, striking off to the left over the bulk of Skyhill (the Norse named it Skógarfjall – the wooded hill). Follow the path up through the plantation, which was the site of a battle in 1079 when Godred Crovan overcame the native Manx and assumed kingship of the Island.

From the plantation the track opens out on the level near some rugged flat-topped pine trees at Park ny Earkan (pasture of the lapwing). Stop and look back over the northern plain, formed by the outwash from the retreating ice sheet at the end of the last ice age. The Point of Ayre is in the far distance.

Carry on to the top mountain gate and enter the open moorland. The track is still discernible and there are waymarkers which you follow to a very wet boggy area. Cross by

Looking towards the Point of Ayre from the high ground above Ramsey

means of the planked walkway and be careful to follow the waymarkers off to the right, heading for a cairn on the skyline in the saddle between Slieau Managh (mountain of the monks) and Snaefell (snow mountain).

The original kings' road veered off to the left here and followed the line of the mountain road for some distance, travelling around the east flank of Snaefell. The Millennium Way favours the west flank to keep away from the traffic on the mountain road and at the same time introduces you to some of the more inaccessible places in the Island.

Pass the cairn and carry on over the saddle a short distance to join the mountain wall above Block Eary Reservoir (from blakkärg meaning black shieling). Follow the mountain wall where it turns steeply down below the massive bulk of Snaefell. Cross the wall at the bottom by the stile and over the river.

The way strikes off steeply from the river and at right-angles to it. It can be wet here at all times of year but only for a short distance. As you climb it is worth looking back across the valley at the route you have just walked.

You should just be able to make out the shape of some circular mounds. These are the shielings where the young men used to live with their animals on the mountain pasture during the summer months – another remnant of a past way of life and the best example of such structures on the Island.

Follow the waymarkers across the mountain until you pick up a stone wall and sod dyke which is part of a large earthwork known as Cleigh yn Arragh (stone rampart). Follow this until you reach a forestry department track and then the Tholt y Will

Road.

Cross the road at the signpost and strike diagonally down the mountainside towards the mountain ahead, which is Beinn y Phott (very loosely interpreted as turf peak). At the bottom of the valley cross the river by means of an old stone bridge, built and used by the miners who operated the mine a short distance upstream. The stone structure you can see is the remains of the wheelcase of the waterwheel. The mine closed in 1867.

Climb up on the left-hand bank of the gulley, being careful at the top to take the left-hand fork, and head for the signpost which you should be able to see on the Brandywell Road.

This is where the Millennium Way joins the route of the old ridgeway again. Cross the road and follow the track over the saddle between Beinn y Phott and Carraghyn (meaning scabby, with reference to its stoney top) as far as the mountain gate giving access to a rough track, which you follow for almost two miles. As you skirt the shoulder of Carraghyn, the views open up over the Baldwins and on towards Douglas in the distance.

The track starts to drop down at Cronk Keeil Abban (the hill of St Abban's church) where an old keeil was located near an ancient Tynwald site on your right. At St Luke's Church, built as a chapel of ease to Kirk Braddan, join a surfaced road taking you downhill into West Baldwin.

At West Baldwin, cross the bridge and the road to follow the signs up a track through Ballagrawe (Balla ny Groa - farm of the cotes or coops) and across the fields of Ballalough (farm of the lakes). After passing the farm, cross the stone stile and follow the lane for a short distance before crossing a ladder stile. Follow the waymarkers across two fields on the eastern flank of Greeba.

There are superb views to the left over Douglas as you head for the saddle between Greeba and Cronk ny Moghlane or Mucaillyn (hill of the sows) and the signpost on the skyline. After the next stile there is a diversion around the edge of the field before reaching the narrow road leading to Cronk Brec (hill of many colours – literally piebald). You must now make a left and right to follow a rough stone track down to Ballaharry. Just before you reach the cottages, look to the right and the sign pointing to an ancient monument. This is the site of the remains of Keeil Vreshey (the church of St Bridget) and is an example of early Celtic Christianity. There were many such sites on the Island.

At Ballaharry the track joins a surfaced

road which takes you into Crosby village at the crossroads with the main Douglas to Peel highway. Here you can finish the walk and return to Douglas by public transport – or if you have the energy, carry on along the southern section to Castletown.

SOUTHERN SECTION: 12 MILES

The southern section of the Millennium Way is totally different in character, and the old ridgeway passed to your left to cross between the Mount and Slieau Chiarn (the Lord's mountain). It has been incorporated into the present road network, and in order to keep the walk more attractive the Way takes a slightly different but parallel route.

The start of this section is tough. Make your way down Station Road in Crosby: you will see where it gets its name as you pass the small crossing keeper's house where the railway went over the road. Then it is a stiff climb up School Hill, passing the old school built in 1874. Its bleak location may seem a little strange when you look around and see where the centre of population is now. When it was built, however, the school was in the centre of the parish serving numerous remote farmsteads as well as the village. The same factors applied to the old parish church which you will pass at the top of the hill. The church is dedicated to St Runius and dates from the 12th century, although the remains of a keeil dating from the 7th century can be seen on the site.

Continue along the road under the avenue of trees towards the Garth crossroads. Look out for the ancient monument sign on the right as you start to climb the next hill. It directs you to the site of St Patrick's Chair - a small group of stones which according to tradition is the spot where St Patrick first preached and intoduced Christianity to the Isle of Man.

Carry straight on over the crossroads, passing Ballanicholas and drop down the hill to Campbells Bridge, which marks the boundary between the parishes of Marown and Malew. Stop at the bridge ,spanning the Santon River, to read the interesting plaque. Look over the bridge and you may just be able to make out the remains of old mine workings.

Continue on past Shenvalley (old farm) and in the distance you will be able to see the tower of the church at St Mark's. The church is a good landmark and you will need to turn left and then right at St Mark's and around the old schoolhouse. The church, school and adjoining houses were built in the 18th century at the instigation of Bishop Hildesley as a chapel of ease to Malew parish church.

You need to be careful here and look for the waymarker beside the old parsonage. The path follows the lane beside the parsonage to the Awin Ruy (red river) and crosses it on an old stone slab. The path meanders through the fields of Upper and Lower Ballagarey (farm of the river thicket), crossing hedges through kissing gates and eventually arriving at a surfaced road.

Cross the road and follow the waymarkers through two fields before entering

Ballamodha Mooar farmyard and following the farm road through Ballamodha Beg to its junction with the Ballamodha Road (Ballamodha meaning farm of the dog, Mooar meaning big, and Beg little).

Turn left and walk along the road for approximately a mile, taking care as there is no footpath. The Ballamodha straight was used in the past for hill climb and reliability trials when the motor car was in its infancy.

Continue to the bottom of Silverburn Hill and at the Atholl Bridge turn left to Silverdale and walk on the path alongside the river. Approaching Silverdale you will come to a children's playground, boating lake and cafe. The boating lake gives the clue as to the function of the old building adjoining the cafe. Creg Mill was one of two built by the monks of Rushen Abbey, and the lake powered the waterwheel. The little waterwheel which now turns the children's carousel is worth more than a passing glance as it came from the Foxdale Mines when they closed.

Continuing downstream you pass Ballasalla

Windy Corner, looking south

Monks Bridge, Ballasalla – one of Britain's last surviving examples of a 14th-century packhorse bridge

Ochre & Umber Works – an old industrial site now converted into a private residence. The company was a substantial one and had warehousing in Castletown, from where shipments were made. The north quay still carries the name Umber Quay.

Leaving the wooded glen you emerge through a gate at Monks Bridge, dating from the late 14th century and probably the oldest bridge in the Island, built by the monks of Rushen Abbey.

Approaching the site of the abbey, look left

to the opposite side of the river to Abbey Mill, now converted to private apartments. It was a substantial mill with an internal waterwheel and gives an indication of the importance of the abbey. The whole area of the abbey has been acquired by Manx National Heritage and archaeological research is further revealing the unfolding *Story of Mann*.

Follow the boundary wall of the abbey to the right and walk around the perimeter – on the way you may be able to catch the odd glimpse of abbey remains through a gate. Cross the road and almost opposite, the waymarkers direct you down a narrow lane and then left to the river again. The Way follows the river into Castletown on a pleasant walk through river meadows. Cross the river on a wooden bridge, continuing on the other side nearer to the steam railway. Look for the weir that took water from the river for the Golden Meadow Mill, visible from the path as you pass Poulsom Park. The railway station is across the park and you can return to Douglas from here or continue into Castletown and finish your walk at the castle.

SHORT WALKS

THE FOXDALE LINE (2.5 MILES, 1 HOUR)

This short walk follows the disused railway line which connected the Foxdale lead mines to the rest of the Island's railway network at St John's. The best option is to take a bus to Foxdale and start from the old station, which is adjacent to the primary school.

The Foxdale Line was built in 1886 by the Foxdale Railway Company, an offshoot of the Manx Northern Railway, as an opportunist venture to win lucrative mineral traffic from the Isle of Man Railway.

Prior to the building of the line to Foxdale, all the ore was taken by horse and cart to St John's for onward transmission by the Isle of Man Railway to Douglas station. It then had to be loaded again into horsedrawn carts and hauled to the harbour at Douglas. The contract for the carriage of the ore came up for renewal and the Manx Northern bid was successful, creating a direct rail link between the mines and Ramsey harbour. But it was to prove a financial disaster and resulted in the eventual downfall of the Manx Northern, everything coming into the ownership of the Isle of Man Railway.

When mining came to Foxdale it brought with it a tremendous increase in population. Public houses sprang up in its wake and it soon supported a constable and a jail.

Methodism found a strong footing in the area as in Laxey. The established church appointed a chaplain to Foxdale in 1850 but it was to be 1881 before Foxdale had its own church. Public subscription and a handsome donation from the mining company resulted in the foundation stone being laid in 1874 by Mrs Cecil Hall. The church, designed by James Cowle, was consecrated by Bishop Rowley Hill on Whitsun Tuesday, 7th June 1881 as a chapel of ease to Kirk Patrick Parish Church. The village became a parish district in its own right some years later. The church can be seen on the opposite side of the valley beyond the old school.

It is hard to imagine now what this area was like at the height of the mining boom, lead and silver produced to an annual value of £50,000 at the time the railway was built. There were 350 people employed in the mines. The three main shafts were Potts, Beckwiths and Bawdens. The deepest, Beckwiths, reached a depth of 320 fathoms (1,920 feet) by 1902, yet by 1911 the industry had declined and the Isle of Man Mining Company had ceased working.

The walk starts by the old station building which is opposite the school in Mines Road, and is all downhill at a steady gradient of 1 in 49. There is quite a wide defined track which runs from the road beside the school. This is the start of the track bed, and the building on the left is the station building. There was a shallow platform with brick edging served by a single line with a run-round loop. The area presently occupied by the school was the site of the principal spoil heap from the Beckwiths mine.

A temporary siding was built into this area in the 1930s to assist with the removal of the spoil, which was mostly used in the construction of the playing fields at the National Sports Centre in Douglas. The spoil from the Bawdens shaft formed a massive heap and the station was hemmed in between these two mountains of waste – a scene very very difficult to imagine today.

Beyond the station building was a small brick structure supporting a water tank for the locomotives. A single line climbed behind the back of the station at a gradient of 1 in 12 to cross the road and enter the mines yard. Here the ore was loaded into wagons for Ramsey via St John's. This line was always referred to as 'the back of the moon' – which was exactly how the area looked after the mines had ceased working.

Before starting the walk, go up Mines Road a short distance and you should just be able to see the remnants of the crossing, with the running rails and check rails in the road surface – the only visible remains of the Foxdale Railway.

Return to the station and start to walk down the line. While the first part near the school is somewhat changed, you soon come on to the old track bed, which is quite unmistakably railway as it skirts behind the miners' cottages in Higher Foxdale. On the hillside to the right there is still visible evidence of the oldest mine in the area, particularly near the river.

Now you are very close to the road. The line ran on a high stone-built embankment before swinging left to cross the road on a steel girder skew bridge (Luke's Bridge), the road prescribing a double corner as it dropped under the bridge to continue to Lower Foxdale (the name Foxdale is an anglicised corruption of Forsdalr, a Scandinavian word meaning waterfall dale). The bridge was removed when the track was lifted in the early 1970s. You must climb through the stile in the boundary wall and cross the road to the opposite side where there are steps leading up the old bridge abutment and back to the track bed.

Now the formation can be really appreciated and you continue on an embankment towards Lower Foxdale with a view of Slieau Whallian ahead. Cross over the accommodation road to Ballamore farm (from an Irish family name – More's farm) on a small bridge. The line entered a cutting

through rock as it curved left and approached Waterfall Halt, which was the only intermediate stop. Little remains of the halt. Originally planned to have a passing loop, it was completed with only the single line and a small wooden building on the flat area to the right.

You have to walk out of the station area on to the Ballanass road to bypass the small bridge, now demolished, which carried the line over the Gleneedle stream, a tributary of the Foxdale River. You will be able to see the abutments of this bridge from the road you are on before rejoining the track bed. The halt served the community of Lower Foxdale and also attracted visitors to the Hamilton Falls, where the stream cascades down a rock face before joining the main river.

Back on the line, walk under the bridge which carries the Ballanass road over the railway (Balla n eas is Manx Gaelic meaning farm of the waterfall). You are in a short cutting under trees and can probably hear the sound of the waterfall below you on the right. You emerge to curve around the hillside with lovely views towards the central valley dominated by Greeba Mountain. The line was built on an embankment and followed the natural lie of the land. There was an old mine on the left, but nothing remains except a very overgrown spoil heap. The occasional telegraph pole is a reminder of the railway's existence.

You are now approaching Slieauwhallian farm (an obscure word which could refer to a personal name, possibly Mc Aleyn, or it could refer to hill of the whelps) and entering a wooded area. Pass under the bridge which carries an accommodation road associated with the farm and you will see that the construction was of a very simple nature and used concrete for the abutments. After the bridge the line passes through a very attractive section before curving left alongside the plantation – part of the larger Slieauwhallian plantation, neither of which existed in the days of the railway.

Unfortunately you have to leave the line at the end of the plantation and veer off to the left to join the Slieauwhallian back road. Follow it to the right, downhill to the Patrick Road and right again to the next junction.

Before leaving the track bed, note where the track continued on an embankment almost forty feet high. Although now much overgrown, it still gives an indication of the amount of material needed for its construction. The line curved to the right to cross the Foxdale River on two steel spans carried on a central stone pier between two abutments.

If you like you can turn right at the junction. Walking a short distance towards the Hope Inn will show you where the line crossed the river, after which it curved in a left-handed sweep to cross over the Peel Line and into St John's. If you return to the Patrick Road junction, you can carry on towards the village to a car park - the site of the St John's station originally built by the Isle of Man Railway.

Walk further up Station Road and cross over the Foxdale Line just before the post office. You can look over the right-hand parapet wall and see where the line came into St John's behind Pretoria Terrace, with the embankment climbing away towards Foxdale and over the Peel line. Look over the left-hand parapet and you can clearly see the St John's terminus of the Foxdale Railway. The station was a grand building by comparison with that belonging to the Isle of Man Railway, and similar in style to the station building at Foxdale. There was a passing loop at the station, with goods sidings and the connection to the Manx Northern Railway beyond.

Finish the walk here and use public transport to go on to Peel or Douglas.

DOUGLAS TOWN WALK

Starting in front of the Sea Terminal forecourt, it is worth taking time to look at this building, completed in 1962. Now offices, the circular part of the structure immediately below the spire was originally a restaurant commanding unrivalled views of the bay and harbour. The unusual roof earned it the nickname of the lemon squeezer. The building was formally opened by Princess Margaret in 1965.

The short walk around what is now the lower part of Douglas commences along Bath Place towards the bus station. Keep to the left-hand side of the road and head around the corner towards the inner harbour and the new harbour bridge, which replaced an earlier swingbridge. The accumulator tower and control room for the old bridge can still be seen on the other side of the harbour.

Cross the road at the swingbridge to the harbourside and read the inscriptions on the plaques, which have been fixed to blocks of Foxdale granite. The inner harbour was until recently a commercial harbour and was tidal. When the new bridge was installed a tidal flap was built and the enclosed basin became a yacht marina, part of an overall plan to redevelop the harbour as a focal point for Douglas.

Walk along the side of the harbour behind the parked cars and cross the road opposite the Clarendon Hotel and continue along the North Quay. The old Fish Market (now the Royal British Legion Club) and the market are the next buildings you pass before reaching the British Hotel.

The harbour frontage is gradually changing but much of its past can still be traced on this part of the quay. At the junction of Ridgeway Street is St Matthew's Church, dating from 1895 and built at a time when the old heart of Douglas was being redeveloped and new streets were being driven through the town.

Continue along the quay and look for the plaque on the building on the right just before arriving at Queen Street. You will see that it was the first electricity generating station for the town. At the junction with Queen Street are the last vestiges of the old character of the area. The Liver Hotel formerly stood directly opposite the building which is part of the Newson Trading block. Opposite is the Saddle Hotel, and the old narrow alignment of Queen Street, winding round the rear of the quay to Quines Corner, completes the picture.

The area had many more public houses then than it has now, earning it the reputation of the 'Barberry Coast'. As you walk along the quay to the top of the harbour you will see that the old and the new have blended together to keep some of the character of the old harbour frontage.

Cross Bank Hill and walk into the railway station forecourt and across to the steps on the right leading up to the clock. At the top of the steps pause and look back at the grand building in red facing brick, built at the start of the 20th century at the time that the Isle of Man Railway Company acquired the other two railway operators.

Go through the entrance gates and cross into Athol Street and walk along the street on the right-hand side. By the start of the 19th century it represented the upper limits of Douglas, the Georgian-styled houses being the residences of merchants and the wealthy. As the town expanded this area quickly became its business centre, and still is. Much of the street has been redeveloped but here and there you can still see some of the original buildings.

Walk as far as Lower Church Street and turn right past the now derelict old Court House which is about to be redeveloped. Note on your right the new multi-storey car park. At the bottom of the hill turn left by Scotts Bistro. It is probably the oldest surviving building of old Douglas. Opposite is the John Street elevation of the Town Hall and the site of the original fire station for the town.

Turn left and head up Prospect Hill, passing several of the national banks before

Castletown's harbour and castle are indeed a picture

reaching Athol Street again opposite the Italianate-style Isle of Man Bank headquarters. The opposite side of Prospect Hill has been redeveloped, new office buildings presenting a stark contrast in styles.

Continue as far as Hill Street and pause before turning left to look at the 'wedding cake corner' buildings - part of the administrative and parliament buildings of the Isle of Man Government. On the opposite side of the road is St Mary's Roman Catholic Church, designed by Henry Clutton and opened in 1859.

Walking along Hill Street you will note more new office development reflecting the new-found wealth of the town. At the end of Hill Street turn right into Upper Church Street and opposite is St George's Church, from which the street gets its name.

Walk up as far as Circular Road and turn right, crossing over to walk on the left-hand side of the road to its junction with Prospect Hill again. Opposite, at the other end of Government Buildings, are the Rolls Office and the new Court House. Now turn left and continue up Bucks Road, once the main route out of Douglas to the north.

Carry on as far as Rosemount, pausing to admire the fine spire of Trinity Methodist Church. Continue straight on past Prospect Terrace and the shops which were originally built as private houses, the extent of the original terrace framed by the pediments. At the junction with Hawarden Avenue is Woodbourne Square, laid out in the late 19th century and one of several which retain the Victorian character of the town.

Walk through the square and emerge opposite the Masonic Lodge. Cross the road and walk towards the next town square which you will see behind the Lodge. Hillary Park is totally different from the square you have just seen. Walk through it and emerge opposite the terrace of yellow brick houses and turn right, walking as far as Derby Road, where you turn left.

After a short distance look for the right turn to Derby Square opposite the Bowling Green Hotel and walk to Crellins Hill, at the top of which is the Manx Museum. Walk down the steep hill to St Thomas Church, completed in 1849. Keep to the left-hand pavement, cross the road and walk down Church Road to the promenade. Turn left, walking past the Sefton Hotel to the Gaiety.

If the Gaiety Theatre is open for conducted tours you shouldn't miss the opportunity to see it. The theatre is described in detail elsewhere in this guide, so suffice to say it will be time well rewarded. Otherwise, cross the promenade to its seaside walkway and return to the Sea Terminal.

CASTLETOWN WALK

The walk around the former capital of the Island starts at the railway station. This will give you the ideal opportunity to arrive at Castletown by train and sample the delights of Victorian travel.

From the station, go over the railway lines into Poulsom Park and cross the park adjacent to the children's play area, through a gate directly opposite on the bank of the Silverburn River. Turn left and walk beside the river.

Pass under the railway bridge, where you will almost certainly be accosted by the resident population of geese and ducks. Walk up to Alexander Road and cross it to join Victoria Road, continuing beside the river. Straight ahead is the imposing grey bulk of Castle Rushen, around which the town grew to become the ancient capital of the Island.

The castle beckons – but first, a detour. Cross the road at School Lane and walk past Victoria Road Primary School and the unusually named Smetana Close, so called because of the town's close association with many continental musicians and through an annual music festival held in the town.

Emerge past the gates of Lawn House, a former residence of the Governors of the Island, on to Douglas Street and turn right. Look out across Castletown Bay at the long

peninsula of Langness, its prominent
lighthouse at the southernmost tip. Walk
along the pavement to the corner with
Bridge Street and past the Nautical Museum,
a part of the *Story of Mann* which presents a
history of the Island's fishing industry and the
story of *Peggy*, the oldest surviving Manx-
built ship. Continue as far as Bridge House.

As you join the harbour turn left, cross the
swingbridge and there's the castle in all its
glory. Straight ahead on the corner is the
local police station, designed in keeping with
the castle by Baillie Scott. Across the road is
the castle barbican and entrance. The castle is
a must on your list of places to visit. It is one
of the best-preserved medieval castles in the
British Isles, largely because of its limestone
construction, and it has remained in use
throughout most of its life.

For now though, leave the castle behind by
turning left and walking along the quay. Then
turn right up narrow Quay Lane, leading into
what is now a public car park. Ahead is the
old Grammar School, one of the Island's
oldest buildings, incorporating part of the
medieval chapel of St Mary and its structure
pre-dating most of the castle.

Turn immediately right and walk into
Parliament Square, which forms the forecourt
to the old House of Keys building. This is
where the Island's Parliament met until
Douglas became the capital. It too is part of
the *Story of Mann* and merits a visit.

Turn left into Castle Street and into the
Parade. Cross the road and catch the best
view of the castle. Note also the unique one-
fingered clock presented to the Island by
Queen Elizabeth I in 1597. The castle as it
stands now dates from the latter part of the
16th century but parts of it were built as early
as 1250. The dominant features are the
massive keep and four flanking towers.

If you look to the right, the other end of
the Parade is Market Square, which has as its
backdrop the former garrison church of St
Mary's, dating from 1826 but now
deconsecrated and converted into offices. In

the centre of the square you will also see a
fine Doric column built to commemorate
Cornelius Smelt, the first Governor of the
Island. Unfortunately the column never
received a statue of the Governor.

Continue along Arbory Street, the road to
the left off the Parade. The shops in this street
have changed little over the years and are
much sought after as sets and locations by the
Island's developing film industry.

When reaching the Crofts turn right and
admire the part of the old capital where the
wealthy of the day lived. Half way along the
Crofts go in through the gate on the right to
the municipal bowling green and walk past
the cafe and green to emerge in Malew
Street. Turn left and then right to walk down
Mill Street.

This area has been redeveloped under the
guidance of the local Commissioners to bring
people back into the centre of the town. At
the end of Mill Street turn right into Hope
Street and walk back towards the town
centre. At the end of the street is a limestone
building, formerly the National School and
now converted for use as a replacement for St
Mary's Church.

Turn left and cross the bridge over the
harbour to return towards the starting place
at the railway station.

PEEL TOWN WALK

The walk around Peel starts outside the
Creek Inn in Station Place – formerly the
Railway Hotel and part of the town's railway
heritage, though trains no longer run here.
Directly opposite is the House of Manannan,
which incorporates part of the old railway
station.

To start the walk head away from the
harbour and turn right into Mill Road.
Passing the back of the House of Manannan,
you will see that the goods shed of the
railway has also been incorporated into the
museum.

To some extent this is the 'industrial heart'
of Peel, with the gas works on the left

together with the kipper yards and the site of the old brickworks. Peel Heritage Trust has in fact established a small museum in the brickworks weighbridge office, and the former station yard opposite is now a boat park, though the railway's water tower has been preserved.

Where Mill Road joins the harbour, Moore's kipper yard still preserves herring in the traditional manner and in season operates conducted tours of the establishment. Turn right here and walk alongside the harbour, back towards the Creek. Peel is dominated by the bulk of Peel Hill and Corrin's Hill, worthy of a walk to the top.

You join East Quay after passing the impressive entrance to the House of Manannan. And continue along the quayside for a short distance, passing the remains of warehousing which serviced the fishing industry – for so long the mainstay of Peel's economy.

At St Peter's Lane turn right and walk up the narrow street past grand stone-built houses, originally the homes of fishermen. At the top of the hill turn left, skirting the whitewashed wall which enclosed the churchyard of St Peter's Church, built as a chapel of ease to the original St German's Cathedral on St Patrick's Isle. It was demolished in 1958 but the clock tower remains and the grounds are retained as a place of quiet reflection.

As you walk along the lane, the architecture of the tower gives an indication of the style of the former church. Turn left into Castle Street and then right into Love Lane and left into Market Street. Continue down the hill to the double corner. On the second corner walk through the opening on the right into Charles Street – a charming part of old Peel. Many of the buildings in Peel are built of sandstone and here the beauty of the stone can be seen to advantage.

Continue through Charles Street and Strand Street into Beach Street and turn left on to the promenade. Here you will pass

some of the oldest fishermen's cottages still remaining in the town. Turn right on the promenade, pausing to admire the castle on St Patrick's Isle, which has its origins in a Norse settlement.

Continue along the promenade as far as Stanley Road. Turn right and half way up the hill turn right again into Circular Road. Walk up the hill to the corner at the top and cut through the alleyway into Christian Street, turning left and then right into Mona Street. Peel had many Methodist churches, nearly all of which are no longer places of worship, but their spirit remains in their architecture.

Walk up Church Street to emerge opposite the courthouse and police station. Cross the road and enter the grounds of the new St German's Cathedral. Although the church dates from 1884 and was built as the parish church, it was not consecrated as the new cathedral until 1980.

Continue through the grounds and walk

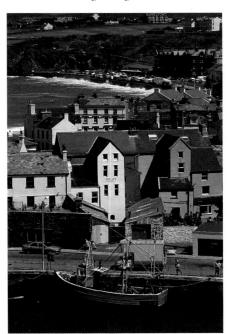

Peel, home of Manx kippers

down to emerge through the grand entrance gates into Atholl Street, opposite the Methodist church. Turn right to Atholl Place and left down Michael Street, which is the town's main shopping thoroughfare.

At the end of the street turn right into Douglas Street and then left at Market Place. Now you can imagine the commanding position which St Peter's Church held overlooking the old part of the town.

Cross the square and follow the church wall to Lake Lane and walk down to Station Place and the completion of the walk.

RAMSEY TOWN WALK

Your tour of the town of Ramsey starts in Market Place, opposite St Paul's Church. This dates from 1822, when it was spawned from the parish of Maughold as the town grew and the population centre gradually shifted.

In earlier times Market Place was the focal point of the town and the location of an open-air market selling predominantly fish. Some stalls still open here on certain days.

Leave Market Place by way of Dale Street, passing the municipal swimming pool and the Roman Catholic Church of Our Lady of the Sea, designed by Giles Gilbert Scott and built in 1900.

Arriving at the promenade, walk in the direction of the Queen's Pier. Dating from 1886, it is one of the surviving classic Victorian piers, constructed to allow passing liners and vessels of the Isle of Man Steam

The tall buildings lining Ramsey harbour are reminders of the port's past wealth

Packet Company to call at all states of the tide. It is now the subject of a preservation campaign.

Opposite the pier, turn right up Queen's Pier Road and then right again into Waterloo Road to return towards the centre of the town. You will pass the old Cross on your right – the site of the Old Town Hall and the point at which one arm of the Sulby River originally discharged into the sea. Just after the Old Cross note the distinctive Mysore Cottages built in memory of Sir Mark Cubbon, Commissioner General and Administrator of Mysore in India. Adjoining is the old Grammar School dating from 1864 and replaced by the present school in 1922.

At the end of Waterloo Road turn right

into Bourne Place and Parliament Street, opposite the terminus of the Manx Electric Railway. The courthouse and police station are on the left as Parliament Street curves around in that direction.

As you continue along Parliament Street, note the facades of the buildings and the dates when they were built. The town still displays a good variety of shops in its main street despite the pressures of supermarkets.

Walk along as far as Christian Street before turning left, but pause at the junction and look ahead at the classic buildings of Auckland Terrace – now more than ever the business centre of the town. To the right the old warehouses, still in use, are a reminder of the wealth and importance that this northern

Ramsey — once a centre for shipbuilding, now a home for boats

town once possessed.

Turn left and on the skyline ahead of you is the Albert Tower, built to commemorate a surprise visit by Queen Victoria's consort when their ship was unable to land at Douglas. Walk as far as the junction with Albert Road and turn left again. Here, on the right, is another reminder of the royal visit, in the shape of Albert Road School. It was built at the turn of the 20th century at the instigation of the then newly-formed School Board.

At the junction with Tower Road, turn right and at the end of the terrace turn left down the narrow lane, emerging in the station of the Manx Electric Railway. After protracted negotiation this was the rather ignominious end of the line when it reached Ramsey, rather than the grand entrance the

MER envisaged along the sea front to connect with the Queen's Pier. In the event the railway seems to have faired better than the pier as a visitor attraction and still provides a unique travel experience.

Walk through the station – but be mindful of tramcars moving through the area – and turn right into Parsonage Road, continuing as far as its junction with Queen's Pier Road. Turn right again and proceed past the bus station into Parliament Square. The newly-built Town Hall replaced two earlier buildings on the site and was completed in 2003.

Continue along the road, which now becomes Bowring Road, and at the first roundabout pause to look across to the left at the area occupied by Ramsey Bakery. This was the site of the station for the steam railway which once connected Ramsey and

Peel, but the line has long since closed and no trace remains of the station. Carry on past the second roundabout and you cross the Bowring Road Bridge, going straight on as far as Windsor Road.

Turn right and walk along Windsor Road. The style of the properties belies the opulence that the merchants and entrepreneurs who originally developed the town enjoyed when Ramsey was in its infancy. At the end of the road turn right into Windsor Mount. Stop at the house on the corner and read the plaque on the wall proclaiming that this was once the residence of celebrated Manx poet T.E. Brown.

Walk down Windsor Mount and Ballacloan Road to North Shore Road. To the left is Mooragh Park, created on land where the second arm of the Sulby River discharged to the sea. On the right you pass the ground of Ayre United Football Club – not be confused with the Scottish club of the same name!

Turn left on North Shore Road to Mooragh Promenade. Turn right along the promenade, which was a late development in the Victorian guesthouse boom and never really realised its potential in the way that Douglas promenade did. All of the houses were built to a very similar design and have come to represent the symbol of the Victorian era on the Island.

Continue back towards the centre of the town and cross the swingbridge – a major feature of the harbour. The harbour frontage ahead gives further clues to Ramsey's past wealth. Many of the old warehouse gables remain but only a few retain their original use.

On reaching the other side of the bridge turn left on West Quay to return to Market Place – your starting point.

this **island's** made **FOR WALKING**

DAY
DRIVES
6 LEISURELY TOURS

As Toad would have it, you can't beat the freedom and pleasure of the open road – or touring the Isle of Man by car or motorcycle!

The six circular routes chosen here cover all regions and can be enjoyed at a leisurely pace, giving ample opportunity to visit points of interest along the way.

The accompanying maps should be sufficient for the purpose, but more detailed information can of course be found in the Ordnance Survey Landranger Map 95.

TOUR I: 35 MILES

DOUGLAS — SIGNPOST CORNER — THE BUNGALOW — RAMSEY — MAUGHOLD — PORT MOOAR — PORT CORNAA — DHOON — LAXEY

This tour starts in Douglas at the foot of Broadway, which is adjacent to the new Villa Marina and where the Harris Promenade merges with Central Promenade.

Climbing up Broadway you leave the tourist part of town behind and as Broadway

day **drives:** six **LEISURELY TOURS**

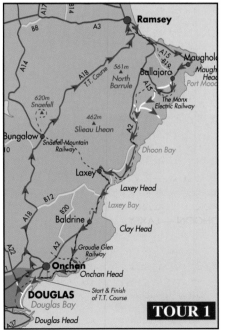

becomes Ballaquayle Road you come to the
Bray Hill traffic lights. Turn right and head
past the TT Grandstand (on your right).

Some three quarters of a mile along
Glencrutchery Road you arrive at Governor's
Bridge. Be careful here that you don't turn
too quickly, and take care at the double
roundabout before following the road marked
Ramsey, turning up – left – by the white-
painted stone wall.

For the next few hundred yards on the
right you are passing the home of the Island's
Governor. Head on up the A18 to Signpost
Corner. Leaving Cronk-ny-Mona behind,
there is a distinct change of scenery as the
road winds upwards to the famous TT
viewing spot of Creg-ny-Baa.

Over to your left, as Kate's Cottage comes
into sight, are some very good views of
Douglas, and the panorama of the southern
half of the Isle of Man lies before you. Take
great care in choosing where to stop to take
in the views, especially on the TT course as it

is a very fast road.

Passing through Keppel Gate you are now in the mountains and some of the finest scenery on the Island. Still on the A18 descend to Ramsey at Brandywell, just past the junction with the B10.

Directly in front of you stands Snaefell and if time permits it is well worth stopping here and catching the electric railway to the summit, from where on a clear day you can see England, Wales, Scotland and Ireland – not to mention the Isle of Man itself, of course! In 1995 the Snaefell Mountain Railway celebrated its centenary and the original rolling stock is still in use.

Past Snaefell the magnificent mountain scenery continues with the views on your right of Laxey and its valley, and the impressive sight of Ramsey and the northern plain spreading out before you. Ramsey is well worth exploring – and if you have still not picked up your free parking disc, call in at Ramsey Town Hall, they will fix you up.

Quiet lane near Maughold

Maughold is the next stop. Drive along Ramsey promenade and past the Queen's Pier, watching for the signs directing traffic to Laxey (A2).

Shortly after, bear left on to the A15. A good tip on these roads is to watch out for the unmanned railway crossings as you will be criss-crossing them for the next few miles.

About half a mile past Maughold there is a small road which takes you down to the peaceful beach at Port Mooar. It's an ideal place to stretch your legs and have a picnic. Back up from the beach turn left on to the A15 and travel to Cornaa.

There is a well-preserved burial ground just past the Ballajora crossroads. Look for an old chapel on the corner, keeping it to the left, and travel uphill on the minor road (which in more recent times became the last resting place for those Quakers who remained on the Island, the majority of their fellow believers escaping persecution by seeking a new life in America).

Take care approaching Cornaa as the roads are very narrow. Turn off the A15 at Cornaa railway halt and turn down the minor road to the left.

Pass the Ballaglass Glen car park on your right and drive on until you reach a small ford where you turn sharp right for Port Cornaa. The drive down to the beach is well worth the effort, but be careful where you park, it is a popular spot with locals and sometimes the stony upper beach can cause problems if you pick the wrong place.

When coming back up this lovely wooded valley continue past the ford – on your right – and climb back up to the A2, watching out for the signs to the Dhoon and Laxey. If you are feeling energetic park opposite Dhoon station and enjoy a walk down to the shore, but remember to leave extra time for the return journey ... it can fool you! The A2 soon takes you to Laxey and there are great views all along the coast.

There is a choice of how you leave Laxey. If you are in Old Laxey then the steep road up from the harbour soon comes out on the A2 at Fairy Cottage. Or if you have been exploring around the mines then rejoin by the Electric Railway station.

On through the picturesque villages of

Maughold Lighthouse, completed in 1914 and automated in the early 1990s

Lonan, Garwick and Baldrine and over the railway crossing just out of Baldrine, take a left turn and over a second crossing in the vicinity of the Halfway House to Laxey (Liverpool Arms) – the road A11 is signposted to Groudle and Douglas. Groudle has a beautiful natural glen and the revitalised miniature Groudle Glen Railway.

TOUR 2: 38 MILES

DOUGLAS — EAST BALDWIN — INJEBRECK — DRUIDALE— BALLAUGH — KIRK MICHAEL — PEEL — ST JOHN S

This journey takes its starting point at the bottom of Broadway and proceeds in just the same manner as that

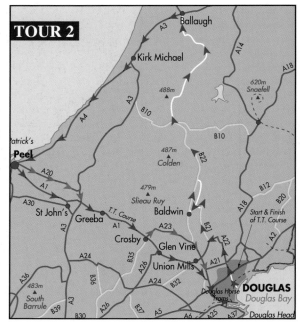

described in Tour 1 until the traffic lights at Parkfield Corner (St Ninian's Church) are reached. Get into the left filter lane and enjoy the run down Bray Hill to the bottom of the dip where you take a right turn. (TT racers speed down this hill at over 150 mph – but only on race days!)

The road now winds along through an area known as Port-e-Chee, which translated from the Gaelic means Haven of Peace. Cronkbourne Village is the next destination and this is soon reached. Turn right and go up the steep Johnny Watterson's Lane (A21), turning left at the halt sign, then drive along Ballanard Road (A22) towards Abbeylands for just over a mile. At the crossroads turn left and, heading over Sir George's Bridge, make a right turn on to the B21 – the East Baldwin Road.

Between 1900-05 a three-foot narrow-gauge railway wound its way around these small valleys, carrying workers and building materials for the Injebreck Reservoir.

Keep on the B21 and move in a northerly

direction until you reach the old and disused East Baldwin Chapel. Park here awhile and see if you can spot 'The White Man of East Baldwin' – a figure built into a mountain wall on the hillside as a memorial to a deemster, who perished with his horse in a snowstorm whilst on an errand of mercy. The walk up to the cairn from the bottom of the valley is strenuous, and mind you don't get your feet wet when crossing the Baldwin River, but the views are worth the effort.

Retrace your track back to Algare Hill – the small connecting road between the two valleys – and a right turn at the top brings you along to St Luke's Church, on the site of an ancient Tynwald. Drop down to the valley floor and join the B22 by heading once more in a northerly direction. There are lots of good picnic spots around here but be careful where you park as the roads are narrow. If you like fishing, Injebreck is a good spot. From the reservoir the road climbs up between the peaks of Colden and Carraghan, eventually bringing you out on to the

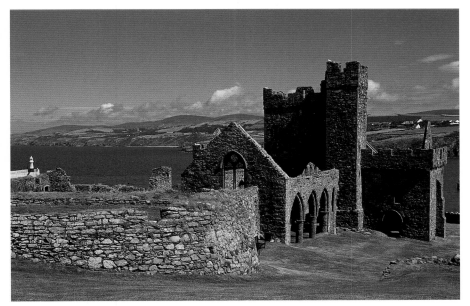

The ruins of medieval Peel Castle on St Patrick's Isle

Brandywell Road (B10).

Just before the junction there is a small slip road which you should turn into and, by turning right and then almost immediately left, you are now on the Druidale Road. This is a single-track road for its entire length. A short drive down Ballaugh Glen brings you to the village.

Turning left at the famous Ballaugh Bridge – where TT racers become airborne for some distance! – you head south-west towards Kirk Michael, home of runic crosses and the last resting place of five bishops. Take the right fork here as the A3 becomes the A4 and head down towards Peel. This is a good road, but if you are not in a hurry stop off at Glen Wyllin, Glen Mooar or the Devil's Elbow.

It's worth spending some time in Peel. This is the only 'city' on the Island, with two cathedrals, and there are some interesting shops, narrow streets, a harbour and a very fine castle. If you are out on an evening run, stay for the sunset, you won't be disappointed!

Leaving Peel behind, take the A1 to St John's, a village of great political importance to the Island. An alternative route to the village is via the A20 and the connecting road through Tynwald Mills, which is well signposted from Peel. Alongside Tynwald Hill lies the Royal Chapel of St John. The village is little changed in the best part of a century.

The last part of the drive takes you along the central valley. Ten thousand years ago this was the sea bed, dividing the Isle of Man into two main parts. Moving along the A1 towards Ballacraine you come up against an Island rarity – a set of traffic lights. Carry straight on towards Douglas, but just after Greeba Castle look to your left and there is the ancient roofless church of St Trinian standing in splendid isolation in its own meadow.

From here there is a choice of routes back to the capital. The main road follows the A1 to the Sea Terminal via Glen Vine, Union Mills, Braddan Bridge and the Quarterbridge. Alternatively, if time permits, why not take the A23 (the Nab Road) by turning left at

Crosby and heading towards Douglas via
Eyreton, the Nab, the Strang and Braddan.
The A23 rejoins the A1 at the Jubilee Oak
Braddan Bridge.

TOUR 3: 38 MILES

RAMSEY — POINT OF AYRE — JURBY — THE CRONK — THE CURRAGHS — SULBY — THOLT-E-WILL — THE BUNGALOW

As you wander around the northern plain
the scenery changes frequently, from the fine
sands of the Lhen, gravel beaches of the Point
of Ayre and up to the wooded slopes of Sky
Hill, Glen Auldyn, Carrick, Rock and Mount
Karrin, and St Ciaran's Mount. Coupled with
the winding lanes of the Curraghs it is one of
the best places to tour.

The drive starts on Ramsey promenade,
but before setting off be sure to take in the
lovely sight of the bay and the slopes of
Lhergy Frissel (Frissel's slope) – the hill with
the tower set on the summit.

Driving along Mooragh Promenade you
may get a glimpse of St Bees Head in
Cumbria, the nearest mainland point to the
Isle of Man. At the end of the promenade
bear left up the hill and join the A10 by
turning right. Follow this road to the lovely
village of Bride. The church acts as a good
landmark for miles around.

At Bride take the A16 marked for the
Point of Ayre. Again it is an easy place to find
because the lighthouse stands as a sentinel.
This landmark was built in the early years of
the 19th century by the great-grandfather of
Robert Louis Stevenson. Definitely not the
place to go swimming: the waters
surrounding the Point are extremely
treacherous.

On now to the Lhen, so reverse the route
back as far as Bride and turn right and west
at the church. Lovely country here with good
farming land rolling down to the coast. Watch
out for the sign to the Ayres Visitor Centre,
well worth a visit but only open mid-May to
mid-September, 2pm-5pm., Wednesdays to

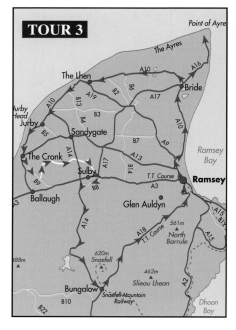

Sundays. Stay on the A10 and the Lhen is
reached after a pleasant drive of a few miles.
Watch out for the sharp turn at the Lhen
Bridge. The little park close to the shore is
ideal for a picnic.

Just a couple of miles further on is Jurby.
Long ago this village was important to the
Vikings and although it has lost something of
its old eminence it is nonetheless a pleasant
part of the Island, and well worth exploring
for its beaches, church and crosses.

Carrying on still further on the A10, look
out for The Cronk (The Hill), such as it is.
Go straight on here at the crossroads,
following the B9, and turn left at the second
road down from The Cronk crossroads – but
not counting any farm tracks or lanes. If you
have it right, it's the road coloured yellow on
the map taking you towards Dollagh Mooar,
Black Lake and the Curraghs (mire or
marsh).

Caution here because the roads are
extremely narrow and there are lots of ditches
awaiting careless drivers. Cross the A14,

approximately half way between Sandygate to the north and Sulby to the south – and you are still following the yellow road to Kella and West Sulby.

Turn left at the junction and for a brief distance you are on the TT course, on the famous Sulby Straight (A3). Just past Sulby Bridge is the Ginger Hall public house and you should turn right here on to the B8, which will bring you on to the Sulby Claddaghs, the river meadowland.

Drive through the Claddaghs to the A14 or the Sulby Glen Road and begin the ascent of the glen towards Tholt-e-Will. This extremely scenic route brings you up past the Sulby Reservoir, built in the early 1980s to secure water supplies well into the 21st century. The upper reaches of the road roll across the shoulder of Snaefell and the scenery is typical of high moorland interspersed with plantation.

The end of the A14 joins the A18 TT

course at the Bungalow. There is a Manx Electric Railway station here and during summer the Snaefell Mountain Railway operates regular services between Snaefell summit and Laxey, far below at the bottom of the valley.

Turn left and travel the 'wrong way' around the TT course – it is still a fast stretch of road. In clear weather, summer or winter, there are fine views of the Ayres, Scotland, England and Ireland. Take care on the final descent into Ramsey – there are some sharp corners. Once into Royal Ramsey it is easy to find your way around and the A18 takes you right into Parliament Square. Turn right just through the Square and you are into Derby Road and West Quay. Cross the swingbridge and on to Mooragh Promenade.

TOUR 4: 40 MILES

PEEL — ST JOHN S — CRONK-Y-VODDY— WEST BALDWIN — BALLASALLA — CASTLETOWN — FOXDALE

Peel is a must and if you are not actually staying in the town a visit should be a priority. This tour takes you from Peel through the Island's lovely hinterland and moorland, valleys and glens.

The starting point is the north end of Peel promenade in the vicinity of the Empire Garage. From here proceed up Stanley Road, turning right then almost immediately left into Church Street.

At the halt sign (the police station is across the road) take a left and head into Derby Road and the A20, signposted for St John's.

You'll know you're on the right road when you pass the Poortown quarry, and after about a mile and a half turn right down the small road marked Tynwald Mills Centre, which is well worth a visit.

Leave the Tynwald Mills Centre complex by the opposite end and bear left on to the TT course (A3). The exit on to the main road is narrow, and sometimes approaching cars from your right-hand side may be

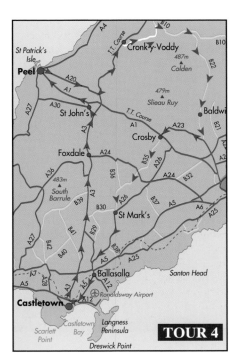

travelling at speed, so take care.

Now you are heading up the beautiful wooded Glen Helen road and if you feel like stretching your legs, stop and stroll up the glen. From opposite the glen car park the road climbs steeply for a short distance, passing the famous TT landmark Sarah's Cottage and on up Creg Willeys Hill, Willy Syl's (or Sylvester's Crag) and on to Cronk-y-Voddy, which translated from the Manx means the Hill of the Dog. Here at the crossroads turn right for the undulating drive to Little London.

Long ago Little London was famous for fishing but nowadays its peace and tranquillity are disturbed only by the occasional passing car or walker. Before the Second World War the Old Smithy was the home of the renowned flyer Captain Pixton, who was the first British winner of the prestigious Schneider Trophy and the holder of many flying records. The road out of Little London skirts the south-west slopes of Sartfell, which is old Norse for Black Mountain or Dark

Slope. In Manx it is known as Slieau Dhoo and joins the B10 about half a mile above Bayr Garrow (Rough Road).

Just before the minor road joins the main road is Sartfield Farmhouse Restaurant. The views from here are superb and at night you can see various Irish and Scottish lighthouses.

Turn up the hill and on the way look back at the view; on clear days there are fine panoramas of the Mountains of Mourne and the Mull of Galloway. You are now heading along the Brandywell Road with Colden Mountain ahead and to the right. There are a lot of cattle grids in the mountains, so be sure to take care crossing them and if you have to use the gates, please don't forget to close them after use.

Keep a lookout for the B22 turning; it should be easy to spot because it is just before Brandywell Cottage – the only building on your left since you started on the B10. Turn off to the right and head along the Injebreck Road, and if you want a good idea of what the centre of the Island looks like, pull in just

Close Sartfield Nature Reserve is a carpet of wild orchids in early summer

before the crest of the hill and you will see a countryside little changed in thousands of years.

Head down into the West Baldwin valley – an area not unlike the Scottish Highlands. At the upper end of this green and tree-lined cleft is Carraghan, which translates in English to rough, craggy or rocky place. It was chosen as an ideal spot for the Injebreck Reservoir, which has served Douglas and much of the Island for many decades.

On down the valley, keep to the B22 all the way until the Mount Rule halt sign, where a right turn puts you on to the A23 bound for the central village of Crosby. The road follows what was the edge of the south coast of the larger of the two northern islands that made up the Isle of Man at the time of the last ice age.

Go straight across the Crosby crossroads and up the B35 towards St Mark's. It is likely that at one time a cross stood somewhere near the site of the present-day village, because its name is derived from the Scandinavian word for Cross Village or Farm. The tour now follows one of the driveable parts of the Millennium Way.

St Mark's is a quiet little backwater and lies peacefully on a rise and is visible for a good distance around the parish of Malew. Once a year it comes to life with the holding of the ancient St Mark's Fair.

A couple of miles or so further on you come to the busy village of Ballasalla. In more recent times there has been an upsurge in commercial activities here. There is plenty to do in Ballasalla, including a visit to Silverdale Glen, which is well signposted.

Go straight on at each roundabout, looking for the airport and Castletown signs (A5). Pass the airport on your left and drive into Castletown. The old capital is described in detail elsewhere in this guide, and when visiting remember that the town is a disc parking area.

The journey back to Peel is fairly straightforward. Retrace the route back along the harbour in Castletown to Victoria Road and the first roundabout, where you should turn left into Alexander Road and cross over the Alexander Bridge. Carry on for a quarter of a mile and turn right into Malew Road and the A3.

Stay on the A3, climbing up the Ballamodha Straight before dropping down through the old mining villages of Upper and Lower Foxdale. Approaching St John's, the road divides at a small hamlet called The Hope (not shown on many maps). Take the left branch and follow the A30 past the Forestry Department's nurseries, bearing right until you reach the halt sign in the middle of the village. A good guide as to whether you are on the correct route is that Tynwald Hill is across the road. Turn left at St John's for Peel and follow the A1 and the signs all the way to Peel promenade and the end of Tour 4.

TOUR 5: 42 MILES

PORT ERIN — THE SLOC — NIARBYL — GLEN MAYE — FOXDALE — BRAAID — UNION MILLS — DOUGLAS — BALLASALLA —PORT ST MARY — CREGNEASH

Pretty Port Erin is a good place to base yourself for a motoring holiday. Parking is easy and although parts of the village are disc zones, they present no real problems.

This drive starts on the Upper Promenade and covers the southern part of the Island. It takes you from the steep cliffs and hills of the south-west, through the gentle rolling hills of Glenfaba, Rushen and Middle Sheadings to the capital, and on to the old Manx hill village of Cregneash.

Drive up the hill away from the hotels and look for the signposts to Bradda. The village nestles on the slopes of Bradda Head and is divided into west and east, although the exact boundary between them is now somewhat blurred. This is the A32 and it brings you along a gradually widening road to Ballafesson, which appears on the ancient

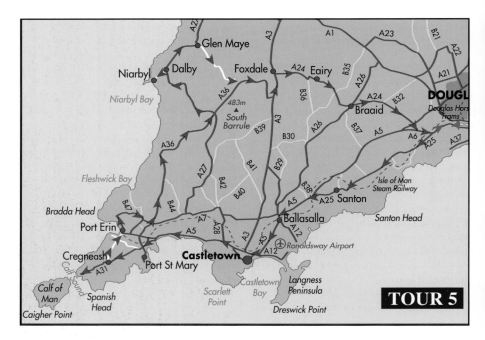

On the map: Glen Maye, A27, A3, A1, A23, B21, A22, Niarbyl, Dalby, Foxdale, A24, Eairy, B35, B26, A21, Niarbyl Bay, A36, B36, A24, B32, **DOUGL**, 483m, South Barrule, A3, Braaid, Douglas Hors Trams, B39, B30, A26, B37, A5, A6, A25, A37, A36, A27, B41, B29, A5, A25, Santon, Fleshwick Bay, B42, B40, B38, Isle of Man Steam Railway, Bradda Head, B47, B44, A5, Ballasalla, Santon Head, Port Erin, A7, A28, A3, A12, Cregneash, A5, Ronaldsway Airport, A31, Port St Mary, **Castletown**, A12, Calf of Man, Spanish Head, Scarlett Point, Castletown Bay, Langness Peninsula, Caigher Point, Dreswick Point, **TOUR 5**

manorial roll as MacPherson's Farm.

At the junction you pick up the A7 for a short while and at the next crossroads – marked as a roundabout – turn left on the A36, up through Ballakillowey (McGillowey's Farm). It should be noted that the Manx usually exchanged the prefix Mac for the prefix Balla as far as place names were concerned.

Just before the junction with the B44 there is a nice open picnic area, with fine views over Castletown Bay and the sweep of the coast right round to the villages of the Howe and Cregneash high up on the Mull Peninsula.

Driving on upwards on the Sloc Road, there are continually changing views of the landscape around almost every corner. There are many fine walks and picnic sites.

The Sloc Road takes you to the Round Table crossroads. Turn sharp left here on to the A27 and down to Niarbyl. Descending the hill into Dalby village, it is easy to see where the name Niarbyl is derived. Jutting

out into the clear waters of the Irish Sea is a tail of rocks, which is how Niarbyl translates into English. Take the minor road down to the shore and spend some time on the rocky beach at the foot of the cliffs.

From Dalby the A27 continues on to Glen Maye, loosely translated meaning Yellow Glen on account of the muddy, almost clay-coloured waters of the streams running down the glen. There are a number of easy walks here.

From here carry on to the village post office. To the side of the building there is a narrow country lane which takes you up towards Garey, translated as rough or rugged river-shrubbery. If there ever was a river up here on the high ground it has long since disappeared; perhaps the road was the river, because in wet winter weather the road does seem to double as a stream. The road is also known as the Back of the Moon Road.

Rushen Mines soon loom up and even the isolation of the mines has a particular beauty of its own. Back on to the A36 and a left turn down the mountain to South Barrule Plantation and the junction with the A3.

Head left towards Foxdale, where you take the first right and join the A24. Skirt the edge of the Eairy Dam – watch out for the ducks crossing the road – and on to the Braaid, which literally translated means throat or windpipe, as applied in the sense of a glen or sheltered vale. Carry straight on at the roundabout, head up the hill for about half a mile, and look down and across into the central valley to the view known as the Plains of Heaven.

Carry on along this road until you arrive at a major road junction where the A24 bisects the A5. Cross over and drive to Kewaigue, which translates into Little Hollow. If you would like to revisit Douglas, continue on into town; if not then just past the headquarters of Isle of Man Breweries turn through an acute right-hander and head for Santon on the A25.

Santon – in older times it was spelt Santan – derives its name from Saint Sanctan. This road is known as the Old Castletown Road and there are a number of roads leading off it down to rocky bays and isolated coves. Try them when you have time, most are off the beaten track and are not accessible by public transport.

The road takes you in the direction of Ballasalla and rejoins the A5 at a spot where the railway line passes under the main road. Stay on the A5 by turning left at the Ballasalla roundabout – the Whitestone Inn faces you directly ahead as you approach it.

Drive past the airport and skirt the edge of Castletown. Leave the town behind by using the bypass (still the A5) and drive all the way along the edge of Bay ny Carrickey (The Bay of the Rock). Turn right up past the tall stone building along Beach Road, heading for the crossroads, where you go straight on using the A31. Ignore any other roads and make for Cregneash. From here carry on down to the Sound to enjoy the totally unspoilt scenery of the Isle of Man's equivalent of Land's End.

This cottage in Onchan is at one with its' garden

For the final stages of the drive you return back up the hill from the Sound towards Cregneash again. Just before entering the village from the south, turn sharp left on to the minor road leading past Mull Hill and its stone circles. Dating from Neolithic times, this unspoilt area remains much as the earliest inhabitants would have known it. This is a single-track road with passing places. Port Erin nestles quietly below as you drive down Dandy Hill and back on to the Lower Promenade.

TOUR 6: 49 MILES

ONCHAN – BALDRINE – LAXEY – GLEN ROY – THE BUNGALOW – SULBY – ST JUDE'S – ANDREAS – BRIDE – RAMSEY – THE GOOSENECK – THE HIBERNIAN – DHOON – LAXEY

Onchan started life as a small village to the north of Douglas and in recent times its growth has outstripped that of the capital. You could be forgiven for thinking that it is a suburb of Douglas, but the village has its own local government and is very much a separate community.

The drive starts at Onchan Head, just above Port Jack. Follow the A11 as it runs parallel to the track of the Manx Electric Railway and passes Groudle Glen. There is a minor road off to the right, approximately half a mile past Groudle station, and a detour up this road will bring you to Old Kirk Lonan Church, well worth seeing. Completing the detour brings you out on to the A2 just to the south of Baldrine village. Carry on towards Laxey via Fairy Cottage and Old Laxey Hill – bear to the right at the filling station – to the attractive harbour.

Laxey owes its origins to the Norsemen, who named it Salmon River. Give yourself time here as there's plenty to see. From the harbour travel up the glen beside the river and when you reach the woollen mills go up the hill, under the railway bridge and straight on at the stop sign looking for the Creg-ny-Baa signpost.

You are now on the Glen Roy Road (coloured yellow on the OS map) and about to experience one of the best glen drives on the Island. The glen was formed by the waters cascading down from Mullagh Ouyr, Slieau Meayll, Dun Summit, Bare or Bald Mountain and Windy Corner respectively. Care on this road is required as there are a number of blind corners, and the road is extremely narrow in places.

Eventually you rejoin a wider road, the B12, just above Social Cottage, and by turning in a south-west (right) direction, the road brings you to the well-known Keppel Hotel at Creg-ny-Baa. Turn right and head the 'wrong way' round the TT course (the A18), aiming for the Bungalow. Just past Brandywell is the highest point on the course at almost 1,400 feet.

The Bungalow actually bears no resemblance to a modern building of that name and the current site was home, until fairly recently, to a magnificent hotel made of wood and galvanised sheeting – very popular with TT fans. Watch out for the directions to Sulby and turn left on the A14.

If your passengers fancy a walk, pull up at the top entrance to Tholt-e-Will Glen. Allow them half an hour or so to walk down the glen and pick them up just outside the inn at the bottom of the hill. Alternatively, Sulby Reservoir car park makes a good location for a picnic. The name of the glen translated from the Manx means Hill of the Cattlefold, and the inhabitants of the lower end of the bigger glen have traditionally been known as the Sulby Cossacks. At any time of year Sulby Glen has a beauty all of its own. In spring the

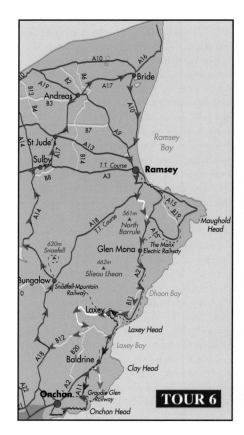

east side of the glen is coloured with a haze of bluebells. At other times the heather and gorse lend their own particular splash of colour and the light always creates a special atmosphere.

A quarter of the way down the glen from the inn lies Irishman's Cottage and, high above the nearby waterworks, is the small feeder reservoir of Block Eary. The reservoir was built by German POWs and although it is a strenuous walk to reach it, it's well worthwhile. The name has changed somewhat from the original Scandinavian spelling Blakkarg but the meaning is still the same, Black Sheiling, from the peaty colour of the stream.

Carry on down the valley towards the Sulby Straight. Passing Sulby Mill go straight on to the main road and turn right on to the TT course at Sulby Methodist church. At the end of the straight, turn off the A3 on to the St Jude's Road (A17). From the West Craig crossroads stay on the A17 to Andreas. There is a subtle change in the scenery here as the landscape changes from moor and glen to low-lying well-drained marshland.

Andreas has a fine church dedicated to St Andrew, from whom the parish takes its name. The village is very much the centre of local agricultural activities. Leave Andreas by continuing on the same road, which takes you to the Island's northernmost centre of population, Bride. The village lies in a little hollow of the Bride Hills and is one of the sunniest places on the Isle of Man.

Leaving Bride, travel along the A10 in the direction of Ramsey. The Bride road takes you right into Parliament Square and if you are not breaking your journey in Ramsey then carry on following the route marked for the TT course and Douglas. High above the town at the Gooseneck there is a minor road leading off behind the TT marshals' shelter. Careful negotiation of the turn is required to get on to what is known as the Hibernian Road. This is a delightful run across the lower slopes of North Barrule and whilst there

seems to be no trace of the name's origination, it is most likely that it takes its form from the same meaning as South Barrule – Ward Mountain.

As you come off this road at the Hibernian, turn right on to the A2 – the coast road – and head for the Corrany. This name is a variation of Cornaa, which means Treen, the modern version of homestead. At the Dhoon is the glen, running down to the shoreline of Dhoon Bay, and the nearby earthworks of Kionehenin. It's an ideal place to stop – and if your passengers happen to be annoying you, send them back to Onchan on the Manx Electric Railway!

Leave the Dhoon car park area by the B11, the Ballaragh Road. This is an interesting name and although its derivation is doubtful, there is reason to believe that perhaps its original meaning was Farm of the Spectre or Apparition. Just before the end of this road, King Orry's Grave is reached.

Turn right here and you are once again back on the A2. At Laxey, turn right and cross over the railway lines into Dumbell's Terrace, known to the locals as Ham and Egg Terrace, and park the car. Looking up the valley you will see the largest working waterwheel in the world – Lady Isabella, the Great Laxey Wheel (which incidentally has its own adjacent car park).

The final leg of your journey takes you from Laxey along the A2 to just south of Baldrine village, where you veer left after the railway level crossing lights and on to the A11 Groudle Road (watch out for trains!).

Passing through Groudle you may catch sight of the popular Groudle Glen narrow-gauge railway as it chugs around the headland. Soon the road grants you a fine view of Douglas Bay and then Port Jack is in sight – and so is your journey's end.

ALL
ABOARD THE MANX
ELECTRIC RAILWAY

Does the prospect of travelling at 18 miles an hour fill you with raw excitement and anticipation? Probably not. But then, the journey you are about to undertake has nothing to do with speed. It has everything to do with...well, step aboard and find out. The Manx Electric Railway awaits your pleasure.

In case you're wondering, you're at Derby Castle, at the northern end of Douglas promenade. This is the railway's southern terminus. The rustic booking office has been here since 1897. Some of the rolling stock is even older, built in 1893 but still in perfect

working order. They don't make 'em like this any more. In fact, the most recent rolling stock on this extraordinary and unique line was made in 1906 – positively brand spanking new compared with the originals.

You'll be pleased to know that the guard and driver are of much younger stock. And before the driver draws current to get the show on the road, and the guard checks your ticket, a brief word about terminology – often a point of contention on the quirky but definitely addictive Isle of Man.

The fact is, although this is called the Manx Electric Railway, there are those who would have you believe that it's actually a tramway. True enough, it is a tramcar – or trailer – you're sitting in. And, in the tradition of trams from the Victorian and Edwardian era, it is driven by electricity from an overhead power line. On the other hand, nobody can dispute that it runs on rails. Or that the words 'Manx Electric Railway' are emblazoned over the sides of the err... tramcars. So, in these pages at least, a railway it is, and no argument.

Now, are you sitting comfortably? Good. With a ting-tinging of the bell, one of Britain's great railway journeys – all 17.5 miles and 75 minutes of it – is about to begin. It's a gentle and graceful departure from the station, passing over the pointwork at the entrance to the car sheds. In busy holiday periods a good selection of the vintage rolling stock is here. Trainspotters note: there are 17 power cars and 19 trailers still in regular use.

A gradient of 1 in 24 takes you and the train up towards Port Jack – the first of 63 possible stopping places between here and the railway's northern terminus at Ramsey, your destination.

You can't fail to be struck by the novelty of road and railway running beside each other like this, in parallel, on the same level and so close together. This will change. Before long, the track will cut its own and more spectacular route that car travellers can only dream about.

So far, so good – and already, a clue as to the coming excitement. A right turn reveals impressive views over Douglas Bay; alas, all too quickly interrupted by a turn the other way to level off past Onchan Head station, and then lost completely with a sharp left past Howstrake station.

Not to worry: the descent towards Groudle brings more superb coastline into view, including Clay Head (300 feet above sea

Laxey, where boats and trains are just two of the attractions

The Queen's Pier, Ramsey, was built in 1886 to provide a deep-water berth for visiting steamers

level). On the other side of the glen from Port Groudle is the Groudle Glen Railway, which runs on track only two feet wide. This little line opened in 1896 to transport visitors to a small zoo at the seaward end, just past the reinstated and clearly visible station building at Sea Lion Rocks.

Now, already 12 minutes into the journey, it's inland to Groudle station, the original terminus of the line in 1893. A Railway Centenary plaque is mounted on a stone monument just past the station on the left. And to prove that those 1890s were a busy old time on the Isle of Man, you'll soon be passing the Groudle Hotel (1893), designed by Mackay Hugh Baillie-Scott, and the three-span Groudle Viaduct (1894), built by Mark Carine.

The Groudle coast road's still there beside you as the landscape on the left levels off and presents you with lovely views of the central mountains and up to Snaefell summit (that's

it, with the pylons on top).

It soon becomes pretty obvious that you're half way to Laxey, courtesy of the Liverpool Arms (Halfway House), a pub dating from the 1860s. As the train crosses over the Groudle road and then the main Douglas-Laxey road, a single white light between the tracks tells the driver that the road traffic signals are operating.

It's not long before the village of Baldrine sneaks up besides you. On the other side are more views up to the mysterious and enticing Snaefell. Baldrine is derived from the Celtic Balla-Drine meaning place of the blackthorns. The village has a new millennium clock which is illuminated at night.

Bye bye, Baldrine and hello, Garwick. It's about 18 minutes into your journey when trees on either side of the track form a virtual tunnel and you emerge at this once-busy station. The remains of a gatepost mark the

old exit from the station to the glen. Garwick comes from the Norse, Gjar-vik meaning cave or creek.

More stunning views open up before you – this time of Laxey Bay and the cliffs beyond Laxey to Maughold Head and lighthouse. The bay stays in sight as you pass a station with a very Manx-sounding name – Ballabeg.

Is this a rollercoaster you're riding, or a railway? You could be forgiven for wondering; not because of any stomach-wrenching ups and downs or breathtaking sharp turns, but because you're definitely riding (albeit sedately) along a rolling coastline, and a pretty spectacular one at that.

Soon you can see Laxey beach, with Laxey Head on the opposite side of the valley. Poles carrying the railway's overhead wires are also visible to the point where the line disappears over the headland on its way to Ramsey.

The intriguingly-named Fairy Cottage station is next, on the approach into Lower

(or Old) Laxey. Fairy folklore is a serious matter on the Isle of Man – scoff at it at your peril. On the other hand, you can certainly take the next station with a pinch of salt; at least, the optimistic claim that South Cape is the station for Laxey beach. In reality it's an energetic walk down, let alone back up!

You are now 25 minutes into your unforgettable journey. Spanning both sides of the valley below you is Laxey village. The line ahead is relatively straight, soon passing Laxey car shed and electrical sub-station. Just before you cross the impressive Glen Roy viaduct into the station, you pass the point which was the terminus of the line when it first reached Laxey in 1894. Crossing the viaduct presents super views – down through the village and glen on one side, and the road bridge and Laxey Flour Mills on the other. Opened in 1860, the mill supplies all the flour for Ramsey Bakery as well as to local supermarkets.

Cornaa station: the gateway to walking the North Barrule and Snaefell ridge

Just when you thought your great railway adventure couldn't get any better, it does. At least, it could. Your arrival at Laxey station gives you the perfect opportunity to switch trains – and to experience the delights of the very uplifting Snaefell Mountain Railway, of which Laxey is the lower terminus. If you decide to go for it you can easily resume your journey to Ramsey on a later train; this is summer and they run every hour (every half-hour between Douglas and Laxey). But no, in the event you decide to give the summit of Snaefell a whirl on some other day – tomorrow maybe. Today's journey is far too enjoyable to interrupt.

However, your appetite is whetted and your curiosity demands to know more about the Snaefell Mountain Railway. Well, to begin with the train buff stuff, the 5-mile line opened in 1895 after just seven months of construction. All six of the original 1895 tramcars still operate the summer-only service. At a gauge of 3 feet 6 inches, the track is 6 inches wider than the one you're travelling on. The overall gradient is 1 in 12,

the tramcars using normal wheel-on-rail adhesion and the centre rail providing an emergency braking system.

It's a tiny exaggeration to say that the railway will take you to the very summit of the highest mountain on the Island (at 2,036 feet), but it'll certainly deliver you to within 46 feet of it – a short walk – and what's that between friends?

Besides the mountain railway there are other sights and points of interest for you to absorb here in Laxey. Take the parish church for example. It was completed in 1856 and built on land that was formerly part of the garden of the Mine Captain's house – now the Mines Tavern. Then there are attractions such as the woollen mill, the Great Laxey Wheel, Laxey Glen and gardens – and not forgetting the cafe in the station building. Laxey, by the way, comes from the Scandinavian word Laxa, meaning Salmon River.

With all aboard who are coming aboard now seated, it's time to leave Laxey, passing the tavern and the former goods shed and crossing the main road. Visible on the right of the valley is the famous giant waterwheel with its 168 buckets, and also on the right are the Valley Gardens – the old washing floors of the mines.

The climb to Laxey Head is rewarded with another good view of Laxey beach and Old Laxey, and you can see how tastefully many of the older buildings have been restored. More superb views come your way, this time of the coastline ahead, as far as Maughold lighthouse. Clear days bring the Lake District into view – even Sellafield can be visible on the shoreline.

Still climbing, and beyond the main road – now on the left – you can see the village of Ballaragh. It's known for a Bronze Age stone about five feet high and decorated with spiral patterns. Looking forward you have a view towards the north of the Island, along some of the most magnificent coastline in the British Isles.

Another intake of breath comes as the train reaches Bulgham and runs along a relatively narrow ledge 658 feet above that big, wide blue-green sea. This is the highest point on the line – and most definitely one of the highlights. In early 1967 an earthslip here blocked the line for several months while repairs were carried out.

The dramatic scenery continues as the train rattles on through a short cutting to run alongside Dhoon Glen and present you with a view of North Barrule (1,854 feet in height). Barony Hill, crowned by a stone circle and tumulus known as Carnane Breck, is on the opposite side of the glen.

You've now been travelling for 45 minutes and Dhoon Glen is the next station (almost 600 feet above sea level), complete with tearoom and the entrance to the glen. The walk down through the glen to the sea is effort well rewarded but deceptive – it takes longer than you'd expect.

It's onward ever onward, through farmland to Dhoon Quarry station. This is now a track storage facility for the railway but in

quarrying days the siding layout was considerably more extensive, with various narrow-gauge lines and ropeways serving the two separate quarries, one each side of the MER line.

The climb out of Dhoon Quarry is steep and you can see North Barrule again. Looking forward and right you also get your first glimpses of Lewaigue and Port e Vullen (Port of the Mill), villages lying on the north coast of Maughold Head.

A long straight run takes you now to Glen Mona. The station building is on the right and the village is up on the left. Then it's into a cutting to pass under Ballagorry Bridge – the only overbridge on the whole line.

Now North Barrule is on your left and there are views up the valley towards Snaefell. The ridge has three other summits. Two are unnamed (at 1,749 feet and 1,804 feet) and at the far end is Clagh Ouyr (1,808 feet).

If you enjoy hill walking, you'll really want to take steps to explore this ridge at some point. The place to begin your ascent would be The Hibernian (easily found on OS Landranger map 95), which would mean leaving the line at Cornaa station and walking along the A15. And the exciting bonus is that whether you finished the walk on the A18 mountain road at Bungalow or on the summit of Snaefell, you could then experience the joy of descending to Laxey by the mountain railway.

Note that this enticing scenario is described as a possible future event, because today you've already decided to complete the journey to the end of the line without interruption. So, about 55 minutes after leaving Douglas, it's on past the former Ballaglass Power Station – now a private residence – to Ballaglass station and the entrance to the glen of the same name. This too is an area awaiting your discovery. Look out for the small single-arched bridge that carries the railway over the river shortly after the station.

The line heads back towards the coast,

CYCLING
6 ONE-DAY
TRAILS

These designated circular routes vary in terms of length and the type of terrain you will encounter, and each is rated accordingly as **easy**, **moderate** or **challenging**, with two trails in each category – so there's something here for everyone.

The easy trails, on mainly flatter roads and lanes, are suitable for all, while the challenging rides tackle steep climbs and descents and require a much greater degree of physical fitness and cycling experience.

You should take as much care when cycling on the Isle of Man as you would anywhere else. Although many of the Island's country lanes are often quiet and traffic is light, other roads and lanes can be deceptively busy.

The nature of the landscape also means that roads tend to be winding and narrow, with high hedges limiting visibility, so approaching traffic can sometimes appear unexpectedly.

You're welcome of course to bring your own bike, and cycle hire is available on the Island. Details are available from the Tourist Information Centre in Douglas.

Happy cycling!

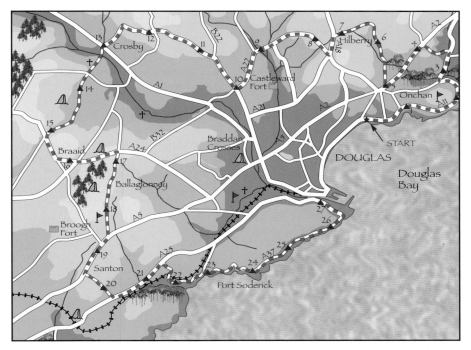

TRAIL 1: DOUGLAS (27 MILES)

Rating: challenging.

Major climbs/descents: Eskdale Road or Bibaloe Beg, River Glass valley at Sir George's Bridge, Ellerslie Hill at Crosby, Braaid, Crogga.

Attractions en route: Manx Museum, Douglas horse trams, Manx Electric Railway, Groudle Glen and railway, Molly Quirk's Glen, St Patrick's Chair, Port Soderick, Marine Drive.

This demanding but rewarding tour takes you out of the Island's busy capital and into the tranquil countryside which surrounds it. Cycling is an ideal way to explore the small glens such as Groudle and Molly Quirk's, and the coastal road of Marine Drive provides a stunning end to the day.

The majority of the route is on quiet lanes, but you will also encounter busy main roads in and around Douglas and need to take care, particularly during morning and evening peaks. You should exercise the same caution

along the promenade, which has tram lines running its entire length, and on roads around the Sea Terminal.

Start the tour at Derby Castle, at the northern end of the promenade, passing the terminus of the Manx Electric Railway and climbing towards Onchan.

After King Edward Bay Golf Club at Howstrake you come to the lovely Groudle Glen, with its miniature steam railway (seasonal). Continue alongside the MER track in the direction of Laxey, and take the first available road on your left (Bibaloe Beg Road – a short but very steep climb).

On reaching the main A2, turn left towards Onchan, but beware: the A2 is a fast, busy road, and your visibility of approaching traffic will be poor.

Cross the Whitebridge into Onchan and take the third right turn (School Road) – Onchan village, shops and pubs are 300 yards ahead.

Pass the Dowty factory, and a hairpin turn takes you down into the glen past Little Mill and steeply up the other side. Continue to Hillberry and the intersection with the TT course. Caution: traffic here is very fast.

Go left on to the TT course, right after approximately 300 yards, and immediate right again into Scollag Road. This takes you to Abbeylands Crossroads and down the steep slope into the River Glass valley at Sir George's Bridge. Follow the A22 into Strang, passing Strang Stores. At the mini roundabout turn right and follow the A23 to Crosby and the crossroads, where you cross the main A1 Douglas to Peel road. Continue up the steep hill, passing St Runius Chapel and, a quarter of a mile further on, a footpath sign to St Patrick's Chair (an ancient monument about 400 yards off the road).

The long climb brings you to Garth Crossroads, where you turn left towards Douglas. A mile further on, cross the mini roundabout at the Braaid. There is another long climb, passing Chibbanagh Plantation, and go next right towards Mount Murray Hotel, which is about a mile and a half further on. Another half a mile beyond the hotel, turn right at the T-junction on to the A5 – a busy main road linking Douglas and the airport. After a mile turn left into Oatlands Road, and go another mile and left on to Castletown Old Road towards Douglas, descending into Crogga dip and climbing out on the other side.

Take the next right turn to Port Soderick, soon passing under the steam railway at the station. Turn left shortly afterwards. Half a mile further on, go next right on to Marine Drive and proceed along its dramatic length to Douglas Head and down the hill towards South Quay – the end of the route. To return to the Sea Terminal you can either go left around the landward end of the harbour, or use the new harbour bridge.

TRAIL 2: CASTLETOWN (13 MILES)

Rating: easy.
Major climbs/descents: *none.*
Attractions en route: *Castle Rushen, Nautical Museum and Old Grammar School (all Castletown); Hango Hill, Derbyhaven, St Michael's Fort, St Michael's Chapel, steam railway, St Mark's Church; Rushen Abbey and 14th-century Monks Bridge (both Ballasalla); Shebeg Pottery, Silverdale Glen.*
Optional: *rides to St Michael's Isle and Langness, both of which run close to the shore and give panoramic sea views, and to Silverdale Glen.*

Far less demanding than Trail 1, this relaxing ride shows you the gentler slopes of the Island's south and is suitable for all age groups and levels of fitness. The total distance of 13 miles does not include the optional

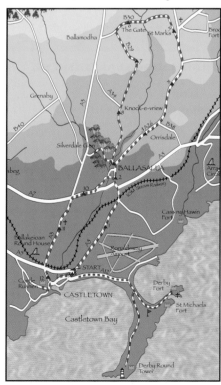

routes, for which you should allow a further
7.5 miles.

Start at Castletown station (Isle of Man
Steam Railway), turning right where the
station approach reaches the A5. Go left at
the mini roundabout and alongside the
harbour, passing the Nautical Museum, and
along Douglas Street.

Where College Green forks off to the
right, you have the opportunity to take the
optional route (as marked on the map) to the
lovely Langness peninsula – a spectacular,
level expanse of coastline in the Island's
south-east corner. This will also enable you to
cross the causeway to St Michael's Isle
(another optional route) and see St Michael's
Chapel and the fort overlooking the bay at
Derbyhaven. However, be aware that for part
of the way you'll be riding alongside the
Castletown links course, so look out for
flying golf balls!

If you decide not to take these options,
ignore the right fork to College Green and
continue straight on to join the main A5
Douglas Road (which you can join from the
Langness detour by retracing your steps
towards Castletown, turning right into Shore
Road and right on to the A5).

Go past the airport and over the level
crossing to the mini roundabout at Ballasalla,
leaving the A5 by going straight on along the
A26 through the village centre. At the second
mini roundabout you must bear right to
remain on the A26 towards St Mark's.

On reaching St Mark's, take the left-hand
fork at the church to join the B30 and then
left again almost immediately. In about a mile
you will pass the pet cemetery.

Turn left down the B29 and continue,
joining the A34 back towards Ballasalla. Both
of these roads are quiet country lanes running
between high Manx sod hedges, so take extra
care as limited forward visibility means that
traffic from either direction can be really
close before you're aware of it. The terrain is
almost entirely downhill.

Once back on the outskirts of Ballasalla,

The coastal views are as breathtaking as the cycling!

you have a third option (see map): turn right
along a leafy lane for just under a mile and
you'll reach Silverdale Glen and its variety of
family attractions. Return on the same
narrow lane and at the junction where you
detoured off the A34, turn right and right
again shortly afterwards.

You are now back on the outward route,
but just before the mini roundabout turn
right, approaching the ford, and cross the
Silverburn River over the bridge. Rushen
Abbey is on your right and the road follows
the abbey wall.

After a quarter of a mile turn right at the
T-junction (a busy road, so take care.) Turn
left at Cross Four Roads on to Malew Road.
Pass Malew Church on the Z-bend, where
Manx martyr Illiam Dhone is buried.

Continue back into Castletown. Cross over
the main road into the old town and,
dismounting, walk along Malew Street into
Market Square, where Castle Rushen stands
with its one-handed clock.

To get back to the station, leave by Castle
Street and The Quay, cross over the bridge at

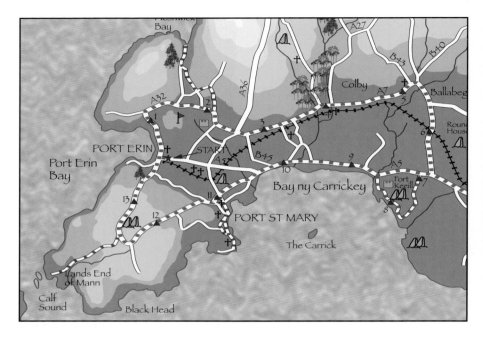

the harbour, and along the opposite bank of
the inner harbour. At the mini roundabout
turn right for Douglas and, a quarter of a
mile further on, go left and into the station.

TRAIL 3: PORT ERIN (14 MILES)

Rating: moderate.

*Major climbs/descents: Port Erin to
Cregneash, Bradda East, the Sound to Cregneash.*

*Attractions en route: Port Erin Railway
Museum, Mull Circle, Cregneash Folk Museum,
Viking ship burial ground at Balladoole, Milner's
Tower (Bradda Head).*

*Optional: rides to Fleshwick Bay, Port St
Mary and the Sound.*

You can really go wild on this eye-opening
ride! The magnificent coastal scenery of the
south-western corner of the Isle of Man rises
dramatically at Bradda Head, and you have
the opportunity to see the seals and seabirds
which inhabit the Sound (the Island's
equivalent of Land's End) and to enjoy a
cuppa at the visitor centre and cafe.

Start at Port Erin station (the steam
railway's southern terminus), turning left
along Station Road (one-way street) towards
the bay. Stay on this road (which turns right
to become the promenade), passing the turn
to Bradda Glen Cafe. The road climbs round
to the right, becoming Bradda Road, and 2
miles further on is Ballafesson.

Here you can exercise your first option:
turn left for a 1.5-mile (each way) detour to
Fleshwick, a rugged cove hemmed in by
towering cliffs.

A quarter of a mile after Ballafesson, turn
left on to the A7 Port Erin to Douglas Road.
Go straight on at the mini roundabout at
Ballakillowey and on through the pleasant
villages of Colby and Ballabeg.

Remain on the A7 until A7 Douglas is
shown as a left turn. Go straight on, which is
the A28 to Castletown, passing close by
Ballabeg railway station (a modest structure)
and on to the junction with the main A5 (a
fast road, so take care), where you turn right.

After a quarter of a mile, turn left through

stone gate pillars signposted Poyll Vaaish, and
you will pass the gate leading to Balladoole
Burial Site – a Viking ship burial ground
dating from prehistoric to Norse times.

The road continues to the coast, where you
turn right at a T-junction to follow the rocky
shoreline until rejoining the fast and busy
main A5 at the bottom of Fisher's Hill, where
you go left. The A5 runs alongside the coast
of Bay ny Carrickey, before swinging right
and inland, at which point you leave the A5
by forking left. Half a mile further on you
come to a crossroads. You can either go
straight on, or take your second option by
turning left to visit the popular seaside village
and harbour of Port St Mary.

This option runs along Bay View Road to
a right turn. After a quarter of a mile, turn
left and left again shortly to the harbour.

To return, go along Athol Street (one-way
street) and before long you will rejoin the
crossroads, where you turn left into Plantation
Road to continue on tour 3.

The road climbs steeply for a mile and a
half, eventually reaching the interesting
thatched-cottage village of Cregneash – a
living museum with a farm which still uses
traditional Manx farming methods. Here you
can take a third option – route 3C down to
the wild attractions of the Sound, with views
across to the Calf of Man islet. It's a detour
well worth making (there's a visitor centre
and cafe) but the climb back up to Cregneash
is quite severe.

After Cregneash, go on past the hilltop
Meayll Circle (a unique megalithic ritual and
burial site) to return to Port Erin. When you
reach the promenade (called Shore Road at
this point), turn right, which is blind so take
care. Go uphill to one-way Station Road,
opposite the Isle of Man Bank, where you'll
have to dismount for the short walk back to
the railway station.

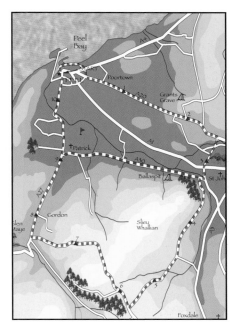

TRAIL 4: PEEL (10 MILES)

Rating: moderate to easy.

*Major climbs/descents: St John's to Snuff the
Wind lead mine, and Garey to Glen Maye.*

*Attractions en route: Peel Castle, St German's
Cathedral, Leece Museum, House of Manannan
(all in Peel); Tynwald National Park &
Arboretum, Manx Wild Flower Garden, Tynwald
Hill, Royal Chapel, Tynwald Mills Centre (all in
St John's); Snuff the Wind leadmine, Glen Maye
waterfall and beach.*

*Optional: an alternative easier route (4A on
the map) between St John's and (Kirk) Patrick.*

Peel and its surrounding area have to be
high on the list of everyone's Isle of Man
cycling plans. As well as showing you the port
and its impressive castle ruins, this trail takes
you through the picturesque villages of St
John's and Glen Maye, with spectacular views
on the climb up to Snuff the Wind leadmine.

Start at the House of Manannan and go
along the quay and the promenade to the
Creg Malin Hotel, turning right up Walpole

Road. Go right at the T-junction at the top of the hill, shortly turning left into Church Street, signposted Douglas and South. At the far end of Church Street turn left into Derby Road and follow it out of Peel.

Passing Poortown Quarry on your left, and round the double bend, turn right into a narrow lane going steeply downhill to a stone bridge over the River Neb.

A short deviation to the right immediately after the bridge takes you to the Tynwald Mills Centre (shops and two cafes in the old mills).

Returning to the trail, continue on the narrow road through the trees and after half a mile you'll see Tynwald Hill close by on your left.

At the crossroads go straight on, across the Peel to Douglas road and through the village of St John's. After the Central Hotel take the sharp right turn into Patrick Road and cross the stone bridge, where the route turns left up the hill. If you wish to take the alternative easier route (4A on the map), go straight on at this point, rejoining the trail further on at Patrick.

The main suggested trail continues up the hill – very steep in some sections – for 2 miles. At the junction on the brow of the hill, near the old leadmine known as Snuff the Wind, turn right. A mile and a half later you begin the 2-mile descent into Glen Maye, emerging by the Post Office, but take care – the road is narrow and winding.

The trail turns right here on to the A27 road to Peel. However, a short detour to your left takes you to Glen Maye and its waterfall and beach.

Return to the trail at the Post Office and take the A27 to Kirk Patrick (2 miles), where the easier route 4B rejoins from the right. Stay on the A27, over the River Neb, and climb to the Peel boundary. Half a mile further on brings you to the top of Station

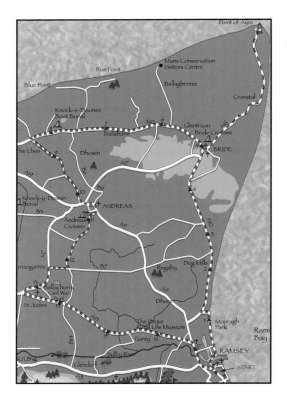

Hill. Turn left and shortly right and you are back at the House of Manannan – your starting point.

TRAIL 5: RAMSEY (16 MILES)

Rating: easy.
Major climbs / descents: none.
Attractions en route: Ramsey Pier (closed), Grove Rural Life Museum, Point of Ayre, Ayres Visitor Centre, Knock y Doonee (Viking ship burial site), Andreas crosses, Kerroogarroo Fort (Civil War – formerly known as Ballachurry Fort).
Optional: *Bride to the Point of Ayre.*

This relaxing ride can be enjoyed by all – particularly if the idea of rural tranquillity and flat, quiet, unhurried roads appeals to you. Set against the backdrop of the Manx hills, the gentle landscape of the northern plain is in stark contrast to the rest of the Island. In other words, it's perfect holiday cycling country!

The gateway to it all – and your starting point – is Ramsey, a pleasant town with a busy shopping centre and harbour. So take care in the traffic.

Start at the Manx Electric Railway station and cross over Albert Street. Turn into Peel Street and take the first right opposite the police station into Market Hill – a short road leading directly into Market Place.

Turn left, then left again, on to West Quay. Follow the quayside and go right over the swingbridge, bearing right and then left along Mooragh promenade. After a mile the road swings inland and gradually climbs the cliff.

Go right at the T-junction beside the Grand Island Hotel and follow the A10 through the small village of Bride – a distance of about 4 miles.

At the mini roundabout you have the option to take a detour to the Island's most northerly place – the Point of Ayre, marked by its distinctive red and white lighthouse. But beware of big lorries which use this road for access to the tip site and gravel pits.

The source of the Sulby is high in the Snaefell ridge

Cregneash village is well worth taking a break for

Returning to the mini-roundabout, the trail continues on the A10 (to The Lhen), heading west. Follow it for 4 miles and turn left into the Leodest road (which will take you past Leodest Farm) to Andreas, a further 2 miles.

In the centre of the village, turn left at the T-junction and right at the Y-junction. Then turn right at the T-junction past the church. A quarter of a mile further on, again turn right, into Bayr ny Harrey (Manx for Road to the Ayres) and follow this quiet country lane for 2 miles.

Go left at the crossroads for half a mile and then left at the T-junction. After a mile this brings you into the village of St Judes, where you turn left at the crossroads and pass St Judes Church. Proceed along this pleasant road for 5 miles back into Ramsey.

Turn right at the T-junction into Bowring Road and cross the bridge into the centre of Ramsey. Go straight on at the two mini-roundabouts and then left (signposted A2

Laxey and Douglas) back to your starting point – Ramsey station.

TRAIL 6: LAXEY (6 MILES)

Rating: challenging.

Major climbs / descents: Laxey to Ballaquine.

Attractions en route: King Orry's Grave, Laxey Wheel & Mines Trail, Laxey Glen gardens, Fairy Cottage, Laxey Woollen Mills (all in Laxey) and Ballalheannagh Gardens.

This is by far the shortest of the 6 designated cycle trails, and one of great scenic beauty, but the initial climb is definitely not for the faint-hearted! And following this are several steep ascents and descents into pretty river valleys, where the road is very narrow and demanding.

You will also encounter some traffic over the first mile or so after leaving Laxey.

Start at Laxey station and New Road (A2), taking the steep hill next to the filling station in the direction of Baldhoon. This is extremely steep to begin with before climbing more steadily.

The road is narrow and cuts a tortuous path through numerous tributary valleys until it reaches the B12, where you turn left.

Follow the road round to the right (signed Laxey) and down the hill towards the coast.

Half a mile after passing the church on your left, turn right at the T-junction and almost immediately go sharp left on to the main coast road.

Pass Fairy Cottage and South Cape and fork right down Old Laxey Hill. Within half a mile you will reach Old Laxey at the Shore Hotel, where turning left into Tent Road will show you the old harbour and Laxey promenade.

You can return to the Shore Hotel along Shore Road. Cross the old bridge over Laxey River and go left up Glen Road, at first following the river.

Cross the river and proceed up Church Hill and under the railway bridge, turning sharp right to return to Laxey station.

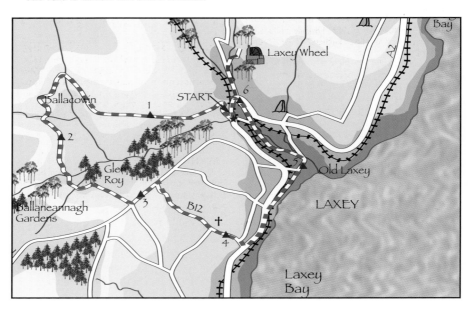

CLASSIFIED ADVERTS

DOUGLAS & THE EAST

ALL SEASONS, DOUGLAS, ISLE OF MAN. Small, well appointed licensed, non-smoking hotel. Indoor heated pool, free broadband internet. Close to all amenities. From only £24.00 pppn. Tel: 0871 855 0603. Web: www.hotels-iom.com.
◆◆◆   ▥✕👢♀♨☐☐🖭🌐♻〜🕈 TSL **12**

ARRANDALE HOTEL & APARTMENTS,
24 HUTCHINSON SQUARE, DOUGLAS, ISLE OF MAN, IM2 4HW. Tel: 08700 46 09 46.
Fax: 08700 46 09 56. Email: mail@arrandale.com. Web: www.arrandale.com. Comfortable, central Douglas, serviced & self-catering accommodation. High guest satisfaction rating. Contact us direct for the best possible rates.
◆◆◆/★★★   ▥👢♨♀☐🖭🆂🅱🖳 TSL **MW 12**

BISHOP'S LODGE, QUARTERBRIDGE ROAD, DOUGLAS, ISLE OF MAN IM2 3RF. Tel: (01624) 671094. Email: n.cooper@bgc.co.im. Superb lodge set in grounds of fine gentlemens residence. Secure covered garage for mountain bikes. Excellent shower facilities and quality accommodation to relax in. Run by keen mountain bikers. Non-smoking/pets.
★★★★   ▥🍴✕🅿☐♻🆂🖳🖳 **12**

BROOKVALE COTTAGE, MAIN ROAD, UNION MILLS, ISLE OF MAN IM4 4AJ. Tel: (01624) 650216. Fax: (01624) 852983. Lovingly restored coach house with fully fitted kitchen, TV/VCR/DVD, Gas c/h. Bed linen and towels provided. Convenient to bus route and local shop, P.O. Provides the perfect retreat from the cares of the world.
★★★   ▥🍴✕🅿♻🖳🖳 **1-11**

CALEDONIA HOTEL, QUEENS PROMENADE, DOUGLAS, ISLE OF MAN IM2 4NE. Good location. Well maintained property. Friendly. High cleaning standards. Full English Breakfast. Chinese Restaurant open in evening. Open all year. Tel: (01624) 624569. Email: caledoniahotel@hotmail.com.
◆◆◆   ▥👢♨♨♀☐☐🖭🆂🖳 TSL 🅿🖳 **12**

THE EDELWEISS HOTEL, QUEEN PROMENADE, DOUGLAS, ISLE OF MAN IM2 4NF. Tel: (01624) 675115. Fax: (01624) 673194. Email: edelweiss@manx.net. Web: www.isleofmantravel.com/edelweiss. STAY ON THE WORLD FAMOUS PROMENADE, A STEP AWAY, EASILY ACCESSIBLE WITH NO STEPS TO FRONT DOOR. IT S A STAY FOR LIFE.
◆◆◆   ▥🍴🔲♀♨☐☐♻♨‼🖳 TSL **2-11**

THE GREAVES, SUNNYCROFT, RAMSEY ROAD, LAXEY, ISLE OF MAN IM4 7PD. Peace, tranquility. Magnificent views. Situated in Laxey Village. Near Electric Tram, bus stop, shops. Homely guest house. Good home cooking, evening meal optional. Walkers paradise. Tel: (01624) 861500.
◆◆◆   ▥♿♨♨🅿♻✿🖳🆂 **12**

GROUDLE GLEN COTTAGES, ONCHAN, ISLE OF MAN IM3 2JP. Self-catering cottages for up to 6 people with panoramic views. Colour TV, DVD, double glazing, central heating. Washer/dryers, microwaves, deck area. Travel arranged. Tel: (01624) 623075. Email: groudlecottages@manx.net.
Web: www.groudleglencottages.co.im.
★★★   ▥♿🍴♨👢☐🅼🖳🖭 TSL 🅿🖳 **12**

HOLLY COTTAGE, MINORCA HILL, LAXEY, ISLE OF MAN IM4 7DP. Charming detached Manx cottage. Fully equipped, private parking, close to beach. More details available. Mid-week bookings accepted. Tel: (01624) 862091. Email: henthorns@manx.net.
★★★   ▥♿🍴✕🅿✿♻🖭 **12**

INGLEWOOD HOTEL, QUEENS PROMENADE, DOUGLAS, ISLE OF MAN IM2 4NF. Tel: (01624) 674734. Web: www.inglewoodhotel.net. Email: inglewoodhotel@manx.net. Excellent location. Renowned for superb service. Quality breakfasts including vegetarian options. Personally operated by the proprietors and licensed for residents. Ideal for those wanting a quiet, relaxing break.
◆◆◆◆   ▥♿🍴✕👢♀♨☐☐🆂 TSL **12**

ISLAND HOTEL, 4 EMPRESS DRIVE, DOUGLAS, ISLE OF MAN IM2 4LQ. Tel: (01624) 676549. Email: island@manx.net. Web: www.visitisleofman.com. Centrally located quality accommodation. Competitive prices and family suites with child reductions. Licensed Bar. All rooms en-suite with TV and central heating. Warm friendly welcome awaits you.
◆◆◆   ▥♿🍴👢♀♨☐♻‼🆂 TSL 🅿🖳 **12**

LAVENDER COTTAGE, QUEENS TERRACE, LAXEY, ISLE OF MAN. Come and stay at our beautiful four star cottage in Laxey village. Fully equipped including colour TV and Video. Sleeps four. Central Heating. Tel: (01624) 679607. Email: petergilbertson@manx.net.
★★★★   ▥♿🍴✕✿♻🖳🖭 **12**

OLD LONAN CHURCH FARM COTTAGES, BALDRINE, ISLE OF MAN. Tel: (01624) 614441. Email: sue@manxcottages.com. Web: www.manxcottages.com. Five star self-catering accommodation with a hint of luxury. Just a few miles from Douglas. All cottages fully equipped to a high standard. Please phone for a brochure.

★★★★★ 　　　　　×🖐✂🗆🎏⚓ SB TSL **MW 12**

SANTON MOTEL, MAIN ROAD, SANTON, ISLE OF MAN. Tel/Fax: (01624) 822499. Email: santonmotel@manx.net. Good quality en-suite rooms and suites. Convenient parking for all clients. Countryside location 3 miles from the Airport, 4 miles from Douglas. Please contact us for further information.

◆◆◆ 　　　　　🖥♿×🖐🅿📞♨🗆☞♨ **12**

SEACLIFF APARTMENTS, 6 CHURCH ROAD MARINA, OFF HARRIS PROMENADE, DOUGLAS, ISLE OF MAN IM1 2HQ. Newly refurbished apartments appointed to a high standard. Located in heart of Douglas, close to all attractions and business centre. Tel: (01624) 624465.

★★★★ 　　　　　🖥×⬆✂♨🗆🖥🗐TSL **6-9**

SILVERCRAIGS HOTEL, QUEENS PROMENADE, DOUGLAS, ISLE OF MAN. Manx owned. Close to all amenities and seafront. Lift. All Bedrooms En-Suite. TV, tea/coffee facilities. Central Heating. Tel/Fax: (01624) 677776. Email: silvercraigs@manx.net.
Web: www.silvercraigshotel.com.

◆◆◆ 　🖥♿×⬆♨🗆☞🎏🛏🎵TSL🖥🗒 **12**

THIE-NY-HAWIN, 5 RIVERSCOURT, GLEN ROAD, LAXEY, ISLE OF MAN IM4 7AG. Tel: (01624) 880237 or 07624 489600. Fall asleep to the music of the Laxey River. Modern two-bedroom house with a sunny riverside patio. Sleeps four. Sky TV. We accept dogs. Non-smoking. No children under nine.
RATING PENDING 　　　　🖥×✂🅿🗆SB🗒🗐 **12**

WELBECK HOTEL, MONA DRIVE, DOUGLAS, ISLE OF MAN IM2 4LF. Blending the style and elegance of a Victorian building with the modern luxuries required by the traveller of today. The Welbeck Hotel is ideal for business and pleasure stays. Tel: (01624) 675663. Fax: (01624) 661545 or Email: mail@welbeckhotel.com. The Welbeck is a no smoking hotel.

★★★ 　　　　🖥♿×⬆🅰📖🗒♨♨🗆 **1-11**

PORT ERIN & THE SOUTH

BALLAQUINNEY FARM, BALLABEG, CASTLETOWN, ISLE OF MAN IM9 4HG. Award-winning Manx Farmhouse accommodation. Own private entrance, lounge, conservatory and parking. Evening Meals. Welcome Break for couples. Working Dairy Farm. Tel: (01624) 824125. Email: PaulineCoole@manx.net.

◆◆◆◆ GOLD 　🖥×✂🅿♨⚓🗆✿S SB **3-10**

BLACK HILL FARMHOUSE, ST. MARKS ROAD, BALLASALLA, ISLE OF MAN IM9 3EF. Tel: (01624) 823667. Email: jeanette@mcb.net. Comfortable B&B accommodaton in scenic countryside. 0.8 miles outside Ballasalla, 3 miles from Castletown and 7 miles from Douglas. Close to airport. Pets welcome.

◆◆◆ 　　　🖥♿×✂🅿♨🗆✿ **3-10**

CHERRY ORCHARD APARTHOTEL, BRIDSON STREET, PORT ERIN, ISLE OF MAN IM9 6AN. Tel: (01624) 833811. Reservation Freephone 0800 6344321. Email: enquiries@cherry-orchard.com. Web: www.cherry-orchard.com. Leisure Centre. Chequers Bar and bar meals. In the heart of this friendly, charming seaside resort. Self-catering with all the extras.

★★★ 　　♿×🄝📖🅿🗆🎏🛎SB🗐🎵TSL🖥🗒♨ **MW 12**

CNOC TAIGH, ST MARYS ROAD, PORT ERIN, ISLE OF MAN IM9 6JL. 5 Bedrooms, 3 en-suite, 1 bathroom, sleeps up to 10. On country road, 5 mins walk to Port Erin or Port St Mary. Tel: (01624) 833133. Fax: (01624) 836664. Email: mkeggen@manx.net.

★★★★ 　　🖥♿×🖐✂🅿🗆✿♨🗐🗒 **MW12**

FALCON'S NEST HOTEL, THE PROMENADE, PORT ERIN, ISLE OF MAN IM9 6AF. Offering superb cuisine, scenic views and overlooking the magnificent Port Erin Bay. The Falcon s Nest Hotel is a friendly, traditional family-run hotel, committed to a value for money policy. Tel: (01624) 834077. Email: falconsnest@enterprise.net.

★★ 　　🖥♿×🅰⬆♨🗆🗆🎏🎵TSL🖥🗒 **12**

HARBOUR VIEW, CORRIS LANE, PORT ST MARY, ISLE OF MAN IM9 5DX. 3 bedroom apartment (all en-suite), spectacular views. Harbour, beach, shops, restaurants, bus station, p.o and bank all within 5 mins walk. Tel: (01624) 833133. Fax: (01624) 836664. Email: mkeggen@manx.net.

★★★★ 　　　🖥♿×🖐✂🅿🗆✿♨🗐🗒 **12**

KNOCK-E-VRIEW BARN, ST MARKS ROAD, BALLASALLA. Recently converted 5 star self-catering accommodation. Sleeps four. Conveniently situated for airport and ferry. Tel: (01624) 829513. Web: www.knockevriew.com.

★★★★★ 　　　🖥×✂🅿🗆✿♨🗐🗒 **12**

MANX MEWS, NR. PROMENADE, PORT ERIN, ISLE OF MAN IM9 6LH. Tel: (01624) 832273. Email: manxmews@porterinhotels.com. Modern self catering just a stones throw from Port Erin Beach. Three bedrooms, one en-suite, family bathroom, g/f cloaks. Spacious split-level lounge/diner and kitchen with secluded rear garden. Ample parking. Sleeps seven. Travel packages available.
★★★★   MW12

PORT ERIN HOTELS, PROMENADE, PORT ERIN, ISLE OF MAN IM9 6QN. 3 Star Royal Hotel - a friendly, family-run establishment. Comfortable en-suite accommodation, full Manx breakfast, optional evening meals, free airport transfers, regular entertainment and sporting extras. Travel Packages available (ATOL 3366). Tel: (01624) 833558. Web: www.porterinhotels.com.
★★★   MW 2-11

UPPER SCARD COTTAGES, ISLE OF MAN. Tel: (01624) 832927 Evenings. Panoramic views of sea and hills from lovely converted barn. Breakfast and transport to walking/cycling routes or local pub arranged by request. Garage, pressure washer and planned routes available for bikes.
RATING PENDING   12

WESTWOOD, BALLAGALE AVENUE, SURBY, PORT ERIN, ISLE OF MAN IM9 6QN. Tel: (01624) 836228. Email: westwood@enterprise.net. Well-equipped and comfortable family chalet bungalow. Home from home, large garden. Electricity, gas, bed linen inclusive. Shops, beach, golf, harbour and Steam Railway 1.5 miles. Contact Mrs Vicky Taggart.
★★★   1-12

PEEL & THE WEST

CRONK-DHOO FARM CAMPSITE, CRONK-DHOO, GREEBA, ISLE OF MAN IM4 2DX. Open all year. 10 acre site, mature trees in meadowland overlooking central valley. Good facilities. New FLAT terrace. Hardstanding for motor homes. Very neatly presented to a high standard. Pub 8 mins walk and Manx sheep breed. Tel: (01624) 851327 or 07624 454416.
APPROVED   MW12

THE FERNLEIGH HOTEL, MARINE PARADE, PEEL, ISLE OF MAN IM5 1PB. Well appointed, comfortable beds. Excellent breakfasts, good tastes catered for. Location ... non better, sea front. See you there - June. Tel/Fax: (01624) 842435. Email: fernleigh@manx.net.
◆◆◆   1-11

GLEN HELEN INN, GLEN HELEN, ST JOHNS, ISLE OF MAN, IM4 3NP. Tel: +44 (0)1624 801294. Email: info@glenheleninn.com. A small comfortable friendly inn situated in a mile of beautiful glen alongside the River Neb. All rooms are ensuite with countryside views. Visit www.glenheleninn.com for the best available rates and details of seasonal special offers, with hyperlinks to online ferry and airline services.
◆◆◆◆   12

THE OLD STABLE, BERK, PEEL ROAD, KIRK MICHAEL, ISLE OF MAN IM6 1AP. Tel/Fax: (01624) 878039. Web: www.theoldstable.net. Email: info@theoldstable.net. Five star cottage. Quiet rural location, sea views, village half mile. High standard facilities. Two bedrooms **(both en-suite)**, dining room/lounge, sunroom, luxury kitchen. Parking, garden.
★★★★★   12

THE STONE BARN, SHENVALLA, PATRICK, ISLE OF MAN IM5 3AP. Tel: (01624) 843023. Email: sam@shenvalla.co.im. Five star, spacious, converted barn with three King size bedrooms, all en-suite. Set in private grounds in a stunning rural, peaceful location overlooking beautiful, well-stocked private lake.
★★★★★   12

WILLOW NOOK COTTAGES, COOIL SHELLAGH FARM, KIRK MICHAEL, ISLE OF MAN IM6 1AU. Tel: (01624) 877745. Web: www.willownook.com. Email: info@willownook.com. Three beautiful five star cottages sleeping four, four and two people. Sea views, sunny patios, gardens. Situated amongst farmland, half mile from village.
★★★★★   12

RAMSEY & THE NORTH

CORRODY COTTAGE, THOLT-Y-WILL, SULBY GLEN, ISLE OF MAN. Tel: (01624) 898095. 5 Star Romantic period Manx Cottage set in pictuesque seclusion. Four poster bed, Ingelnook fireplace, 10 private acres with river frontage. Fully equipped for your home from home comfort. Discounted travel package available.
★★★★★   12

THE COTTAGE, WHITE GABLES, CURRAGH ROAD, BALLAUGH, ISLE OF MAN. Something special. Four Star self-catering for two, en-suite bedroom, sitting room, fully fitted kitchen. Superb countryside location. Parking. Tel/Fax: (01624) 897926. Email: whitegables@manx.net.
★★★★   12

OROTAVA, 14 WESTLANDS CLOSE, RAMSEY, ISLE OF MAN, IM8 3PU. Friendly, comfortable accommodation. Excellent breakfast. Situated in quiet cul-de-sac 10 minutes from Ramsey town centre. Ideal for golf, walking and fishing holidays. Tel: (01624) 814233.

◆◆◆ 12

ROSELEA COTTAGE, GLEN ROAD, SULBY, ISLE OF MAN IM7 2BB. Tel: 0113 256 0858. Email: pask@btconnect.com. Manx cottage sleeping four people. Sky colour TV, CD, Video. Outdoor seating front/rear. Delightful rural setting in quiet old Sulby village. Quarter mile from local amenities. Contact Jude Pollard.

★★★ MW 12

KEY TO SYMBOLS

TOUR OPERATORS

- Everymann Holidays
- Magic Holidays
- Premier Holidays
- TSL Travel Services

DISABLED SYMBOLS

- Accessible One
- Accessible Two
- Accessible Three
- Partially sighted

SELF-CATERING

- Electric hook-ups
- Gas/Electricity charged extra
- Linen provided
- Showers on campsite
- Washing machine/drying

SERVICED & SELF-CATERING

- Central heating
- Children welcome
- Dogs welcome
- No dogs
- Guest laundry/laundry service
- Gym/Leisure facilities
- Lift
- Ground floor bedrooms
- Non-smoking
- Private parking
- Public telephone available
- Residential liquor licence
- Tea/coffee making facilities in all bedrooms
- Telephone in all bedrooms or sc units
- Television in all bedrooms or sc units
- Accepts major credit cards
- Garden
- Group rates on application
- Public Liquor Licence
- Swimming pool (indoor)
- Modem point in bedroom
- UL Unlicensed (alcoholic drinks not served)
- S Special diets provided
- Conference Room
- SB Short breaks offered
- 12 Open all year
- MW Mid week bookings

Red Arrows at Ramsey

USEFUL
INFORMATION

The information given in this alphabetical listing, relevant to many of the articles in the guide, is useful for checking out opening times, admission prices, what's on and other details which can help you to plan and make the most of your visit to the Isle of Man.

ARTS & ENTERTAINMENT

■ Villa Marina & Gaiety Theatre Complex. Enquiries 01624 694566. Box office 01624 694555. *www.villamarina.com*

■ Arts Council (for details of what's on and to obtain a copy of the Ten-Year Strategy). 10 Villa Marina Arcade, Douglas. 01624 611316. *www.gov.im/artscouncil*

BUS AND TRAIN SERVICES

■ For up-to-date timetable and fare information, contact Isle of Man Transport on 01624 662525 or the Tourist Information Centre on 01624 686766.

CIRCA – SHOP MOBILITY

For information about disabled facilities, contact either the Manx Foundation for the Physically Disabled (01624 628926) or CIRCA (01624 613713).

FERRY SERVICES

For details of routes, services, fares and special offers contact the Steam Packet on 01624 661661 or visit *www.steam-packet.com*

FLYING TO THE ISLE OF MAN

See page 10.

FURTHER READING

■ Other books published by Lily Publications:

Spirit of Mann (new second edition)
Air of Mann (an aerial photographic survey)
Manannan's Kingdom (the coastline in photographs)
Lucky Little Devil! (Norman Wisdom's Island home and life)
Wild Flowers of Mann

■ Isle of Man books by Lily Publications' sister company Ferry Publications:

Life & Times of the Steam Packet
Ferries of the Isle of Man Past & Present
Steam Packet 175
Steam Packet 175 - The Album
King Orry
These titles are all available direct from Lily Publications at PO Box 33, Ramsey, Isle of Man IM99 4LP. Tel: 01624 898446. Fax: 01624 898449. Email: *LilyPubs@manx.net*
Website: *www.lilypublications.co.uk*

■ Many other books about the Isle of Man, and a comprehensive list of Manx titles, are available from Lexicon Bookshop in Strand Street, Douglas.

Tel: 01624 673004. Fax: 01624 661959. Email: *sales@lexiconbookshop.co.im*. Website: *www.lexiconbookshop.co.im*

HARBOURS

■ *Douglas*. Good shelter except in NE winds, very heavy seas in NE gales. Harbour Master 01624 686627.
■ *Laxey*. Sheltered except in strong NE/SE winds. Harbour dries out. Port

Summerhill Road, near Jurby

Manager 01624 861663.
■ *Peel*. Good shelter except in strong NW to NE winds, when entry should not be attempted. Harbour Office 01624 842338.
■ *Port St Mary*. Very good shelter except in E or SE winds. Inner harbour dries out. Port Manager (also for Port Erin and Castletown) 01624 833206.
■ *Ramsey*. Very good shelter except in strong NE/SE winds. Harbour dries out. Port Manager 01624 812245.

ISLE OF MAN LAW

The Isle of Man has a strong anti-drugs policy and illegal possession of banned substances can lead to imprisonment.

ISLE OF MAN STAMPS

You can buy Manx stamps online at *www.gov.im/stamps*

ISLE OF MAN WEBSITES

The main visitor website gives details of accommodation, events, attractions, activities,

TT and motorsport, travel information, special offers and more. Visit *www.visitisleofman.com*

The Isle of Man Government website at *www.gov.im* has a comprehensive index and is also a mine of information.

LICENSING LAWS

Liberal new Isle of Man legislation has introduced 24-hour opening for pubs, bars and off-licences. This means that all licensed premises, including nightclubs, restaurants and the Douglas casino, now have the option to serve alcohol 24 hours a day but only within their stated pre-arranged opening times.

MANX NATIONAL HERITAGE

■ For opening times, admission prices (where applicable) and other information about Manx National Heritage sites call 01624 648000. Or visit *www.gov.im/mnh* or either of the Isle of Man websites.

MANX WILDLIFE TRUST

Manx Wildlife Trust is based at the Tynwald Mills Centre in St John's. The shop here has a wealth of leaflets, books, maps and other information about Isle of Man wildlife and habitats. Call 01624 801985 or visit *www.wildlifetrust.org.uk/manxwt*

MOTORING LAWS AND INFORMATION

■ *Careful drivers*. Isle of Man roads and lanes are narrow and should be negotiated with care.

■ *Mobile phones*. It is an offence to use a hand-held mobile phone while driving.

■ *Parking discs*. These are required in some of the larger towns and villages and are available **free** from Isle of Man Steam Packet vessels, the Sea Terminal, airport, car hire companies and local Commissioners Offices.

■ *Seatbelts*. Similar seatbelt laws to those in the UK and elsewhere apply.

■ *Trailer caravans* are not permitted on the Isle of Man without a permit, but tenting campers and self-propelled motor caravans are welcome.

OKELLS BREWERY TOURS

■ Heron & Brearley tours of the Falcon Brewery, Kewaigue, Douglas can be arranged by appointment. 01624 699400.

TOURIST INFORMATION CENTRE

■ Address: Sea Terminal, Douglas, Isle of Man IM1 2RG.

■ Telephone: 01624 686766.

■ Open throughout the year: April–September 7 days a week, October–March Monday to Friday.

TOURIST INFORMATION POINTS

Open all year:
■ Airport 01624 821600
■ Castletown 01624 825005
■ Onchan 01624 621228
■ Peel 01624 842341
■ Port Erin 01624 832298 & 835858
■ Port St Mary 01624 832101
■ Ramsey 01624 817025

Summer only:

■ Ballasalla 01624 822531
■ Laxey Heritage Trust 01624 862007

TYNWALD

The Tynwald Parliamentary website is at *www.tynwald.org.im*

Mooragh Park, Ramsey